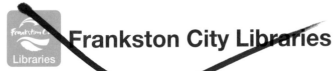

EASY STREET

Center Point
Large Print

Also by Richard S. Wheeler and available from
Center Point Large Print:

The Two Medicine River
Richard Lamb
The Fate

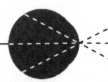

EASY STREET

Richard S. Wheeler

CENTER POINT LARGE PRINT
THORNDIKE, MAINE

This Center Point Large Print edition
is published in the year 2016 by arrangement with
Golden West Literary Agency.

The text of this Large Print edition is unabridged.
In other aspects, this book may vary
from the original edition.
Printed in the United States of America
on permanent paper.
Set in 16-point Times New Roman type.

ISBN: 978-1-62899-839-9 (hardcover)
ISBN: 978-1-62899-845-0 (paperback)

Library of Congress Cataloging-in-Publication Data

Names: Wheeler, Richard S.
Title: Easy street / Richard S. Wheeler.
Description: Center Point Large Print edition. | Thorndike, Maine :
Center Point Large Print, 2016. | ©2012
Identifiers: LCCN 2015037823| ISBN 9781628998399 (hardcover : alk.
paper) | ISBN 9781628998450 (pbk. : alk. paper)
Subjects: LCSH: Large type books.
Classification: LCC PS3573.H4345 E17 2016 | DDC 813/.54—dc23
LC record available at http://lccn.loc.gov/2015037823

Easy Street is dedicated to Brian McCoy. Over the years, he has always encouraged me, finding merit in my work and sharing my novels with others. I sometimes think I would not have succeeded as a novelist without his many blessings. So this one is for my friend and mentor, and his family too.

Chapter One

Free at last. Yesterday Jay Tecumseh Warren had graduated from college. Today he would begin a life of leisure. He paid the driver of the hack, collected his bag, and approached his parents' New Haven brick pile.

It seemed oddly solemn. He had expected them to pour out of the door, welcoming him with a homecoming celebration. Instead, he found a deep quiet that seemed almost ominous. Well, no matter. He was done with school. He had drifted through, with gentleman's grades, mostly Cs and Ds. It was unseemly for the privileged to appear too ambitious.

He entered the red brick manse and found the foyer shadowed and silent. An odd thing. There, at the foot of the stair, was a suitcase he recognized as his own, and on it, a white envelope. Ah, a surprise graduation gift! He set down his bag, opened the envelope, and extracted a note written in his father's spiky handwriting. The note was wrapped around five one-hundred-dollar bills and a lengthy train ticket. Frowning, he read the note.

My dear son,
I have prepared you for life as best as I am able. Now it is time for you to enter the adult world. It is my deepest belief that

each man should advance through life on his own merit, and make his own way, as I have done. I would do you no favor by indulging you now. In fact, life as a rich man's idle son would be your ruin. You will find here five hundred dollars, a sum adequate to sustain you while you find employment. I enclose also a rail ticket to Cheyenne, Wyoming Territory, which I consider an excellent place to find yourself and shape your destiny.

Your loving father,

Tecumseh Warren.

Young Jay, Harvard graduate, rich man's boy, was shocked. He read the note again. He studied the somber house, noting the absence of the man-servant Joseph, the maid Matilda, and Agnes the cook. He wandered through the quiet rooms, saw motes of dust in the sunlight but no life, and knew at last that his father meant it. He was being banished. He was being disowned. Well, not disowned.

He scarcely knew what to do. He was a mile from the Hartford station, with two bags to carry and no servants to help him. He opened the suitcase that had been left in the foyer, found his clothing neatly packed. Impulsively he raced up the stairs to his room, and found it empty. Not a memento, not a tintype, not a book.

Maybe this was his father's little joke; a graduation jest. But he dismissed that. His father had built a shipping fortune with no help from anyone, with wits, courage, and a genius to see opportunities. He was a self-made man and never failed to let the world know it. No, this was no little joke.

In the foyer, he weighed taking both bags, decided on the one left for him, and headed for the railroad station, fear and a little petulance building in him. The June day was pleasant, but he had never carried a bag any distance; servants had always been eager to relieve him of the task.

He found a shiny oak pew at the station and waited for the next local, both fuming and desperate. What of his summer at Martha's Vineyard? What of his rendezvous with Rosalita, exotic daughter of the Spanish ambassador? What of the three invitations to Newport Beach? What of sailing on the sound?

The train chuffed in, hissing steam, and he climbed into an odorous coach, sitting as far as he could from a mother with a hiccupping brat. A summer shower descended, running streaks down his grimy window. The conductor ripped the bottom off the yard-long ticket, and returned it to Jay. The ticket was a yellow monstrosity, patching together rides on several lines that would eventually dump him out in the middle of nowhere. Cheyenne had barely existed a few years earlier, and was nothing more than a wild railroad town. Heading there seemed like descending into hell.

And what was he supposed to do there? Watch the buffalo? Study wild Indians? Well, he'd stay until his cash ran out and then his father would relent. But maybe not. Tecumseh Warren was a tough old bird, with a trimmed beard, sharp eyes, and no stomach for fraud, lies, or nonsense. Could the old man possibly believe that his one and only son should be subjected to the grimy world of the frontier?

Jay sighed. The answer was yes. The baby hiccupped and then howled, and Jay swore a new odor drifted through the battered coach. A dread seized Jay; he would never see home again; never see his mother and father; never see his friends; never court a real lady; never have a moment's entertainment.

What a lousy trick. The old man was out of his stinking mind.

The young man peered longingly at the forested New England countryside, with its settled towns, civilized life, and amenities. What would Cheyenne be like? Indeed, why had his father chosen the place? Well, he'd see. Of course he didn't have to stay. He could go somewhere else, but that was a little vague. Cheyenne it would be until his old man released him from prison.

New York, Scranton, Cleveland, Chicago. His father had made the trip easy for him: there were berths in George Pullman's sleeping cars for him and porters to shine his shoes. Some of the express trains had diners, where a man could order a steak and get himself some spirits. He'd had trouble cashing one of the hundreds but a stationmaster in Cleveland helped him. A hundred could support a family for a month. The trains rocketed west, a mile a minute in some stretches, and Jay felt the coaches weave under his feet.

Maybe the whole thing wouldn't be so bad. He'd tour the wild west, meet some of the local gentry, and head back to Hartford all the better for it. He'd take tea with his mother, Aloise, who was usually indisposed mornings, and tell her about all the ruffians he'd encountered, and she would smile sweetly and nod.

These were summer days, and he wore his light cream suit and straw boater, his two-tone oxfords, and his newly-acquired Harvard class ring of 1876. The suit had a waistcoat but he didn't wear it. He had his Waltham pocket watch on a long woven gold watch chain, which he dangled conspicuously down his middle as a badge. He had innocent blue eyes, a ruddy complexion, and stiff brown hair, a little like his father, but all of it subdued by what he had gotten from his pale and elegant mother.

He met various sorts on the train, most commonly drummers, swarming out to sell sewing machines or whiskey or ready-made shirts. They were a crass lot, brimming with profane comments, and he loathed them all. They, in turn, eyed him warily, taking in his status, which he wore plainly. As much as he wished to meet young ladies, there were none in sight except a few who were carefully escorted by glowering fathers whose gaze settled on his gold watch fob.

Chicago took a deal of trouble, with a hansom cab to a different station, but he got it all squared away. What an awful city, full of immigrant barbarians. He doubted there was a decent restaurant in the whole place; nothing like Delmonico's at any rate.

Now the countryside changed; trees were fewer; horizons grew. Grass stretched into infinities. He hadn't known the world was so large. It was also boring. He much preferred life where there were lots of people and they were all doing things. If this was the West, he'd gladly turn it over to the cattle, or return it to the tribes.

He sighed, stared at the endlessly boring plains, and lamented that he'd ever been born into an eccentric family. What a sad fate to have a father like Tecumseh Warren. It would have been much better to be born into old wealth, like the Astors. Only now, as the endless prairie crept by, did he understand what a burden it was to be the son of a self-made man.

But maybe his ordeal wouldn't last long. After a few weeks his father might relent, bring him home, and his happiness could be renewed. But somehow he doubted it would happen. It was no good to indulge in wishful dreams. No good would come of this, and he would suffer.

The train had no diner, and stopped periodically for meals and refueling. The food in these rude stations was abominable, and he suspected that what was billed as chicken was more likely prairie dog or gopher. He ate glumly, aware that the indignities were piling up. What good did it do him to get a degree from Harvard when he had to eat prairie dog for dinner?

By the time they reached Omaha, the world was changing again; trees were scarce; grass was shorter. The torpid Missouri River drifted by, rather muddy and uninviting. There the passengers were transferred to the storied Union Pacific, one of the two great rail lines that had completed the transcontinental route. But that was of little interest to Jay Warren. The bright, empty country only made him melancholic. Whatever was his father thinking?

One morning they passed a vast herd of buffalo, so distant that they seemed to form a single black mass. That didn't prevent the barbarians in the coaches from opening the windows and banging away at the herd with any firearms that came to hand. Judging from the noise, most of the travelers had a weapon of some sort in their duffel. No one hit a buffalo, which grazed serenely on the horizon, and the train labored on, ever westward.

The line followed the miserable Platte River valley. A drummer enlightened him, saying it was a mile wide and an inch deep, and the water was so thick with silt it should never be mixed with whiskey. Jay Warren no longer cared. He was now a thousand miles from women, and two thousand from people worth knowing. Indeed, the passengers had thinned out, and women were no longer on board, except for a few headed for California. All of this country was a part of the Louisiana Purchase negotiated by Thomas Jefferson. He could see it was a grave mistake. Mr. Jefferson had bought a lot of nothing.

Then, finally, days after his rude ejection from Hartford, the conductor announced that the next stop would be Cheyenne. From there one could, he said, find stagecoach passage to the Black Hills gold district, and passage to Denver. The thought of going to the new gold strike in the Black Hills intrigued Jay Warren. Gold! Weren't the Hearsts getting rich fast?

He collected his suitcase, which now had more used under drawers in it than fresh, and waited impatiently while the express train huffed its way across lonely prairies, unchanging and dull, and finally wheezed to a stop in a ramshackle town on Crow Creek. The conductor placed the step stool, and three drummers, a fat lady, and Jay Warren stepped onto dry clay, a grim strip of earth beside the track that divided the false-fronted shacks masquerading as businesses on either side of the rails. The sun beat down hard from a cloudless heaven. The smell of outhouses rose from the main drag. There were a few saddle horses tied to rails located in front of the buildings. Jay stared about him.

This was where his father had sent him? That was to be his place of destiny?

He raged at Tecumseh. Why here? What would it prove? Why did his father suppose that everyone had to prove his worth? Did that apply to women? Would he send a daughter to some god-forsaken place and hand her a few dollars and tell her to make something of her life?

The handful of locals meeting the train had already dissipated by the time Jay Warren had fought another fight with the ghost of his father. But there was one old and no doubt smelly man who sat in an open carriage.

"You want a ride?" he asked.

"What's the best hotel in town?"

"There ain't any but the best hotels. They're all best."

"What's one that's not a bedbug parlor?"

"They ain't but all bedbug parlors."

"What's the best boardinghouse around? With meals?"

"There ain't any best."

"Are there private rooms let by widows?"

"Only private rooms around here are bunked three deep."

"My good man, what would you suggest? I want the best place in town, where I can get a good night's sleep between clean sheets, and not be awakened."

"I got the spot, fella. That'd be the cemetery. They sleep mighty fine there, mighty fine."

Chapter Two

Well, follow the salesmen.

"Take me to wherever the drummers stay."

"That'd be the Dakota," he said. "Hop in, peckerhead."

Jay lifted his duffel into the grimy carriage, climbed in, and the hack driver carried him a block and a half. The Dakota was a false-front, whitewashed establishment with the name painted in black above the door.

"That'll be a dollar, fella."

"A dollar!"

"Two bits for the ride, six bits for the questions."

He'd been suckered but he paid anyway, choosing not to give a tip. He would swiftly buy some humble clothing and hide his pocket watch with its woven gold chain.

Within, the reception area was the size of one of his father's closets, but a mustachioed gent appeared in a window, and the pilgrim succeeded in renting a room by the week for one dollar a night in advance. Outhouses in the back. Meals across the rutted street at Ma's Eats.

The room was also the size of a closet, with a narrow cot and a wooden chair and a makeshift table. A tiny window well above the chair let in wan light. The room stank.

He stared bitterly at the cubicle. Had his world come to this, at age twenty? What was his old man thinking?

He couldn't stand the thought even of resting for a while on that bunk, so he removed his watch and gold fob and hid it in his portmanteau, undid his cravat, switched from his two-tone shoes to plain oxfords, left his straw boater on the battered table, and escaped the hotel. He had one flaming desire: to abandon the West and frontier as soon as he could and never return.

He made his way to the foul outhouse, relieved himself, and set out to explore Cheyenne. It would soon be time for a dinner, and then he'd examine the assorted saloons that crowded the street, each vying to be gaudier than its neighbors. The town stretched several blocks along the Union Pacific track, and petered out a few blocks to either side of the rails. One thing was fine: the air was dry and pleasant, and nature itself seemed to scrub Cheyenne of its dust and grime and filth. The town was only a few years old, all of it built from wood imported vast distances because no forests grew close at hand.

The people Jay observed were ordinary; he could think of no other word for them. Just nondescript males, in dungarees, scratchy shirts, and battered brogans. They wore hats that were as stained as their work clothing. They were a sorry lot; no doubt poorly schooled and ignorant. He supposed they were off the local ranches, though Cheyenne was also a jumping off point for the gold rush in the Black Hills, and some of those burly, bearded men surely were heading for the bonanza country.

If this was a rowdy place, he saw no evidence of it. The males on the clay streets were loading buckboards, toting burlap bags, strapping small purchases to saddles, and knotting in groups to gossip. He assumed he would be spotted for a greenhorn, no matter that he had hidden away the most obvious of his attire. But in fact people paid him no heed. He wasn't a rich man's son; he wasn't a dude; he was nothing.

He chose Ma's Eats for his evening meal, having examined The Beanery and Fogarty's Famous Food. Ma turned out to be the fat lady who got off the train when he did, but now she wore a vast apron and an odd bandanna. Ma, it turned out, levied two bits per plate, and you didn't undergo the agony of choice at Ma's Eats: you got whatever she chose to set before you. Also, one paid in advance. There would be no skipping out on Ma. She dished up a bowl of stuff. He didn't know what it was. A sea of brown gravy hiding small bits of gray meat. He stirred it, trying to learn something about it. But its secrets eluded him. He sampled a bit, felt offended, and quit the place.

He did better at Fogarty's Famous Food:

antelope steaks and boiled potatoes. There might be something redeeming about Cheyenne after all. The males in the restaurant ate seriously and fast, conversing not at all. That annoyed him. Meals were social events in Hartford; half the fun of eating was the company at the table. He would try The Beanery, just to make sure he was eating in the most elevated circumstances in Cheyenne.

He stepped into a soft, velvet twilight. The sun had just dropped below the distant horizon, lighting the clear sky momentarily, and now a purple peace lay upon the rough city. He walked the town, noting its crudeness. It had started as a rail camp, a raucous end-of-the-line camp where the Union Pacific crews lived and fought and drank. Now there were a few sturdier buildings rising, as if some people liked the place and decided to stick around. The railroad had pushed west toward its rendezvous in Utah with the Central Pacific, leaving Cheyenne behind as a ranch supply town and crossroads. He was getting at least an inkling of why his father shipped him there: it might be a fine place to start a business, especially a shipping company.

He put the horrible thought out of his head. He'd scheme some way to escape Cheyenne and return to civilization.

The faint sound of a fiddle caught his ear; it was time to explore some of those saloons that were crowded together along the railroad. He drifted that way, peering into the ill-lit drinking parlors. Most of them had a long bar along one side, and some gambling tables at the rear, lit by double kerosene lamps. They seemed so much alike, from the street, that he wondered what led a drinking man to choose one over another. The rancid smell of beer rose from some; of whiskey from others. Their names hinted at their clientele: the Shamrock, the Highlander, the Prince of Wales, the Pacific, the Mint, the Exchange.

Then he discovered a larger and better lit place called The Stockman. It was more to his liking and catered to a better class. It featured a good mahogany bar and back bar, a brass foot rail, and a well lit gambling area with several games, including Monte, Roulette, and Faro. He knew little about any of them, but resolved to watch. There was also a large round poker table, presided over by a coughing, slick-haired, goggle-eyed gent who plainly had consumption.

He wouldn't play, of course. Only fools would risk their cash on a game loaded against them.

The Faro table was brightly lit, but there were only two players plus the dealer and some gent on a stool operating some sort of abacus.

The dealer exhaled smoke from a cigarillo and smiled. "Have a seat, fella. Ten cents a toss, ten dollars the ceiling."

"I'll just watch for a while," Jay said.

"Ah, fine. I can see you're new to the game. You

just take it in, get the hang of it, and pretty soon you'll be ready to make your bonanza."

They all laughed.

"I need one," he said.

The skeletal dealer eyed him. "Note a couple of things here. The cards are drawn from a box, two at a time, the first a loser, the second a winner. And note this, my friend. The only advantage a dealer has is when two cards of equal value are dealt. Those go to the house. Faro's the right game for those who want to be real careful."

The two players were restless, so the dealer drew a jack, which was the loser, and a five, the winner. The fellow on the abacus shoved two black beads along; Jay realized they represented the jack and five. Players would know exactly what cards had been played and what remained in the spring-loaded box.

The dealer cleaned off a chip that had been bet on the jack, exhaling a stream of yellow smoke. He coughed. Another consumptive, Jay thought. The smoke drifted past the twin lamps lighting the green baize.

The layout had thirteen cards painted on it; all spades, but suits apparently didn't matter in Faro. A player would place his chip on one of the painted cards, and if it won he would double his money. Even as he watched, one sun-stained gray-haired player swiftly built his pile with a series of wins. He was betting heavily, somewhere near the maximum, but Jay couldn't be sure. The other player yawned, sipped an amber-colored drink, and played only occasionally.

The dealer drew the last card from the box, and it was alone, which puzzled Jay. The dealer saw it.

"That's the hock. It doesn't play. The first card is the soda, and it doesn't play, my friend," he said.

He shuffled the deck, his fingers so expert that the red-backed cards snapped into place, and then he placed the shuffled deck into the box, drew the soda, a queen, and put it in the dealer's discard pile.

"You want to try your hand, fella?"

"No, I'll just watch," Jay said.

"Suit yourself," the dealer said, drawing a seven, loser, and eight, winner. No one won or lost. The bored abacus man slid some black beads along the wires.

The old guy who'd won a bunch slid a stack of chips onto the king and then placed an octagonal copper token on top of it.

Jay had no idea what that was about, so the dealer explained. "He's coppering his bet; he's betting the king'll lose. You cover your bet with copper, you're reversing it."

Ah, so players had a few more options. Jay liked that.

The old buzzard let it ride for two more turns, and then the king won, and he lost.

He smiled, shoved the stack toward the dealer. "Time to quit," he said.

The dealer did a swift count; the old guy had won two hundred thirty dollars in spite of losing his last wager. Jay stared. Two hundred thirty dollars was almost half of what his father had given him. The old man stuffed the worn greenbacks into his purse, and eyed Jay.

"Greenhorn, don't be a fool," he said, and wandered off.

Jay Tecumseh Warren didn't like being called a greenhorn. He watched the ignorant old galoot drift out the door and into the soft night.

"You want to try a game?" the dealer asked.

He drew a grubby handkerchief from his pocket and coughed pink scum into it.

"Think I'll watch," Jay said.

But there wasn't much to watch. The remaining player slid single chips onto the layout, won or lost a few dimes, and bored Jay.

"See ya," he said to the coughing dealer and case keeper. He'd watch that game a little more before he'd tackle it.

He drifted to the shining mahogany bar, where the keep eyed him and waited.

"Whiskey," Jay said. "And put a little ice in."

The keep shook his head, and poured a tumbler without ice. Apparently there was no such thing in Cheyenne, Wyoming Territory.

"Some water then."

The barkeep added a little tepid water. Jay eyed the half-dozen male imbibers lining the bar. They were all roughly attired, but he spotted signs of grooming; a carefully clipped beard, or boots that weren't worn at the heels. It seemed oddly quiet; these gents were downing spirits but avoiding talk.

The whiskey had been aged about two days. Jay gasped, waited for his offended throat to quiet, and tried another sip. A drink in Cheyenne was not the same as a drink at the Harvard Club.

He eyed the gent next to him, a black-haired dandy who stared at the picture of a nude above the bar.

"I'm new around here. What's the easiest way to make some real money?" Jay asked.

"Rob a bank," the dandy said.

"Well, what's the fastest way?"

"Rob three or four banks," the gent said.

The patrons all sipped and smiled.

Chapter Three

These yokels were toying with him. His father could buy and sell the whole lot, ten times over. They saw the greenhorn, but they didn't see anything else, and didn't know his name. Maybe he should tell them his name, Jay Tecumseh Warren, and watch the amused faces turn respectful. Anyone who knew anything at all knew who Tecumseh Warren was.

But having a little fun at someone's expense was a two-way street. Jay looked over the rustic standing next to him, a boot on the brass rail, and took him for a local farmer or rancher. His boots looked like they'd been soaked in plenty of manure.

"All right," Jay said. "Tell me this. What's the fastest way to lose money here? You look like you might be able to advise me."

That did get him a smile or two down the line of onlookers, all of them now focused on the conversation at Jay's end of the bar.

"Sonny, I've lost money in more businesses than you have years," the man said. "You want to know how to lose? Let me help you."

"Well," Jay said, "I'd like to know. I think maybe raising livestock might be it."

"You can lose a lot faster than that," the man

said. "Try freighting. That's like opening a vein if the weather's bad or the oxen take sick, or the teamsters quit, or no one pays."

So the man was a teamster. That explained the mud-soaked boots.

"Well, I'm looking to start a business."

"I didn't get your handle, fella."

"Jay Warren. And you?"

"They call me lots of things, usually son of a bitch. You come here looking to start up a business, but you don't know what?"

Warren nodded.

"You got any trades?"

"What do you mean, trades?"

"You a blacksmith or an accountant or a teamster like me?"

"I don't need trades. I'll hire people to do that."

"You come from back east somewheres?"

"Connecticut."

"You think maybe you should fetch yourself to the railroad and take the next train east?"

"No, sir, I'm here, I'm ready to run a business, and I'll get some money."

"Well, that's entertaining, fella. That's like me. I'm here and ready to get some money myself. Tell me this, fella. You're going to start a business, with what? Doing what?"

"Well, that's confidential, sir. I'm scouting things out, and when I'm ready, I'll make money."

By this time no one else in the saloon was

27

saying anything, and Jay's conversation was the only thing going in that establishment.

"Okay," the local said, "you must of had some idea what you'll do here. What was that?"

Jay was tempted to tell the whole story; getting stuffed on trains and disowned more or less by one of the richest men around. But he decided there were better things to talk about.

"Gold," he said.

"Ah, Black Hills, right? You heading out there?"

"I'm looking for opportunities."

"There's three ways to make her in a goldfield. One's to work your claims and pan it out of gravel or rip it out of rock. Another's to speculate on mining claims, buy and sell the claims and maybe get lucky. And third, supply all them miners up there, which is how I make my drinking money. I ship britches and boots and drawers and gold pans and picks and pickles and flour, and that's not a half bad way to make a few dollars, if the trail's dry and the weather's decent and the oxen don't croak."

"Well, of course, I'd hire that done. I'll just use my brains and see what I can do."

By then, the others at the bar were listening intently and saying nothing. Even the barkeep, in a clean apron, was listening hard. At the far end of the bar, a well-dressed man picked up his tumbler and headed toward Jay. He wore a cream colored linen suit, suitable for summer, with a waistcoat and black tie. But it wasn't his grooming that caught Jay's attention, but the man's face. It was knotted and weathered, his eyes black coals, his gray-shot beard trimmed fine and close. He surveyed Jay with a single knowing glance.

"Warren is it? That's a familiar name," he said.

"Is it?" Jay asked.

"I'm Foley, Fairweather Foley, sir. What brings you here?"

"I'm ready to engage in business, sir."

"But you don't know what, I gather."

"I just arrived, sir."

"By engage, do you mean invest in a business?"

"Well, I thought more of starting one and running it."

"Well, then you have capital."

Jay said nothing; let the man think it. Beneath that linen suit was another ruffian, and it paid not to reveal much to such a man. "What do you do, sir?" he asked.

"I make money," Foley said.

"Well, that's admirable," Jay said. "I always admire a capitalist."

"That's the last thing I am," Foley said. "I'm saying don't compete with me. You'll regret it."

"You haven't told me the nature of your business, sir."

"If you haven't learned that, you're not learned in business, Warren. It's hardware, men's clothing, furniture, assay services in mining camps, ranch land, mineral claims, the Cheyenne Overland Stage, the Medicine Bow Irrigation Canal, cavalry remount ranches, and town lot developer."

"You're just the man I want to meet, Mr. Foley. I think you need a lieutenant."

"I think not."

"I think we need to have a lunch and talk it over, sir."

"Warren, I don't know why you're here. If you're planning to start a company, you'd better make sure it's not one that competes with me. And before you come looking for a position, you'd better show me some ground-up experience."

"Ah, I'm just testing the waters, sir."

"Is that what you call it? I'll be watching," Foley said.

"Ah, what would you recommend, sir?"

Foley eyed him in the lamplight. "For you? I have absolutely nothing to recommend." Foley set his glass on the bar, nodded, and drifted through the double doors and into the soft evening air.

Jay eyed the staring patrons, suddenly felt worn, and decided to call it quits. He'd traveled far this day, and tomorrow would be better. He smiled, left two-bits on the bar, and departed, aware that every man in the saloon was watching him. At least he had found the right saloon, where men of substance collected. He'd eventually find some sort of berth with one or another of them, but he would have to win their confidence.

There was more to all this than he had imagined.

The dry air was pleasant. The day's heat had abated. Up and down the dim-lit rutted street he could see light spilling from saloons. A few saddle horses stood at hitch rails, some with legs cocked. There wasn't any visible traffic. Cheyenne might be a rail town and the jumping off point to a major gold strike, but one wouldn't know it this quiet evening. He could already see what made the town tick: it was the supplier of all sorts of goods to the surrounding hinterlands, and the transfer point for thousands of men flooding to the Black Hills nearby.

He strolled the street in the quiet dark. Saloons on one side; a string of dark boxcars and flat cars on the other, waiting to be unloaded into freight wagons. The saloon doors were open; inside, a lamp or two lit knots of ruffians, men who toiled long hours and employed their muscles rather than their brains. He had no particular sympathy for them. They toiled, drank away their day's wage, and toiled again. Far from being noisy, the railroad street was engrossed in silence. One scarcely even heard conversations. He doubted they had much to talk about; their lives were small and narrow.

He drifted toward the hotel, worrying that he couldn't sleep in that hot little box of a room. And maybe there would be bedbugs after all. No sooner did he step into the stifling heat of the building than he realized his worst fears were real. He found his room in virtual darkness, unlocked with the skeleton key, and let himself in. The place was oppressive. It was his new prison.

He undressed in the dark and lay on the iron cot, staring into the blankness above him. He wanted space, air, cool, the things the rich took for granted and the very poor had too much of. His father's money had given him a proper bedroom, light, airy, with leaded glass windows, fresh linens, and safety. There were none of these here, and he wondered whether he would ever enjoy domestic comforts again.

But he abolished that notion. He was young. Life was just beginning. He'd show these hayseeds a thing or two. This day he had learned for the first time that he was ill-fitted for the business world. He had no trade and no experience. He had a liberal arts education, but what would knowledge of a few of Shakespeare's plays get him in Cheyenne?

He slept not at all that night, his mind restless, his fears lubricated by every noise in the corridor, the passage of unknown feet. He doubted that the flimsy bolt would slow down anyone who wanted to shoulder his way in and steal what little he possessed.

But looming over the restless night was fear. The clock was ticking. His funds were flowing relentlessly out of his purse. He had a little time, unless foul luck undid him. But he hadn't the faintest idea what to do, where to go, what to ask for, or how to stanch the dribble of cash. He no longer was angry at Tecumseh; he was immersed in dread of starvation, or life lived in unspeakable squalor, or a life of great ordinariness, no different from hundreds of thousands of other ordinary lives. He was Tecumseh Warren's son—but soon he might be nothing.

Still, he made it through the nightmarish night, and welcomed the pastel dawn in the east. He wondered if he'd ever sleep again. He knew the next night would be as bad as this one; he would be tormented by dreams and humiliations. The horror was upon him now: to survive he might have to toil in manual labor, like someone off the immigrant boat.

Wearily, he sat up. He realized he had not been bitten by anything in the night. The place wasn't a bedbug parlor. He poured water from a white vitreous pitcher on the table into a white basin and laved his face, feeling the stubble of his young beard. He would want to find a tonsorial parlor for a shave. And that would cost more money.

He needed to have his underclothes and shirts laundered. And that would cost more money. And apparently he needed to dress the way the locals did so he wouldn't be dismissed as a greenhorn. And that would eat into his diminishing hoard of cash. He hoped he would find one of those drummers. They would know what to do.

He faced the prospect of finding an edible breakfast. Ma's Eats was off-limits to him. He'd find somewhere that served up a decent omelette and coffee. And that would cost money. How could a man who wasn't earning anything afford anything?

Still, a new day was dawning. He slipped into the chill air, breathed deeply, and eyed the Union Pacific station and sidings where a long string of boxcars stood quietly. But even then, there were work crews wrestling large objects, casks and barrels, out of a boxcar and onto a waiting, high-sided freight wagon while six yoke of oxen lolled in their harness. He watched the men a moment. Some were boys, some were desperate, shaky old men, who looked like they were town drunks. Down a way there were more freighters with teamsters hard at work, loading giant crates and rolled up rugs, and iron woodstoves. He counted twenty-two men hard at work in the earliest dawn light, some of them sweating even in the chill. Once in a while one of those heavy crates or barrels would crash hard into a freight wagon, shattering the dawn peace.

He watched teamsters whip the oxen dragging one loaded wagon and it rumbled away from the rails and down the chalky street, stirring up dust from its thick iron-rimmed wagon wheels. The teamsters turned the oxen north, and the rumbling freighter slowly vanished from view. He knew where it was headed: the new gold fields of the Black Hills. That's where wealth could be torn out of the earth by anyone smart enough to find it.

Chapter Four

Every freight wagon along the track had a black F in a diamond painted on its side. These were Fairweather Foley's wagons, then. He seemed to have a monopoly on freighting, or close to it. There were twelve boxcars on the siding, laden with goods destined for the goldfields and ranches of the whole area.

Jay examined the hive of toiling workers as they rolled casks and dragged heavy crates. Chumps, the whole lot. Drones, working for around a dollar for a long day's labor, wrecking their bodies, injuring themselves. Foley's slaves. That's what they were. Slaves. He owned dozens of them. There wasn't much difference between wage labor and slavery. They barely put food in a man's belly or clothing on his back. Chumps, the whole lot. Jay couldn't imagine wasting a whole life hauling barrels and crates.

It was time for breakfast, so he tried a chow parlor called The Beanery made out of an abandoned passenger car, with a counter running the entire length, and stools for about twenty customers. Flapjacks were the thing there; two cooks and two waiters, working feverishly to cook the cakes and sausages, make and pour coffee, and keep restless customers content. Jay ordered the cakes and sausages and watched the waiters and cooks toil away. Chumps every one. Maybe they were not lifting and tugging and sweating, but they were dancing to a different tune, the demands of a lot of customers. He couldn't imagine dishing out hash to people for a living. That would be worse than rolling barrels.

He finished his barely edible flapjacks and left the chump a dime tip out of pity. The man was doomed. Cheyenne was beginning a bright summer day. He saw shopkeepers in white aprons sweeping the boardwalk in front of their businesses. A milliner in a smock was washing the small windows of her store. A wagon loaded with cordwood was parked next to Ma's Eats, and two knuckleheads were dumping stove wood into a bin. Chumps all, willfully squandering their miserable lives on nothing but empty toil. It didn't look good for the human race when drab daily toil was all people could hope from life.

The front doors of most of the shops were opened wide now, the doors propped open with a rock. Within, bored clerks adjusted the stock on shelves or stared at the door, waiting for the first customer. More chumps. What had they come West for? To grind out their lives for pennies each day?

Off a way, a sweating blacksmith was pumping his bellows, heating up his coal-fed fire, turning a horseshoe red. Then he grasped the shoe with tongs, set it on an anvil, and hammered it until it was narrower. Then he doused it in a barrel of filthy water, making the water hiss, boil, and turn to steam. Nearby, a closely tethered draft horse yawned. When the shoe was cooled enough to handle, the smith lifted a rear leg and began tacking the shoe to the filed down hoof, working in a backbreaking crouch. Mean work. The man was scarred from countless injuries, had grimy hands, and wore a sour expression. Another chump, earning a few nickels for miserable work. Why would any sane man do it?

There was a purpose in this close examination of Cheyenne, the town where his father had sent him to make his own way. There was nothing here that made life worthwhile. So far, the only man he'd encountered who had made something of life in this outpost of civilization was Fairweather Foley, who managed to hire many of the dunderheads and pay them a pittance.

There were, of course, other ways of life that Jay had not examined. Ranching was the main one. A man might make a living at it if one was able to endure the utter boredom of the open country, with nothing entertaining about the grasses and creeks and trees and weather. One might, he supposed, graze cattle on public land and harvest the increase. It seemed a business that didn't require much capital; enough to buy some cows and stuff them onto public lands, and then sit back and wait. But cows didn't grow very fast; certainly not fast enough to put a man on Easy Street. Of course there would be moments the rancher would require some slave labor of his own, branding and rounding up his animals, but mostly he could sit in his ranch house and do nothing. At least that was how Jay imagined it.

By noon, Jay had toured the whole of Cheyenne, and had gazed at every street, every home, every business, every road leading into the great West. It was the ugliest place he'd ever seen. And it lacked women. He decided that women had more sense than to come to a desolate place like Cheyenne.

He found the Cheyenne Overland Stage office, actually a small counter in a freight warehouse, and approached a clerk, a skinny, distraught sort with a bobbing adam's apple.

"What's the price of a ride to the gold strike?" he asked.

"Thirty-seven seated, twenty-five on the roof, sir. One way, of course."

"What's the city?"

"There's none, sir. Just some camps. Gold's everywhere they put in a shovel."

"A hotel, or boardinghouse?"

"You'll want a tent and bedroll, my friend."

"What if I choose to buy it there?"

The clerk smiled. "Take your chances, sir. There's plenty of tent stores, tent cities in every gulch. Deadwood gulch, that's the one now. But a proper fellow would ship a tent, bedroll, kitchen, chow, and pickaxe and shovel and gold pan ahead."

"No city? No buildings?"

"Oh, there's a few going up. Log, with canvas roofs, selling goods even while the walls are rising and the roof's getting stretched."

"Surely there must be a place for the finance men, the clerks and recorders."

"A year ago, sir, General Custer was looking around there; now it's swarming with prospectors. And the Sioux, they're a bit upset. In fact, it's our rule that every man on every coach be armed and ready. There's been a dozen ambushes, and they're getting worse and worse. We've got coaches coming back with holes in them."

"Indians?"

"Mad as hornets. That's their ground. Treaty ground, but there's no stopping a rush. Big bunches of Indians are stopping coaches, stealing cattle and anything else. Mostly not killing anyone— yet."

"Maybe it's safer with the freighters?"

"They're carrying scatter guns and rifles, my friend. No, there's two men with each wagon, and spread out, and the Sioux know it. The company's looking for more men to go with the freight."

"What does that pay?"

"Free passage to the goldfields including a man's stuff."

"But no ride?"

The clerk stared at Jay as if he were daft.

"I'll wait," Jay said, adding a smile.

Heading for the goldfields wasn't quite what he had anticipated. But those towns would rise fast; maybe he'd be able to rent good quarters up there soon, and begin speculating in gold claims.

But he knew somehow that wouldn't happen. And just getting there and equipping himself would gouge deeply into his purse. He stared at the little railroad town, bustling now with farm wagons, freight outfits, and people on saddle horses. It all seemed as alien to him as the moon. And sickening, in a way. His cash was bleeding away; it wouldn't last anywhere near the time he needed.

But he was not a pessimist by nature. He was a sunny man, looking at sunshine, and he knew suddenly how to get ahead. He was the son of Tecumseh Warren; that was enough. Mention that name to anyone and it won instant recognition, if not respect. His father's reputation was all he would ever need. Mention his father, mention who he was, and there would be opportunities. Hadn't Fairweather Foley recognized the name at once last evening? Of course he had. He might not be a Rockefeller or an Astor or a Vanderbilt or a Morgan, but his father was right up there, and the name of Warren would pave the way.

He decided to find Foley and take advantage of

who he was. That took some doing. Foley didn't seem to have an office anywhere. He finally discovered that Foley's office was a cubicle in a corner of Foley's warehouse, and the sole clerk guarding the place didn't know where Foley was at that moment.

"Out somewhere," the clerk said.

"Is this his only headquarters?"

"Headquarters? This isn't the army, sir."

"He runs many businesses, doesn't he?"

"More than I can keep track of, sir. Do you care to leave a message?"

"Where can I find him?"

"Wagon yard, most likely."

Jay hurried off to a vast and unkempt yard that held several freighters, two stagecoaches, some wagons, some livestock in pens, and a shop of some sort, apparently used to repair the wagons.

"I'm looking for Mr. Foley," Jay said to a teamster.

The man pointed.

Legs in dungarees projected from under a massive freight wagon. It was Foley, all right, but he wasn't wearing a cream linen suit; he was dressed the way any common man might dress. That faintly disappointed Jay. Foley should hire help, not demean himself.

Eventually the man crawled out from under the freight wagon, wiped his hands, and spotted Jay.

"Busted axle," he said. He motioned to a

mechanic, who began blocking up the wagon to pull the wheels off.

"Have you a minute, sir?"

"I always have a minute."

"We met last evening. I'm Jay Warren. My father is Tecumseh Warren. I'm sure you're familiar with him. A shipping company. I'd like to talk to you about a suitable position."

"Suitable position?"

"Yes sir, based on what my family and I might contribute to your enterprise."

"What's suitable, young man?"

"I'm sure you have administrative or executive tasks that need doing."

Foley stared, his hard gaze taking in everything there was to know about Jay Warren.

"I know Tecumseh Warren. Did he send you?"

"He suggested I come here, sir. Maybe he had you in mind."

"Explain to me what you mean, young man. He suggested what?"

"He, ah, believes that a man ought to acquire some experience; some time prepping for administrative duties."

"Is that what he said?"

"Not exactly, sir, he didn't put it that way."

"Then what did he say? And why are you here?"

Jay flashed his brightest smile. "Oh, he thought the West would be a good place."

"Is that why he sent you to me?"

"Well, sir, it's hard to explain. But yes, he bought me a ticket and included some funds, and I'm sure he wanted me to represent the Warren family in the West."

"Is that what he said, now?"

Jay twirled his straw boater in his hands a moment. "Well, sir, he said that he believes that all men should make their own way, and not depend on family . . ."

"Ah! Now that sounds like Tecumseh Warren. I thought he was going soft."

"Yes, sir, that's my father."

"So you want a job, I take it?"

"Yes, sir. A position."

"Well, you're not worth much. You don't know a thing. But I'll start you as a teamster. I'll apprentice you to some of my best men. You'll load and unload. You'll feed, water and handle oxen. You'll drive my freight wagons. The pay's good, sixty a month and found. I need men, and it's yours, my boy."

"Ah, Mr. Foley, I'll think about it. I'm examining my options, and weighing offers. It may take a few days before I've discussed a position with other concerns, but if yours is the right one for me, sir, then I'll let you know. I should have an answer in a few days."

Foley had an odd, quirky fire in his eyes.

Chapter Five

An ad in the Cheyenne weekly paper brightened Jay's morning. Right there, in the *Weekly Eagle*, was an announcement. The town's first school district was being formed. A grade school teacher was needed. Apply to the chairman of the school board, Wilbur Lockwood.

Well, it was worth talking to the man. Jay finished his coffee at the Beanery, paid up, and headed for a meeting with Lockwood, who was a coal and stove wood merchant. Of course, Jay was overqualified, Harvard degree and all, but the work need not be permanent. It would give him something to subsist on while he looked for a suitable executive position.

Lockwood led him to an office cubicle at the back of his wood yard, and looked the young man over.

"All right, tell me what you'd bring to the position," the man said.

"Well, sir, I have a good education, a degree from Harvard."

"Have you taught before?"

"No, sir. Actually, I'm interested in administration. I would be interested in overseeing the school, a principal or headmaster."

"I'm afraid, sir, you'd be teaching reading,

writing, and arithmetic, to a variety of students in a single room. You'd be working from McGuffey Readers at various grade levels, with other texts the board will select. There'll be about thirty, as far as we can gauge, of all ages ranging to high school levels. You'll mostly be involved in individual instruction; there's no standardized level of education among these children. Are you up to it?"

"Well, sir, that depends on circumstances."

"I see. The pay is forty a month, ten months a year, plus lodging in the teacherage we're acquiring. You'd have custodial duties as well, including maintaining the schoolroom, liming the privy, keeping a supply of stove wood on hand, and so on. You'd maintain regular hours, eight to five, and tutor those who require it after regular class has ended."

"Forty a month?"

"Plus the residence."

"I was more interested in administration, sir. A man with my background, well, this doesn't seem to be an adequate opportunity to employ my skills."

Lockwood stared. "I see," he said. "Well, we'll keep on looking, Mr. Harvard."

Jay Warren found himself in the bright sunlight once again, its harsh glare wounding his eyes. There'd be no point in wrestling nouns and verbs into thick skulls for less money a month than Jay

Warren intended to spend in a day once he was established.

The moment he was back on the streets, the tension returned. All he could think of was the way his cash was dribbling away, and he was no further on the way to a suitable income than ever. He raged at his father, who'd done this thing to him. Not for as long as Jay lived would he forgive his rotten old man. The streets of Cheyenne seemed alien; the world was indifferent to Jay. Did no one care? Where could he find a friend? There were no friends here in this frontier version of hell. There wasn't a man in town he'd be pleased to call a friend.

Back east, things would be different. Jay might lunch with a friend; the friend might put in a good word; Jay would have a comfortable position with a good salary and a very light load and few responsibilities to burden him. There would be time for golf and whist and tennis and tea. He wouldn't need to grub for money like some immigrant off the boat. That's what friends were for. One favor in exchange for another.

The telegraph office was in the railroad station. He would wire his father:

TECUMSEH WARREN
WARREN SHIPPING, NYC.
LOOKING HARD. FOUND NOTHING.
NEED MORE TIME. NEED MONTH
MONEY. REPAY WHEN HIRED. T

47

Yes, that would be it. Let his father know. Help would come.

He found the telegraph office, manned by a frail old clerk with a black sleeve garter and a black cuff-protector. Jay penciled the message onto pulpy yellow paper and handed it to the operator, who eyed it through wire-rimmed spectacles.

"Ninety seven letters, ten seventy, then."

"Dollars? For that?"

The telegrapher nodded. "That's it, fella. Send it?"

Jay dug into his purse and drew a ten dollar greenback and a single. He had no idea telegraphing his old man would cost so much. Another hole in his bankroll.

The clerk made change, sat down at the brass telegraph instrument, and began tapping out the message with a gentle but fast flick of his fingers. Jay immediately felt better. The message was on its way, by modern magic, and soon help would be on its way. His father knew he was looking. That was the main thing. If he kept on looking, he would fulfill his father's peculiar wishes. Tecumseh would understand that and help him along the path.

He stepped back into a hard, sun-beaten day, wondering what to do until he got more cash. The town was busy now. There were crews unloading boxcars for Foley. There was a string of new cars, painted barn red, waiting to disgorge their goods.

Cheyenne was plainly a great transfer point on the Union Pacific.

To the east of town were large livestock pens, and these were teeming with brown and white cattle that would soon ship east to slaughterhouses in Chicago. He drifted that way, intent on seeing how the other half lived. A rank odor rose from the pens, where heat baked the runty looking cattle being shipped for slaughter. Drovers were lounging around, doing a lot of nothing, plainly waiting for something. They shaded their coppery faces under big sombreros, as sweat-stained as their grimy shirts. They all wore filthy boots and battered britches of jean cloth. Mustaches were the big thing among them. Enormous fields of hair drooped from their upper lip, cheeks, and chin. Jay had never seen such a baroque bunch of mortals as these.

After a bit a stubby yard engine, belching smoke and steam, pushed six slat-sided cars into place next to the pens, with the first car's doors aligned with a ramp in the pens. With that, the drovers stirred to life, and soon were whipping and jabbing the bawling beeves into the cars. The wild-eyed animals seemed to know they were doomed, and blatted their terror.

"Nice looking cattle," Jay said to an older man who was watching. The man was cleaner, had a combed beard, and probably owned the buckboard parked nearby.

"They'll all be twenty pounds lighter in Chicago," the man said. "Shipping loss."

"That's where they're weighed?"

"They sure ain't weighed here, my friend."

"So you and your crew'll load and then ride out to your place?"

"Nope, the crew goes with 'em. Those critters got to be fed and watered."

"Where do your men stay?"

"In the cars. Keeps 'em warm at night, but likely full of cow pies."

"How do they get back?"

"Same way. Railroad lets 'em. It's all part of doing business."

"In the same clothing?"

"Naw, they buy fresh in Chicago, hire a bath and shave and some witch hazel, spend their last nickel on drink and dames, and then ride back on clean straw whiles they sober up."

"Ah, what do they earn? If you don't mind my asking."

The old fellow eyed Jay. "Forty and found."

"I guess I'm not quite up on the terminology."

"Forty a month plus room and board. They get all the beef they can eat."

"That's enough to live on?"

"That's enough for their monthly blowout here."

"Who do you hire?"

"All sorts. Never have enough for what needs doing, but there's slack seasons too, when I keep just a few. Most of them just beg chow all winter long."

"And they're happy with that?"

"Don't know and don't care. Take it or leave it. I get new ones all the time."

"But what of their future?"

"Cow hands don't got a future. They've only got the now."

"Don't they save for a rainy day?"

"There ain't any rainy days for a cowboy. He just quits and vanishes. Don't know where."

"You know these fellows, loading up the cars?"

"First names mostly. They come and go."

"I imagine you've got a foreman or two, been around a while."

"Foremen don't last any longer than the rest, my friend."

"Maybe you need a permanent foreman, who'd look after all this, and administer the business. There's a lot of things to look after, I suppose."

"Already got one. Me."

"Other ranchers do the same?"

"Don't rightly know, fella. I do it my way, the next one does it his way. I hear some have foremen, been around the horn a few times, and the owners can go to California for the winter if they like. Me, I'll go to Denver and call it a holiday."

"You interested in doing that?"

"Hell no. California's the worst place on the planet. Warm all the time."

They watched a couple of drovers rope a wild-eyed beast and drag him into the boxcar by sheer force. Finally they leaped out and slid the door shut and bolted it.

"They make it look easy," the rancher said. "Mostly rank steers like that, it'd take six hands to drag 'em in. Those are old mossyhorns, those two."

"You pay good men more money?"

"Why? There's always more coming along."

The last of the cattle were loaded, and in no time a road locomotive was coupled to the string, and the clattering, bawling, thumping shipment tumbled along the rails eastward. A silence enveloped the rancher and Jay.

"See you at The Stockman," the rancher said. "I got some accounting to do with the rail office. They'll try to screw me any way they can. That's shipping outfits for you."

So the man was one of those listening to Jay that first night.

The train rattled east, its whistle shrill on the horizon, and then vanished, save for a plume of white smoke far away. Six cowboys and a lot of cattle, rattling across the prairie day and night. He felt oddly lonely, and couldn't say why. The rancher was the first man to talk to him like a friend. He might be another western rube, but at least he was halfway friendly.

Well, The Stockman, then. Loading had eaten up

much of the afternoon. He drifted to his hot, close hotel, laved his sticky flesh, and then headed for the spacious confines of the best saloon in Cheyenne, where a man might get to know the most influential people in the Territory.

It was far from suppertime, far from evening. But he had nothing better to do, so he headed for the place, found it cool and inviting, and its dark confines cut the glare of the summer day. The mahogany bar glowed under the single kerosene lamp.

There were only two at the bar, and no players at the gaming tables.

"You got some good whiskey?"

The aproned barman eyed him, pulled a bottle of Old Orchard from under the bar.

"This do you?"

"Pour one, with some cold water. Or ice if you have it."

"That's a dollar, friend."

"A dollar!"

"Comes a long way, friend."

Jay paid. He had gone through another hundred. The clock was ticking faster and faster and faster. But of course, by tomorrow there should be a money draft at the telegraph station, so he wouldn't let himself worry.

He drank the bourbon and tried another. The rancher must have decided on a nap. And no one else was around. The other two patrons kept to themselves. The bourbon felt just fine. So Jay had a third, and waited for some company. Maybe he'd tell them he was Jay Tecumseh Warren this time, and watch their faces.

The consumptive gambler arrived, along with his case keeper, and opened shop at the back of the saloon, mindlessly shuffling cards while waiting for some business.

Jay eyed the man, suddenly seeing a chance.

Chapter Six

Jay eyed the gambler, who looked bored, mind-lessly cutting and shuffling and manipulating the deck. A single lamp lit the rear of the saloon, shedding yellow light on the slicked black hair of the tinhorn. The man coughed, spitting up more pink pieces of lung, while the case keeper sat on his little stool, staring at the empty saloon.

Jay took his whiskey with him, and sat down.

"Little game?" the deal asked.

"Learning session," Jay said. "Empty place. Good time for me to pick up some tips."

"Ah, learning. Not much to learn, my friend. The house has an edge when both cards are the same. It's all simple mathematics."

"If the odds are so poor, why do you run a game?"

"Popular game. Get more trade. Now roulette, that pays better for the house. With the green zero, there are thirty-seven pockets on the wheel, but the house pays all bets on a thirty-six basis. That's the edge, one-thirty-seventh, right? But roulette doesn't get the play. Thick-skulled cowboys don't get it. They don't get poker. They don't get Monte. But they get Faro. So I deal Faro."

"All right, I'll buy in."

"You'll want dime chips. Learn the whole

shebang with cheap chips. How many? Fifty? Five bucks?"

"Sure," Jay said, finding some two-dollar green-backs and a single in his purse.

The dealer shoved fifty blue chips at Jay, and stuffed the deck into the spring-loaded case, with the cards facing up and the top card visible. The deck was held in place by a narrow rim. The dealer pulled the top card, the soda, and slid it into his discard pile. It was a seven. The case keeper slid a bead along a wire that accounted for the sevens.

Jay dropped a chip on the king. Nothing happened. The loser was a four, the winner an eight. The case keeper kept track. The game was obviously so dull that it took willpower just to sit there and play.

Jay yawned and played. The deeper into the deck the game went, the more obvious were the choices, because every played card was recorded on that contraption. He won, lost, won, tried some different bets, such as a chip on the win bar pasted at the top of the layout. The yawning dealer showed him how to place a chip between cards on the layout to bet on both, and how to copper a bet. In very little time, Jay had the game down, and found himself a dollar and seventy cents ahead, so he cashed in. In a dull twenty minutes he had gotten ahead a little. And it was easy. The gambler was right. Faro was a game for idiots.

"Say, where do you buy the layout?" he asked.

"You want to deal, do you? Forget it, sonny. You're just buying trouble."

"No, I really want to know. What does the Faro box and layout and cards and that thing with the beads cost? And how much of a bank do you need?"

The dealer sucked a cheroot. "Competing with me, are you?"

"Lots of places to set up a game," Jay said.

"Not many where players have money in their britches, boy. Like here. You just quit thinking you'll run a game. You were born in the wrong slot."

The dealer had collected the cards, and now was expertly riffling them. "Fella, sooner or later someone's gonna break your bank. You got enough?"

"I'll get enough," Jay said.

"Kansas City," the dealer said. "That's where."

"What's the company? How much?"

But the dealer was grinning, sucking his weed, and coughing.

No one approached the table. The bar was bustling, but the gambler had no action. Jay eyed him, eyed his pink-flecked kerchief, and thought he knew why. Other dealers no doubt were making piles of cash, just by sitting quietly through a pleasant evening.

Jay plunged through the double doors into a

lavender evening, with a dry breeze cleaning Cheyenne of its smoke and stench. The night was just beginning, and bored saddle horses lined the hitch rails in front of every saloon. This plainly would be a night with more action than the last one. He strolled down the boardwalk, peering into each saloon, looking for ones that had gaming tables in them. There were plenty. And some of them had lively crowds of cowboys collected around them, sometimes whooping and shouting. Games of chance seemed a lot more popular in these places than in The Stockman.

Some of the games were mobbed; it was all the dealer and case keeper could do to handle the chips heaped across the layout. The case keeper not only kept tabs on what had been played, but kept an eye out for cheats, men trying to slide losing bets away in the hubbub, or slip a winning one in while the dealer was paying someone else. Jay hadn't thought of that, and was glad to see how it worked.

One of the saloons catered to railroad men, while several others catered to ranch hands, and there were others Jay wasn't sure about; maybe teamsters or small-time store owners. There were games in most of them, but none had roulette. He didn't see a wheel in Cheyenne. One place was clearly the favorite of poker players, who crowded silently around tables where a dealer presided. Jay wondered if the saloons rented the table space or took a cut of the winnings. Probably rented the space. It'd be too easy to cheat the barmen.

He became a silent spectator, watching the games. Some of the Faro cases had a tiger enameled on the side; others used cards with tigers printed on the backs. Some of the layouts were new and bright, with good, walnut case boxes; others were battered, and their owners looked worn. The clean layouts sure added to the game; they made their dealers look substantial.

There were too many unwashed bodies in those places for Jay's taste, so he headed into the velvet night. There was one place he hadn't visited, at the far end of saloon row, so he wandered that way, soon finding himself in a very quiet saloon with solid furnishings and a good brass rail along the bar.

He bought a bourbon from the quiet barkeep, took his tumbler with him and headed for the Faro table. There was no case keeper there; just a skinny youth not much older than Jay, who stared morosely at the green baize layout. The dealer eyed Jay without the slightest welcome, which puzzled Jay.

"You mind if I ask a few questions?" Jay said.

"You want to play? Nickle limit."

"No, I was wondering where to buy a layout like this."

"This? A. J. White, in Kansas City."

"What's one cost?"

"You want to buy a layout? I'll sell mine. I'm bailing out."

"I'm not one to dicker. Name your best, final price, and tell me what I get."

"A hundred fifty. You get the layout, six decks, the case box, chips, tokens, coppers, the tally—that's to keep track."

"What do you pay to run a table here?"

"Twenty a month. That's how it is along the row."

"So for a hundred seventy I'm in business?"

"You got a bank?"

Jay nodded. He had something over three hundred left. A hundred-fifty for a bank.

"How come you're quitting?" Jay asked.

"Busted. Cleaned out. The barman, Charley, won't give me credit."

"What do you know that I don't know?" Jay asked.

"I'm tired. Buy or not. I'm folding up."

Jay stared at the layout. It was good, clean, costly, solid. "Hundred forty?" he said softly.

"How you gonna pay me?"

"I'll be back in a few minutes. I'll want a bill of sale listing every item. And say in writing there's no lien against this outfit and you're selling free and clear."

"Sure," the dealer said. "It's all yours, pal."

He kept his big bills in a secret place slit into the lining of his suitcase, collected all three bills, and hurried into the night. This was the break he'd wanted, the fast money he ached for. When he returned, the dealer had the layout all folded up in a carrying case.

"No, I'll play here, at least for a while," he said.

"Deal with the barman, then."

It didn't take long. The dealer got the hundred forty; the barman twenty; Jay got the set-up and a signed receipt executed by Lucky Bob Lilly. The young dealer grinned, pocketed his big bonanza, tipped a hat to the barman.

"I'm off for Arizona," he said. And he was out the door, into the night.

"You in business tonight?" the barman asked.

"I'll set up and look this outfit over," he said.

Jay spread the green baize, stacked the chips and coppers and tokens that indicated what any color of chip was worth in play, set up the walnut box, shuffled a deck of cards, and slid the deck face-up in the spring-loaded box. He drew the soda, an ace, and set it in the loser pile—actually his winning pile, but the players' losing pile—and played through a game, first placing bets on the board, then drawing the paired cards, then paying off bets, while keeping cases as well. It took a little getting into, sort of like working a rhythm, but before long he'd played a deck, pulling the last card, the hock, and setting it in the loser heap. That went pretty well, he thought. A cowboy wandered up.

"What's your limits?" he asked.

"Come back in a while," Jay said. "I'll open a game after I get myself settled in."

What slowed him most was what he could manage with such a small bank. He could pay out a hundred fifty fast if luck ran against him. So he shuffled, and thought, and figured that a real low-level game might be the thing. Dollar tops, ten cents a chip. He could lose a pile of dollars and not come close to busting the bank. But mostly it'd be ten-cent play, even odds, nothing very heavy.

"Where's Lucky Bob?" a burly man asked.

"On his way to Arizona."

"I have his marker for fifty; you got the game, you pay."

"Sorry, that's his debt, not mine."

"Punk, I'm making it yours."

"He just left! Go find him. He's got cash. I just paid him."

"He's gone, pal, and you're it."

The big man loomed over Jay, unruly gray hair jamming in all directions, meatball fists clenching.

"Mister, go get him. I don't owe you a thing."

"That's what you say, punk. Not what I say. That layout'll do."

He reached for green baize, sent chips flying, snatched the Faro box and the several unopened decks of red cards.

"Cut that out, you idiot!"

The big galoot just grinned. Several customers gathered, whistling and grinning.

Jay was watching his hundred fifty vanish, and made a quick decision.

"Fifty, give me the marker."

"I thought you'd see daylight," the man said. "Lay the cash right there, and you'll get the paper."

Aching, Jay spread out the bills, two twenties and some small greenbacks, while the crowd whistled. The barkeep was enjoying the show.

The big man pocketed the bills, crumpled up the marker, and dropped it on the table. Moments later he was out the door and into the night.

The crowd whistled. Jay quietly collected the layout and spread it on the table, arranged the chips and cards, collected the copper tokens that were on the wooden floor, stacked the decks neatly, and set up the case-keeping abacus. His heart was pounding. He hoped no one saw it. He eyed the rubes, who were still grinning, and quietly made his debut.

"The game opens in a minute or two, ten cent minimum, one dollar maximum. Step right up and try your luck. I'm Lucky Jay, new in your fine city of Cheyenne, ready to run a good, fast, clean game of Faro, and may you all be lucky." he said.

No one moved. And then a skinny cowboy, his hat pushed way back, stepped up.

"Let her rip," the cowboy said.

Chapter Seven

The rustics crowded around the table, rough, grinning, dim-witted, and coarse. They wanted to get into the game. The stakes were low, and they could afford it. Swiftly, Jay set up six players with chips; that's as many as he could handle. Most bought twenty chips for two dollars, so Jay was, for the moment, flush with cash. But others crowded in, and began laying coins, and even dollar bills, on numbers, some reaching over to the tokens to copper their bets.

An odd, grinning excitement gripped them all. They were waiting for something beyond Jay's fathoming. He was going to have to keep cases himself, but he understood the contraption, and knew how to slide the beads at the conclusion of each play. A dozen ruffians crowded the table, and a dozen more were watching, most of them with tumblers of whiskey in hand.

"All right then," Jay said, as he drew the soda card.

He drew the first play from the box, a nine, the loser, and a second card, a five, the winner, and set about sliding the beads. There had been three chips and a quarter on the nine, which were now his, but he swore one chip and the quarter had vanished in the moment he was keeping the cases.

And somehow, in the confusion, the winning chips on the five had multiplied. There had been three; now there were two quarters and a fourth chip.

"Hey!" he cried. He slid the losers into his own pile, and eyed the winners.

"Pay up, tinhorn," someone yelled.

Jay decided not to start a fight, but to watch sharply for the sort of skullduggery that was plain here. So he slid out some quarters and chips.

Hands reached out in all directions, stacking chips on various numbers, coppering bets, stuffing dollars and coins onto numbers, and shifting chips from one number to another. It was all happening so chaotically that Jay couldn't keep track of it all. But then he pulled the next pair, a queen loser, a king winner, and this time didn't adjust the cases. Instead, he started to pull in the chips and cash he, the dealer, won and the players lost, but somehow half the pile on the queen had vanished in the confusion, and some of the chips on the king hadn't been there moments before.

They were cheating. They were using the jammed-in crowd, with hands snaking out from every direction to shift chips and cash around, to euchre him out of everything. He decided not to pay out a chip or a coin. He quietly adjusted the cases, running the beads for the king and queen, and waited.

"Hey, tinhorn, pay up," one yelled.

"No one gets a chip. Not until this stops," he said.

"You accusing us of cheating?" one burly lout yelled.

Jay knew he was on dangerous turf. "I will pay in a moment. If I see any hands on this table during or after I draw cards, no one gets paid. Am I clear?"

"You cheating us, tinhorn?"

"I'll pay the last draw, and then follow the rules."

He carefully collected the loser chips and cash, which had dwindled, and paid out the winner chips on the king, one chip for one, one coin for one. Even odds. He had lost a couple of dollars to cheats that time, but now there were rules in place, and he'd weather this.

"All right, put 'em down," he said.

Once again, the players pushed stacks of chips around, put chips in between numbers to play them both, elaborately coppered bets, until the whole layout groaned with chips and cash and exotic bets. Jay eyed the table.

"All right, I'll draw. Not a hand on the table, or all bets are off. I'll say when you can collect your winnings or move chips."

He pulled a two, loser, and a six, winner.

But no one heeded his warnings. A dozen hands slithered across the table, cash vanished, chips got moved, chips wagered on two numbers ended up on one.

"All bets are off," Jay said. "You've been warned."

"You calling us cheats, tinhorn?" the burly one asked.

"All bets are off. I'll draw again, same rules."

"Hey," yelled one, "I got six chips on the king, and you're going to cover my bet right now."

"Where'd those six come from, sir? They weren't there a moment ago."

"So you're calling me a cheat, are you? You want to step outside and see if I'm a cheat, do you?"

Jay decided to hold his ground. "Where'd those chips come from?"

"You crook, you lying, cheating tinhorn, I've had it with you," the tough said. He reached across the table, scooped up Jay's uncounted change heaped before him, and pocketed the whole handful.

"Crook!" yelled someone else. He yanked the green baize layout and sent everything flying. The Faro box crashed to the floor, cards flew, chips sailed, copper tokens thudded, and unopened red decks dropped. And so did Jay's money pouch, which contained his game funds. Someone grabbed it and the pouch vanished into the mob.

"Hey!" Jay yelled.

"Damned crooked tinhorn," someone yelled back.

They were laughing. They were sipping amber fluids from their tumblers. The barkeep was grinning. They ambled to the bar, enjoying themselves, leaving Jay with his debris. The floor was a sea of chips.

"Who's got my purse? Give me my purse," Jay said, but the black sack was nowhere in sight, and whoever had it wasn't even out the door with it.

It was gone. With most of what was left from his father.

He stared at his ruined table, picked up the layout from the floor and folded it, slowly got his chips stacked and stowed away, found whatever coppers he could find in the dull light, got the cards together, picked up the box, scratched now from the fall, and even found some coins in the gloomy corners that the mob had missed. When he got it all together, his forlorn Faro outfit, now missing a few cards and chips, he stared at his own ruin. The ruffians had cleaned him out. He dug into his pants and found a few singles and some coins—all that now stood between Jay Tecumseh Warren and starvation.

He hated this place, rougher than the others on saloon row, full of rotten people without a care for any virtue. A flash of rage filled him. He'd like to shoot the whole lot. But what lay within him, heavy as granite, was the awareness that he had come to the end of everything. He was all but broke. He had nothing, and nowhere to go.

That crushed him so much he could barely stand. At the bar, the toughs were slyly watching, enjoying themselves, studying their drinks but knowing Jay's every move. Jay collected his gear, most of which fit into a shabby carrying case, and headed into the night.

The street was black. He could see no stars or moon. There was no sky, only a mysterious ceiling above him that choked off life and hope. He headed for his hotel room, suddenly aware that a week's rent would be due in two days. He wasn't sure what he had; a few crumpled singles, and he was lucky he still had those.

There was no easy living. Not even when mathematics dictated that he should collect some sort of living from a game of chance. Running a game was as hard and dangerous as anything else, and it was no wonder that the gamblers usually had a weapon, a pocket revolver or a spring-loaded knife, and they cultivated an aura of menace, and they hired case keepers who sat on stools and kept a sharp eye on the board, and every hand and finger and arm that snaked across it. Running a Faro game was no snap. He thought of the consumptive dealer he'd met the first night. The man was working because he had to, instead of convalescing somewhere healthy. The man was as desperate as any. He doubted there were many rich gamblers in the saloons of the West.

He reached his hotel, clattered his way to his dank little closet, left his layout there, couldn't stand the imprisoning walls and close air, and headed out as fast as he could. The night was young. Maybe miracles would befall him. Maybe King Midas would share his gold, or a beautiful woman would bestow her favors on him.

Instead, he found an empty street, save for a few saddle horses still tied to hitch rails. Light spilled from a few saloon doors, open now, but closed against weather most months.

He headed for the railroad station. It was dark now. The telegrapher was gone. Nothing had come of Jay's wire to his father, seeking funds, and Jay knew nothing would be sent him. It was fate. His father had thrown him to the wolves, and thought he was doing something good. All the good it did was to turn him into a bank robber. He couldn't think of any other way to survive. At least any way that escaped dull, grinding toil day in and day out. Which is what he feared most. Not the ache of his muscles, but the ordinariness of it. He'd just be another of the world's anonymous drudges.

The station was open, even if dark, and had some pine pews for passengers. Nothing like the finished oak waiting room seats back east. He settled in one, in utter quietness, peering through grim windows, watching the bleak sky, with cloud curtains that now and then parted, revealing sparkling stars and infinities.

He thought of his burly father and pale mother and the great brick pile in Hartford where he had lived in comfort. All gone now. He felt searing loss and loneliness. If only his parents had had several children, and not just himself, his father's attentions would have been divided and Jay's exile wouldn't have happened.

He heard a clatter outside, and wandered out of the station, looking for whatever was to be seen. There, on the siding, a crew of teamsters was pulling crates out of a boxcar and dragging the heavy stuff into a freight wagon, by the wan light of a single coal oil lamp resting on the ground near the freight wagon. A crew of three men, no doubt Foley's, was emptying the car even in the deep of the evening. Jay drifted closer and saw the familiar F Diamond painted on the wagon wall.

What manner of goods were so important to someone that Foley put teamsters to work in the middle of the night? It took days to get to the goldfields; why bother trying to save a few hours?

"What have you there?" Jay asked.

"Rock crushing machinery," a weary teamster replied.

"Why now?"

"That's how bad they want it up yonder."

"Your boss paying you extra for night work?"

The teamster stared, as if Jay was daft. "Why would he do that? Work's work. I've got to get busy here," he said, as the two inside the boxcar dragged another carton to the door and slid it onto the ramp. There were no loading docks in Cheyenne, it seemed.

Jay drifted back to the station, annoyed at Foley for treating his men badly. No sooner had he settled in the quiet dark than he caught the wail of a whistle far to the west, and knew a train was approaching. The train's whistle sounded again, lonely in the night, and about then the station-master arrived, swiftly lit a lamp at the ticket window, and another at the door. He paid no attention to Jay. No sooner was the station lit than Jay heard the chuff of the locomotive, and after another minute, a four-car Union Pacific passenger train rolled to a stop, dim light spilling from various coach windows. The engine hissed steam, and quieted, except for the thumping of the escape valves.

A blue-clad conductor, barely visible, opened a coach door, settled a step stool, and helped a man to the gravel of the station platform. The stationmaster himself loaded several bags and parcels from the express car behind the engine, settling them on a cart, even as the car's door slid closed.

The train chuffed away, headed for Omaha, Chicago, and points east, but Jay did not have a ticket home.

Chapter Eight

A one-week clock ticked away in the Beanery, its winding key resting on the shelf beside the clock. Jay watched the minute hand creep along as he ate breakfast. When the hands reached noon, he could manage lunch, and when the hands reached six, he could still afford a bite, if he chose the cheapest item, a bowl of soup. After that, the clock would tick toward midnight. And beyond midnight, there was no time left for him. In the morning, he would owe another week's rent, and couldn't pay it. He would want another breakfast and couldn't buy it. And he would soon be hungry, and have no place of shelter, and no future.

He squandered the morning at the Union Pacific station, watching its clock wind slowly toward noon. He decided to forgo lunch, so he would have something for breakfast the doomed next day. He watched the trains come and go, people drift into the station, board westbounds, or board eastbounds, or just loiter, as he was doing. Stations were a place to see the world. By early afternoon he overcame his dread, and headed for the wagon yard of Fairweather Foley, and found him there, deep in conversation with teamsters. They were looking at some oxen that seemed poorly.

Foley eyed him. "You, is it?"

"You said for me to see you if I wanted a job, sir."

"Teamster job?"

Jay nodded.

"You have experience, of course." He was mocking. "I need good men."

"I'll try to learn, sir."

"That's the first solid thing you've said to me. It's hard work, and dangerous. And I require every man on every wagon to be armed. The Sioux are raising hell, now that the Black Hills are full of miners. You ever shot a gun?"

"I've never even held one in my hand, sir."

"Repeaters. Every man on my wagons has a Henry, or a Spencer, or a Winchester repeater. And knows how to use them. I send the wagons out in threes, two men to a wagon, and that means six men with repeaters have to hold off a raiding party."

Jay had scarcely imagined that teamster work might require fighting the Sioux.

Foley surveyed him. "You'd be an extra, a seventh man going out there. Worthless, but maybe you'll do. Here's the deal. My teamsters swear on bibles that they'll make the round trip, but most every time my outfit reaches the gold-field, one or two desert me. They don't keep their word. Lots of men in the world don't keep their word. You want to give me your word that you'll come back here with the empty wagons, Warren? Want to swear it, solemn and true?"

"Yes, sir. I'll return."

"Good. By the time the outfit's ready to come back here, you might be worth something, and maybe replace one or another of the ones that quit me each time. I should add, Warren, that often you pick up travelers going up there, and you band together for safety. But ox teams are slower than most, slower even than walking, so sometimes you may have company, sometimes not."

"I'd welcome the company, sir."

"Pay's good, sixty a month plus feed. I feed you." He eyed Jay carefully. "Not what you're used to, I guess."

"No, sir. But I don't see any way, since I haven't a weapon."

"You don't have clothing, either, or boots."

"No, sir."

Foley studied the sick oxen a moment, and motioned to a teamster, who pried open the mouth of an ox and poured something from a brown bottle into the animal, who licked and spit and drooled.

"That cures 'em or kills 'em," Foley said.

It was dawning on Jay that he knew not a thing at all about this.

Foley eyed him. "Heard you had a little trouble defending your game last night," he said.

Jay marveled that the man knew about it.

"Thing like that, word gets around, boy. Got a lot of people laughing. They shouldn't laugh, robbing you blind."

"They stole everything, almost."

"How much did you pay for the layout?"

"Hundred forty, sir. Dealer wanted hundred fifty."

"You got took. It's nothing but a box, a big piece of green felt, some chips and cards, worth maybe fifty. You want to sell it to me in exchange for I put a good repeater in your hands, a few spare rounds, and maybe a hat to keep yourself from getting fried by the sun?"

Jay nodded, wearily. His spirits were sinking even lower as the afternoon waned.

"All right, you show up at three in the morning at the siding, and load wagons. The men'll show you what to do. Wear old shoes, don't try to break in new. You'll be rolling out at dawn, or close to it. Once you get out of here, it's pleasant going. Oxen don't need much, just keep an eye on things. You'll get paid when you return. If you're no good, you might not get paid at all. Don't take your gear. You got stuff in your room, leave it here, and we'll look after it."

"I'll bring it over, sir."

Foley eyed him directly. "Clear enough?"

"Yes, sir."

"You'll likely do fine, Warren, if you've got something of your pa in you."

Something of his father? The idea startled Jay.

"Three in the morning. There'll be a repeater carbine here for you. Learn how to use it; there's good men to teach you. Aim low. Always aim low, so you hit something."

Foley offered a hand. Jay took it. Foley's was work-hardened and rough.

The clock was still ticking. But Jay Warren, scion of the shipping king, had a job. A job on the lower rung of the lowest ladder in the lowest world of business. A job that might involve fighting for his very life. But a job that paid two dollars a day, and food.

He knew, suddenly, what it really meant: the end of liberty. From now on, he would no longer do what he felt like doing, be what he felt like being. He had been reduced to nothing. He was no better than an ant, doing its predestined tasks.

Foley eyed Jay one long moment, and went back to tending sick oxen.

Yet, in Jay's gloom, there was a tiny thread of brightness: he would eat.

He could think of no way to report at three in the morning except stay up. He remembered his pocket watch, buried in his bag among the dirty underwear, and made sure it was wound up and set. He lay in his hotel bed, waiting, and finally got up, left the skeleton key on the table, and hiked to the railroad station, toting his bag. There, in the quiet dark, he waited for the appointed hour, somehow more comfortable than in his hotel room. When three came, he was ready. He dropped the suitcase in the wagon yard, headed to the siding, found a lit lantern, and reported for work.

"You're the new one? All right, I'm Ike and this is Amos, and we're going to load these three wagons."

"I'm Jay, and I'm new at this."

Both men were wiry and compact, not the burly men Jay had expected. He couldn't see much, not in the light of a single coal-oil lamp.

"What're we loading?"

"Flour, mostly. Beans, oats, barley. These are bags of it, heading for the gold camps."

The wagon had been angled close to the boxcar door, and a ramp of some sort extended across the gap. Jay headed into the boxcar, which was oddly fragrant in a musky way, hefted a bag, felt its staggering weight, and carried it out, dodging Amos, and into the freight wagon, where Ike collected it and carefully settled it in place. Ike was plainly the man to load the wagons evenly.

It didn't take long before Jay was worn and hurting, but there was no stopping. He and Amos alternated trips into the boxcar, each lifting a rough burlap bag, or a smoother cotton one, and staggering out and into the rear of the wagon.

About when Jay thought he couldn't summon any more strength, Ike called a halt.

"We'll break for a bit, kid," he said.

Jay stepped to the clay, feeling night breezes peel away his dampness. The night was bright and clear. A bright half moon shown over the slumbering town.

No one said much; loading heavy sacks didn't invite conversation. The two older men, both bearded, sipped water, using a dipper to drink from a pail, and sat quietly. Jay wondered about the other two wagons, which were nowhere in sight.

Ike, plainly the straw boss here, summoned them back to work, and they were soon wrestling more heavy sacks into the wagon, a task that seemed endless. Somewhere along in there, Jay discovered another freight wagon waiting, with its own crew of two.

Around four, by Jay's reckoning, Ike examined the heavy load, pronounced it well settled, and swung the oxen forward a way. The teamsters with the second wagon swung in, having trouble with the oxen, which seemed uneasy. But soon those shadowed men were loading more sacks into the second wagon.

"Want some beans, boy?" Ike asked.

"Breakfast?" Jay asked.

"All you're going to get."

There was a pot of beans on the ground. They were hot, having been brought from somewhere by someone. There were a few bowls but no spoons. The idea was to slide beans into one's mouth with a tip of the bowl. Jay was too weary to recoil, even if the whole business was barbaric.

"Don't eat heavy, kid," Ike said.

Ike sure didn't have to worry about that, Jay thought. The beans were barely edible. But there was also some coffee, also boiled up elsewhere.

"Try the Arbuckles, boy," Amos said.

For this there were speckled blue enameled cups. The coffee wasn't half bad, and jolted Jay back to life. The second wagon's crew was as quiet as his own, and finished loading around five, when the third wagon showed up, and the whole business was repeated. Now the second two men joined them. Billy Bob and Helmut, they were called. And only Helmut, who spoke little English, could be described as burly.

About first light, the three wagons were loaded, entirely with grains and beans and various staples. This shipment would be vulnerable to weather, so the teamsters stretched tight duck cloth covers over bows and anchored them with cord. But no one started the train rolling, and soon Jay knew why.

Fairweather Foley arrived in a buggy, walked the wagons, checked the loads, tugged on the tarpaulins that would fend off rain, and studied the oxen while the teamsters waited.

Foley handed some papers to Ike, bills of lading, maybe invoices, Jay wasn't sure.

"Warren, come here," Foley said, from the buggy.

He reached to the floorboard and lifted a carbine and handed it to Jay, and then to pasteboard cartons of shells.

"Learn to use it, boy. You may need it. You may be protecting the lives of others here, as well as your own."

The weapon felt heavy in Jay's hands. He had never held a firearm.

"Winchester repeater carbine, came out about a year ago. It has a magazine holds fifteen rounds. You keep it full. Ike here, and the rest, they'll drill you some. Don't waste bullets; you might need them all. These men all have repeaters. Henry, Spencer, and a few like this. With these, a few men can hold off a lot of raiders—if you're careful and use the wagons for cover. Take good care of it, boy, and it'll serve you when you need it badly."

The others gathered around, some plainly envious. A fifteen-shot weapon was as fine as it got.

"He paid for it," Foley said. "He had a Faro layout, and now he's got a Winchester."

The others didn't seem exactly mollified. Jay knew what they were thinking; a greenhorn armed better than the rest; a greenhorn who'd never fired a shot.

Foley collected the beans and coffee pot, and the teamsters hawed and bullied the ox teams, and the small train rumbled and rattled away, Jay walking beside his wagon, going he scarcely knew where.

Chapter Nine

Full daylight found them climbing a gentle grade out of the South Platte valley, the prairie grass still green from late June showers. It was, by Jay's reckoning, the twenty-fifth day of June, 1876. He had won his degree from Harvard in late May; he had arrived in Cheyenne at the beginning of June; it took him three weeks to lose his stake. And here he was, walking somewhere beside three lumbering freight wagons, each hauled by four yoke of oxen, each wagon and its team handled by two teamsters. Jay was attached to the first wagon, the one operated by Ike, the trail boss.

The pleasant dawn breeze was a comfort. Later, the heat would build, but for the moment Jay had no complaints. He didn't have boots, but his well-worn shoes wouldn't bite at his flesh or scrape his heels raw. No man carried his carbine, though Jack Gill, on the third wagon, wore a Navy revolver. The two teamsters on that wagon, Gill and Rathbone, were a little different; both were burly and big-bellied, and their pants sagged under their ponderous stomachs.

There wasn't much talk. He wondered if teamsters ever talked. He had questions, but somehow sensed he should wait to find out a few things. He didn't even know where this outfit was going, other than the Black Hills.

He watched the oxen move easily in the wooden yokes that fit over their necks. The oxen actually pushed, their chests and shoulders pushing into the yoke. The oxen were slow, slower than a man could walk, but they seemed tireless. Maybe that was the virtue of oxen. There was no speed in them, but if they were rested, and fed and watered well, they could go long days, and barely tire out.

But Jay was speculating. He'd observe, try to avoid doing dumb things, and maybe he'd survive this misery. No one was trying to teach him things. No one was drilling him, rebuking him, hazing him. Ike and Amos were walking beside the oxen, and Ike had a small whip in hand to pop at laggards. There seemed to be no problem steering them. The oxen stayed on a worn trail, numerous ruts, some drying puddles, and no grass to impede them.

The sun skimmed the east, so the slightest rise threw long shadows through a dawn haze. It would be a clear day. Some crows took alarm at the wagons, but Jay saw no other life. He felt his own body moving easily, but he knew all that would change.

Ike and Amos often stood while the oxen walked by, eyeing each animal, looking for limping or other trouble, and eyeing the harness. Ike stayed close to the lead yoke, but Amos wandered, sometimes walking many yards away, a sort of outrider. Behind the lead wagon, the others came along but well behind, which minimized dust.

Jay wondered whether these oxen had been used much, and how much of a rest they got, and whether Foley kept herds of them along the trail, to switch with the worn ones. Jay thought he'd learn soon enough. He wasn't sure there was anything worth learning. He couldn't fathom these empty-headed men, who were content to plod their way through life, no different from these lean, muscle-bound, stupid oxen.

What looked to be level prairie wasn't at all. They struck a wide, dry gulch with steep grades in and out. Ike halted the oxen while Amos grabbed a chain and threaded it between the spokes of a rear wheel and then anchored it to the wagon box. The wheel could no longer turn, but could skid. It became a brake. Ike cracked the whip, and the team lumbered down the dusty grade, with mincing steps, as the wagon pushed from the rear, but they made the bottom without trouble, and Amos removed the chain so the rear wheel could turn again. Then he pulled a stick with a frayed brush on it from a small bucket hanging from the rear, and greased all four axles.

At the uphill side, Ike cracked the whip without striking any oxen, and that was enough to get them to lean into their yokes and drag the heavy wagon up the grade. At the top, Ike pulled ahead and waited for the two other wagons to traverse the gulch.

All this while, no one spoke to Jay or asked him to do anything. It apparently was enough for him to absorb the routine, see what went into teamstering, and maybe acquire some notions of a day's work.

"You doing all right, boy?"

"My feet hurt."

"Worthless shoes, eh?"

Jay didn't want to admit he had nothing else.

The oxen rested in their yokes, imprisoned in a way that kept them from moving much, or reaching grass. They were all young, but seemed docile, resigned to their fate in their stupid way. Teamsters and oxen had much the same cast of mind, Jay thought. Both came cheap. Oxen cost around twenty-five dollars; draft horses or mules much more. Chains stretched from rings hanging from each yoke back to the wagon tongue, that was kept off the ground by harness on the beasts closest to the wagon. The whole arrangement seemed uncomplicated, compared to the elaborate leather harness of draft horses.

Moving freight was plainly the dullest job in the world. Jay thought he was a prisoner of his stomach. If he didn't have to eat, he would be a free man. He trudged along, kicking up alkali dust, dodging sagebrush and prickly pear. The heat began to build. He was getting thirsty. Worse, his shoes were abrading a toe on his left foot and the heel on his right, and also rubbing the left foot wrong, so his feet began hurting, and it didn't quit, even as the ox team didn't quit.

A half hour later he had raised several blisters, and every step hurt.

Ike called a halt in a rare shaded area, under some cottonwoods that had tapped water under the rim of a gulch.

"Your shoes eating you up, boy?"

Jay hated to admit it. The rest of the teamsters were fine; they wandered from their wagons, relieved themselves, sat down with their backs against the cutbank, relaxed.

"Take off your shoes, boy," Ike said.

Jay did, and stripped away some stockings worn through. His feet were in worse shape than he had realized. Blisters had raised and broken. They leaked pink fluids.

"Shouldn't have come out with shoes," Ike said.

Jay didn't reply. None of it was his idea.

"Always some damned thing," Ike said.

The other teamsters gathered around and stared at Jay's blistered, bleeding heels and toes.

"Goddamn greenhorn," said Jack Gill. "Go on back. Worthless."

"I'll decide that," Ike said.

"Maybe I could sit on a tailgate," Jay said.

"No, not ever. We're overloaded. We should have five yoke on these."

He wanted to wash his feet, clear away the pulp and tie some sort of bandage over the bad areas, but no one volunteered any bandaging or water. "I'll go back," he said.

The thought of it tormented him.

Ike said nothing, but rose, headed for the lead wagon, found his gear, and pulled out something. He handed Jay a pair of ankle-high moccasins of soft leather.

"Try 'em," he said.

They fit snugly, actually felt good. They didn't chafe at his blisters.

"Walk around a little."

Jay did. Nothing bit at him. He nodded.

"Yours," Ike said. "They don't last worth a damn, but you're good for a while."

Jay wasn't sure he wanted the gift. He just wanted to get back to Cheyenne and put his legs up for a week. But he nodded.

"Also, watch out for cactus. Spike'll go right through a moccasin."

"We should unload him at the next stage stop," Gill said.

The idea heartened Jay. The Foley company could send him back on the next stage south. He'd tell Fairweather Foley his feet couldn't take it, and could he have an administrative job?

Rathbone grinned from a mouth with black caverns between his teeth. "College boy," he said. "Real pretty one."

"Let loose of him, Rathbone," Ike said.

But Rathbone kicked Jay's leg. "Pampered brat," he said.

Jay sprang up and bulled in, his flash temper exploding. Rathbone landed a single fist in Jay's gut, felling him and stopping his breathing. It took a moment before Jay could gasp for breath.

"Just joking," Rathbone said.

"We're three hours out and there's trouble," Ike said. He turned to Jay. "If you can't take it, get out. Just get out."

Jay wheeled away and tried some serious walking in the moccasins. "Let's go," he said.

The caravan started up again, plodding north. A southbound mudwagon, one of Foley's, passed by, the jehu barely nodding to the teamsters. The southbound coaches often carried gold out of the Black Hills, and stopped for nothing.

They nooned at a creek running narrow in a wide gulch. Ike and Amos unchained the yokes and let them wander. Jay wondered if there'd be a meal, but nothing was done, and after a good break, they put the ox teams back together.

"Different wheelers," Ike said. "The oxen closest to the wheels wear out fastest, so we rotate them. The wheelers go to the front now; that's the lightest load."

He handed off the pair of oxen to Jay, who grabbed the iron ring between them and led them forward and waited for further instruction. So Ike was teaching him a thing or two. Maybe that said something.

"All right, boy, here's a whip. Don't lose it. Don't use it hard. They know gee and haw, so you can turn them. You just follow the trail, staying on the left of the lead yoke."

So there he was. Teamstering. He yelled at the oxen, cracked the whip a few times, and the train lumbered to life, pushing through midday furnace heat. The animals slobbered, sunk into their yokes, and dragged the heavy freighter along.

He scarcely noticed his bad feet. There was something to be said for soft tight moccasins. He did remember to dodge anything spiny, including sagebrush.

After a while, Ike relieved him, collected his long tasseled whip.

"I never learned where we're going," Jay said.

"Custer City. South edge of the Black Hills."

"How far is that?"

"Couple hundred from Cheyenne, give or take. We'll be going a while."

"What's there?"

"Gold, boy. Them gulches are full of gold miners. Deadwood gulch, near there, it's a big strike. Ten thousand hungry miners, starved for eats, and we're bringing some."

"This for ten thousand?"

"For now. Foley's got more coming. Every wagon he's got. He's shipping as fast as the rail cars come in, and they still ain't got enough. They eat faster then we ship."

"What'll happen with winter?"

"Oh, they'll weather it. They go hunting. Still some buffalo around."

"I mean the shipping."

"It gets mean, boy. Mire and cold and snow, and nothing wet flowing, and sick oxen, and fingers that don't work. Mire's the bad thing. Wagon sinks in and it's done for."

"You like your work?"

"If the world depends on everyone liking their work, it'd stop still."

"You gonna work in the winter?"

"It beats living in a shanty or a soddy and trying to get through blizzards until it thaws and they can dig for gold again. But we get snowed out sometimes, and then they starve out there, and eat horses or mules. If they ain't eating rabbits or coyotes."

That's how the day went. Ike was quietly teaching Jay a thing or two. Jay was learning not only about the gear, but about resting the oxen, rotating them, checking hooves. And getting along with people. And getting along with his sore feet.

Ike drove deep into the evening. He knew exactly where he was headed, a place he called Chugwater Creek, where there would be grass and water for the oxen, firewood, shelter from wind, and maybe some game to put in the cook pot. The teamsters simply released the oxen, which drifted to water, which they drank slowly, for a long time, and then wandered toward any grass they could find.

"Don't have to round them up, and the Injuns don't like 'em," Ike said. "And that reminds me, boy, get that Winchester out, and we'll learn you something. After that, some supper."

Chapter Ten

The teamsters pulled the yokes off the oxen and freed them, one pair after another. The oxen drifted toward the creek, stuck their snouts in the brackish water, and started tugging grass from the stream banks. The teamsters didn't let it go at that. They circled the animals, studying their necks and chests, their hooves and buttocks, looking for trouble.

"The animals come first," Ike said.

That annoyed Jay. It was obvious. Did Ike think Jay needed to learn the obvious? What there was to know about operating a wagon and team could be learned in fifteen minutes. Ike was acting as if there were some mysterious wisdom that would take months to master.

They watched the twenty-four oxen drift apart, each claiming space, some stepping into the creek and dropping green cow pies into the turgid water.

"All right, bring the carbine and a box of shells," Ike said.

Jay pulled the Winchester and some shells from the wagon. It felt heavy in his hands. It had a solemn purpose and was meant to be used solemnly.

"All right. Shots are scarce and we may need

'em. We'll dry fire, and I'll show you how to lever a new one in, and how to fill the magazine."

He showed Jay the basics of operating a repeating weapon. He had Jay pull trigger. He had Jay lever the repeater. He had Jay lie in the grass, use his elbows for a rest, and aim at a tree. He had Jay use a level cottonwood branch as a bench rest, a way to steady the weapon.

"All right, that's it. Fill the magazine," Ike said.

"That's it?"

"You'll learn to aim low. I can't teach you. The gun'll buck into your shoulder, and you'll jerk it upward, and you'll need to figure that out when it happens. Better save your cartridges. We may need every last one."

"Looks pretty peaceful."

Ike just smiled. It was a strange smile that shot a chill through Jay.

While Ike watched, Jay loaded the magazine.

"Some fellers keep a round in the chamber. You, I'd say not. That way, if you decide to shoot, you've got to jack one in, and there's no accidents."

"I think I can be trusted not to have an accident."

"After a month, we'll see about it."

The rest were watching furtively while doing other stuff. Apparently Gill and Rathbone would be the cooks in this outfit. They had a cookfire going and a pot over it. Rathbone filled it with creek water, and Gill started to boil some beans. They were studiously ignoring the lesson. Amos was greasing all the wagon wheels, carrying his tar bucket with him.

"All those wild Indians everywhere," Jay said.

Ike stared.

They left Jay to his own devices after that. The others seemed to stay busy. Amos was repairing a boot, using some thong and an awl to anchor a sole to an upper. Ike was shaking out a bedroll. Billy Bob and Helmut were collecting firewood. Whatever was in the cook pot was boiling slowly. Beans could not be hurried, apparently. The sun dived suddenly, leaving a sudden chill in the creek bottom. It dawned on Jay that he had no blankets, and he saw no tent going up, and he wondered where they would want him to sleep. The air had changed. Nothing held heat in the prairies, and it fled with the sun.

The oxen grazed quietly in the twilight, gray and black against a brown land, with a few silvery green cottonwoods hanging to life where there was water.

When Gill and Rathbone were ready, they began loading some tin bowls with beans, using a ladle. Jay collected a bowl along with the others, and noted that the rest simply sipped from the bowl, though Billy Bob managed to shovel beans into his mouth with a hunting knife he carried at his side.

Jay tried sipping beans, and got a few into his mouth when the bowl erupted, splattering beans and slime everywhere. The thing was alive. Horrified, he discovered a thrashing garter snake being roasted in the middle of the bowl by the hot beans. At least he thought it was a snake. Something was writhing. He threw his bowl down, spattering beans everywhere, and a dying little snake.

The rest observed this blandly.

"If ye don't like yer supper, then don't eat," Rathbone said.

"I'll start over," Jay yelled, barely controlling his rage.

"All served up, fella, sort of out of luck, I'd say."

They were staring now. The mess of brown beans lay scattered across clay. The snake expired, and lay limp.

"Food," Jay snapped. He picked up the bowl, headed for the kettle, and found it was so: the cooks had divided the whole contents among the seven men. And the rest weren't about to share one bean. So they were going to haze him and keep him miserable. He felt a vast scorn for them all. Were they proud of themselves?

And some serious hunger. He had walked all day, eaten nothing, and now faced a hungry night. In the dusk he scraped up what beans he could find on the ground, some of them covered with ants, and when he had gotten what he could find in the dying light, he took his bowl to the swollen creek and carefully rinsed his miserable supper. The brackish water, carrying the residue of the cowpies, scarcely did the job, but he had no choice. Eat what he had or starve.

He ate. The beans were mush, and not much of that, but he got a few bites of food into him. He could not remember, or imagine, a worse meal, or one more foul.

The teamsters were cleaning their own bowls in the creek, and returning them to Gill and Rathbone, who were putting their kitchen away in the third wagon. The light faded, and no one built up the campfire.

He found Ike. "I don't have a bedroll," he said.

"Then I guess you sleep cold."

"You set up a tent?"

"Under the wagons," Ike said.

"In the wagon?"

"You'd likely bust some flour bags."

Jay remembered that there was a spare tarp in Ike's wagon. He found it, rummaging around in the fragrant and musky dark, and pulled it out. Ike didn't stop him. The duck cloth was tight and heavy, and would do if it didn't get cold. He collected it, sat on it, and pulled his moccasins off. The blistered places were pulpy, and every inch of his feet hurt one way or another. Some places stung, others ached. But he could see nothing that was worse than when Ike gave him the moccasins. He washed his feet in the creek and put the moccasins on and rolled out the duck cloth into a bed. No one talked. He was grateful for that, at least.

It turned black, but the sky was transparent, and stars popped out of the firmament as last light faded. Ike carried his bedroll over to a cottonwood and spread it out there. Amos chose to sleep under the wagon, like Jay. Both men had their carbines with them. Jay wondered if that was necessary. If Indians don't go for oxen, why bother?

The ground was hard and lumpy, and not even the doubled up duck cloth took the cast-iron hardness out of it. He had no pillow. The night was going to be long, and it was only the first of an endless string of them. So there he was, thanks to his father, lying on dirt with some stupid ruffians and stupid oxen.

Oddly, given his exhaustion, he couldn't sleep. It wasn't the hard ground. It wasn't the chill, or the unfamiliar roughness of the duck cloth. It wasn't the lack of a soft pillow. It wasn't his hurts, though he hurt plenty, and hurt where he had never hurt before. It was something else. He was afraid. There were no safe walls around him. No roof to ward off rain. No stove. But that wasn't it either. He was among strangers, and entrusting his life to them. He had yet to speak to Billy Bob and Helmut. What sort of men were they? Gill and

Rathbone were bent on tormenting him. Would that continue? Could he do anything about it? He knew at once he couldn't. Ike and Amos, two more strangers. Ike had little sympathy for him. Amos didn't seem to care. So there he was, caught among rough men he didn't know. But that wasn't all. He lived in a universe without walls or protection. The prairies stretched, unfenced, forever. There were wild creatures there, and the wildest and most dangerous were Indians, and they wanted to stop the migration to the Black Hills, and killed to defend their land.

So Jay couldn't sleep. He lay there under the wagon, staring at the lumps lying elsewhere, barely discernible in the night. He sat up, knocked his head on the wagon bed, and crawled out, suddenly in a different world, an infinitude of bright stars, brighter than he had seen in the East, where the air was moist. But the stars didn't console him. He studied the walls of the gulch, seeing nothing move, and finally crawled under the wagon again. He did not fall asleep, and squandered the night worrying about little things, like a parade of ants, and large things, like tomahawks wielded by men intent on splitting his head open.

He heard the bark of coyotes. Or was it wolves? He scarcely knew the difference. But the howl and yelp were messages. And didn't Indians mimic the sounds of the animals to communicate? Maybe there'd be a party of murderous savages whirling out of the dark.

Dawn was slow to come, but even in first light the rest rose and stretched and immediately began collecting the stock, which had not drifted far. That was a valuable thing about oxen. They didn't run off. No one asked him to help. They threw ropes over the animals and led them in, caught them in their yokes, with the oxbows under their necks, and looked them over. They ignored Jay, and maybe that was just as well. He had no knowledge of gathering the stock, yoking it, and clapping the chains to the yokes.

It was only then that the men settled around the coffee pot, smoke-stained blue enamel hung from a tripod of sorts, over a small, smelly fire. Jay waited for breakfast, but there was none: only a cask of hardtack, rock-textured biscuits one could gnaw on. Barely food. He had a bad night, and now a bad morning. At least no one forbade him to eat more than one, and he saw most of the teamsters pluck up two, and some slid a third into their pockets. Fairweather Foley wouldn't even treat his men to a breakfast worth eating, Jay thought.

He bit into one, found it dry and bland, almost nothing more than caked flour cooked hard to preserve it.

At least there was the coffee. Gill had poured beans from a bag with an Arbuckles label into a small grinder and then poured the ground coffee into the pot, where it settled on the bottom and flavored the boiling water. Jay sipped it, occasionally spitting out grounds, and found the coffee almost curative. His aches disappeared along with his dour mood.

Then, sharp on the morning air, they heard four gunshots. These echoed in from some great distance, but could be nothing else. Ike nodded to Helmut, who grabbed his carbine from the third wagon and hiked north, where the shots emanated. Jay watched him climb the bluff carefully, until he could just barely gaze out on the plains. Then he climbed higher, until he was silhouetted in the dawn brightness, a small dark statue on the lip of the gulch. But then he walked back to the wagons.

"Nodding," he said.

But the shots were real, and had changed the day.

They dumped the coffee grounds, loaded up, and hawed the oxen to life. In a few minutes they topped the northern slope of the gulch, and rode out upon a sea of emptiness.

Chapter Eleven

At Fort Laramie the freight wagons had to be ferried across the North Platte along with the ox teams. It would be a long and tedious business. Worse, Ike was in a hurry; there'd be no time to go to the post and see the sights.

Jay was much put out. After long boring days he was ready for something, *anything,* to relieve the tedium. They had met few people on the trail other than station tenders that Fairweather Foley had scattered along the route to supply fresh teams. Jay wondered what madness would inspire some old man, or dour couple, to live in the middle of nowhere, look after horses, and harness fresh ones when a coach rolled in.

"Beats working for a living," said one, which immediately won Jay's sympathy. Apart from a little harnessing and graining and chopping firewood, the old codger could sleep his days away. Always assuming there were no Indians around. But those days were nearly over.

The ferryman proved to be a muscular old man with a gray beard that reached his waist. The Foley outfit drew up on the south bank, found the ferry waiting, and started loading the first wagon and team. The ferry was a flat-bottomed scow guided by a cable stretched across the stream.

There were pulley on the scow. The ferry was poled across by the ferryman or his assistant, who was nowhere in sight.

"Three wagons, three dollars, twenty-four ox, two-forty," the old man said, holding out callused hand. Ike didn't complain; anyone who complained was likely not to get taken across at all, or made to sit for a few hours while the ferryman doled out his revenge.

Ike paid. The first wagon, that of Billy Bob and Helmut, rolled out, but only after the teamsters whipped the reluctant oxen into stepping on the bobbing wooden platform of the scow.

"I 'magine you've heard," the ferryman said.

"Heard what?" Ike asked.

"If you ain't heard, then I'm not the one to tell you."

Ike ignored the man. Apparently this was some sort of ritual. The ferryman had to be coaxed into telling anything, and usually it didn't amount to much anyway.

So nothing got said, and the ferryman cut loose, poled into the slow-moving North Platte, furrowing the turgid waters across a broad stretch of river that had cut deep into the dark hills, covered with jack pine, that hindered passage in this area.

Jay watched the ferry bump the far bank, where there was a ramp of sorts, and the teamsters drove the oxen and wagon off the vessel. The ferryman slowly poled his way back. A few soldiers watched. They were armed, which surprised Jay.

The ferry bumped the south bank again, and Ike motioned Gill and Rathbone to board the ferry, which the old boatman watched sharp-eyed, making sure he wasn't cheated. A dog cost extra, but the Foley outfit had none.

"Gen'l Custer got whumped," the ferryman said. "And most of the Seventh Cavalry, so it's said."

"What does that amount to?" Ike asked.

"Lotta Sioux on the loose."

With that, the ferryman pushed hard into his pole, and the scow reluctantly left shore and lumbered across the brown river.

When the ferryman returned, Ike wanted to know more. "What happened? Where?"

"Way west, in Montana. They's not much to worry about. Gen'l Terry, he's still got most of his army. Just a couple hundred with Custer, got them self pin-cushioned up. Over at the post, here, they're all lathered up. That's why them soldiers is over yonder, keeping an eye on things. But it don't come to a hill of beans. And that's a far piece. You getting your outfit on, or do I quit for lunch?"

"But what happened to Custer?"

"He got himself a ticket to heaven, fella. Now get rolling or I'll just call it quits for the day."

"Is there an officer I can talk to?"

"You know as much as they know, fella. It don't come to much."

"Who defeated Custer?"

"Who cares? Them chiefs, who can tell one from another? Sitting Bull, and a new one called Crazy Horse, I hear."

Ike didn't like it. But he motioned to Jay and Amos, who whipped the oxen forward. The beasts minced their way onto the barge. Jay wondered what would happen if the oxen panicked in the middle of the river. But then he realized the ferryman was raising a low barrier across the front, some upright planks intended to discourage that. He slid his pole deep into the bank and pushed hard, and the scow slowly edged away, and was caught by the stream and guided by the upstream cable and pulleys.

There were no howling Sioux in bonnets descending on them.

But on the north bank, where steep slopes crowded the trail, a few men and pack mules stood watching. They all wore felt hats, and brown or black britches, and looked to be well shod. If they had been clean-shaven once, they weren't now; scraggly new beard scratched across their faces. They clearly were waiting for something. The mules, freed for a moment, dug at whatever grass they could find beneath the carpet of sagebrush.

The ferryman gave one last shove, and the barge

plowed into a muddy grade and stalled there a few feet from dry land.

"Low water now, dang it," he said. "I plumb hate July."

He dropped the front livestock barrier, and Amos and Jay hawed the mules forward, snapping whips and energizing the slobbering beasts to tug the wagon, which rolled off the barge and into mud. More whip-snapping and the wagon slowly rolled past the mire and onto dry ground, next to the other two Foley outfits.

"Anyone going acrost?" the ferryman yelled.

No one was. He stuck his pole in the mud and pushed and hauled, and finally freed the ferry, which drifted away and caught in the current.

One of the men with the pack mules approached. "You headed for Deadwood?" he asked.

"Custer City."

"That's a bad omen," the man said. "With the General expired. We're heading for the new strike. Lots of side gulches not even sampled yet."

"We've got delivery in Custer," Ike said.

"We heard Custer's a ghost town; everyone's lit out for the new strike. What are you carrying? Must be heavy, four yoke a wagon."

"Flour mostly. Barley, oats, beans."

"Flour! We'll take a bag. Name your price."

"It's all promised to the Custer City man."

"You give us a bag of flour and a bag of beans and name the price."

Ike didn't hesitate. Cash on the barrel head, and less weight to haul. "Twenty-five a hundred-weight, fella. They're fifty pound sacks."

"Done!"

The leader of that outfit paid cash in greenbacks and collected one cotton sack of flour from Ike's wagon and a burlap bag of beans from Gill's wagon. The eleven men began shifting loads around, balancing up the packs and shifting weight to other mules. Jay saw that it was an art, putting loads together, getting them balanced and even on the mules, which were a little skittish about the shifting.

But Ike was in a hurry, and started his wagons rolling. This was difficult country, with twists and grades and it wore out oxen fast.

"Wait," yelled one of the men. He trotted up to Ike. "We'd like to travel with you. There's safety in numbers, and we might need some numbers."

"Sure; we're slow, you know."

"You've got rifles?"

"Every man is well armed. All repeaters, too."

"Then we'll be in good company," the man said. "I'm Jake Bones. These here'll get to know you along the trail. We're out of Fort Leavenworth."

"Veterans? Army?"

"Some, some not. We've got a cobbler, a black-smith, a gunsmith, a couple of farmers, and some young rascals that ain't got a trade and hope never to get one. The idea is to work our butts off in the diggings for a year or so, and never work again."

"Well, Bones, we're all with Fairweather Foley, out of Cheyenne," Ike said. "We've got Amos Boggs there, our new man Jay Warren here, and you'll get to know the men behind."

"Heard good of Foley," Bones said.

"He makes it all work," Ike said. "You fellers now, you'll be eating Foley's beans whiles you dig. That how Foley is, you know. He sees a need and gets there first."

Jay listened carefully. The two leaders of the outfits got along, talked about everything but weather. Mostly they talked about some new digs at Deadwood, and how a man could stick a spade into gravel and come up ten dollars richer, and it didn't take many shovelfuls to put a man on Easy Street, but time counted; a man had to get in there before it was all took up.

Ike laughed. "And when you're all starved, you'll pay any price for Foley's flour, coming along slow and steady."

They were winding through varied country now, not the monotonous plains. Here were slopes black with jack pine and purple wildflowers and occasional sparkling creeks. They continued on most of that day, and camped together in an idyllic valley, rich with prairie grasses, with plenty of deadwood for fires, and out of the wind.

By then Jay knew the whole routine. He unyoked the oxen, looked them over, released them to graze and drink, checked hooves, greased axles, and looked to his clothing, which was starting to fall apart. Over in the other camp, men picketed their mules on good grass, looked for fistulas or hoof trouble, and argued about whether to set a watch now that the Sioux were looking for trouble. They decided against it. Bloody Montana was a far piece west.

Jay met Frank and Louis and Ephraim and Wilbur and Cassidy and Boggs. That turned out to be his only name. Boggs was it. Most of them were carrying firearms now. But these were six-guns in holsters, and mostly not new, either. There were some Civil War Navies. Not a good defense against Sioux. No wonder they were tying up with some teamsters with long guns for a while. Jay thought that having a weapon at hand was a good idea, so he kept the Winchester in the crook of his arm, and the weapon did not go unnoticed among the Fort Leavenworth bunch.

Jake finally approached him directly. "I got a few fellows, they'd like to buy that repeater and any cartridges you got."

Jay shook his head. "It's all I got," he said.

Both companies put out their cook fires as soon as they were done with supper. They were in a sheltered valley, but smoke drifted on the breeze and gave them away. Custer dead? General Custer, Civil War hero? Them Sioux must have caught him taking a crap.

Jay joined the Leavenworth crowd, mostly to ask questions. "What'll you do when you get to Deadwood?"

"We're a company, boy," Jake said. "First we spread out. Whoever finds good ground, he stakes claims for us all, side by side. Then some of us keep looking, while some work the claims to get them in the ledger. And we got the advantage of being a company so we got men prospecting every gulch in the Black Hills. Deadwood now, it's already a city, you know. Half tent, half plank, and half sod, but a city, and it's a lively place. It's already got assayers, dealers, supplies coming in, gold going out in strongboxes in armored coaches. There's already a claims exchange too, boy. You want a claim? You don't like yours? You got a chance to euchre everyone in sight." He laughed. "Half the young ones here, they're itching to squeeze a fortune out of them that want to dig up dust."

That sure tickled Jay's fancy.

The Leavenworth outfit had eaten some beans, and now were cleaning mess kits and stowing them in their packs, and pulling out bedrolls because the night was going to be plenty chilly.

"Boy, we're about ready to pull out early, maybe before your outfit's up. The bunch of us, we'll risk the Sioux. We've got to get to Deadwood before all the gold's took up by people moving quick. We're not well armed, and them Sioux like nothing better than mules, but we'll ride the whirlwind. It's been real good to know you. But we'll be making a run for it." He eyed Jay. "You give her some thought, all right? That repeater's worth a share in our outfit."

Chapter Twelve

In the night, Jay knew what he would do. It didn't take thinking through. He'd have a twelfth share in the Fort Leavenworth company. He'd get to the Black Hills several days before the slow ox teams would drag Foley's wagons there. He'd join some capable men who knew exactly where to go for gold and how to dig it.

He had told Foley he'd stick with his company, and that bothered him. But not a whole lot. The main loss would be the pay he'd earned in two weeks on the trail. But that didn't bother him a whole lot either. Twenty-five dollars? His father spent that in a moment. For that kind of pay, what did Foley expect? A slave?

The mule outfit rose ahead of dawn, and Jay saw the flare of a cook fire. They would have their coffee after packing the mules. These men were using well-made pack saddles and panniers to haul their essentials. By now, they had consumed so much of their food that the mules weren't burdened much.

Jay rose swiftly, washed in the creek, and slid his Winchester and two cartons of cartridges from the back of Ike's wagon. That was it. He started for the mule outfit, which was ahead a piece, when Ike's voice cut through the dusk.

"Where you going?"

"I'm joining them."

"That's what I thought. I was right about you."

"I'm losing pay. So what's your beef?"

"Take off my moccasins."

"Why? You got my shoes for a trade. You come out better than me."

"Take off my moccasins or you'll learn what a bullwhip can do to your hide."

Ike stood in the murky light, a long, mean bullwhip writhing in his grip, almost as if Ike were about to discipline a bull.

Jay headed for the wagon, felt around in the dark, found his shoes, and sat down, untying and tying until he wore his own shoes, while Ike watched, the bullwhip never ceasing to undulate and snake out.

Jay was healed up; the moccasins had protected his feet for two weeks. He remembered that there was a cobbler in the Kansas outfit. There'd be help and relief at once. He eyed Ike, glad to escape the lout, glad to abandon the dimwitted teamsters and get into an outfit with a future. He liked what Bones had said: the mule outfit was full of men who planned to get rich and never work a day in their lives after that. Jay enjoyed it. Maybe in a few months he'd see Ike or other Foley men and they'd have a story to take back to Fairweather Foley about the Warren boy. Tecumseh Warren's boy, a chip off the old block.

He hiked across the bleak field separating the two parties, found the mule men sipping coffee, located Bones.

"I'm in. And I need your cobbler."

The cobbler, it turned out, had no ready remedy, not early in the morning in the middle of Wyoming Territory, but there were moccasins in this outfit too, and Jay's shoes were soon stored away. The cobbler, Bridges, would work on them at the next camp.

And then they were off. They kept an easy, fast stride, walking twice as fast as teamsters with an ox team could move. Three or four miles each hour, with everyone enjoying the progress. These men weren't wasting a minute. He scarcely even knew their names, but it didn't matter. They were moving, and they'd get to the new goldfields, and he'd be right there with them. Two of the mules carried sluice boxes, and another carried shovels and gold pans. These gents would be mining gold the day they put corner cairns on their claims. He had none of this equipment, not even adequate clothing, but they'd share, or charge him a few dollars for things he would need. He knew that in a new digging, things like shovels and gold pans could not be had for any price.

It was amazing, the speed they achieved. Within a half an hour they lost sight of the Foley outfit behind them. Within an hour they were two miles ahead. The trail followed a winding creek, flowing through an unsettled sloping land, and the country was rougher than anywhere near Cheyenne.

He fell in beside Boggs, who turned out to be an Army sergeant who had just left the service.

"That repeater's new. You know how to shoot that thing, boy?" Boggs asked.

"They instructed me, sir."

"Exactly what?" Boggs asked.

"Dry firing. Levering in cartridges. Not enough cartridges to teach me more."

"Boy, if we deal with Sioux, you lend me that piece. I know how to use it, and there'll be plenty of dead Indians when I'm done."

"I'd rather shoot it myself, sir."

"Then maybe there'll be a lot of dead white men. Only two men here got long guns, for hunting. Your repeater, in good hands, evens the fight."

"It's yours then, so long as I have a revolver or something to defend myself with."

"You're a good man to travel with, boy. You got some sense."

After a quick nooning, mostly to rest the mules, he chose to walk with Jake Bones.

"How does this work, this company?" he asked. "Just wondering."

"We signed a compact, boy. Each man brought his own outfit, but the two sluice boxes, they belong to the company."

"Should I sign it, too?"

"Nah. We all know you got a share. We're glad to have you."

"But I don't have my own outfit."

"We'll put one together for you, and you can repay us with dust you'll get as your share."

"The gold, it isn't held in common; it's divided out?"

"End of each week. We got a gold scale for it."

"Then my share's mine after that, right?"

"If you got us paid off, boy."

Why did they call him boy? Why did the teamsters call him boy? They were men, but he was called boy. He didn't like that.

"Tell me about your company."

"Boy, they're the finest men west of the Missouri River, and I'll vouch for it."

"But I barely know their names."

"Ho, fella! They barely know yours."

They pushed hard that hot July day, and didn't quit until full dark. They were traversing a creek and there was no need to stop at a watering hole. The way these gents were moving, they'd be in Deadwood in three days. Four at the most.

Jay never did learn last names, nor did he ever see the instrument that bound them into a gold-mining company, nor was anything more said about his share, his twelfth. But it would all straighten out. These were fine fellows, and he was lucky to get in with them.

They kept watch for Indians, but saw none. At each campsite they sent men out a way to look over the ground. And they took care to build fires only in secluded corners, under cutbanks or deep in bottoms, and they knew the flames were invisible, even to someone close at hand. And they dealt with smoke by dousing the fires as soon as the cooking was done.

There was traffic on the trail; a couple of Foley mudwagons passed by, drawn by plow horses because Foley's stations were so far apart. And they passed some Foley freight outfits returning to Cheyenne. It was always good to exchange information with these men. No one had seen any Indians. Maybe the whole business of George Custer's demise was another rumor.

One of the younger men in the outfit caught Jay's eye. He was cheery, carrot-topped, and walked with a sort of cockiness Jay liked. His name turned out to be Huckleberry Jones.

"Just call me Huck," he said.

"You got born with that name?"

"That's what happens when your old man's been drinking."

"You got plans for Deadwood?"

"Let me tell you something, my friend. I spent three years clerking in the courthouse back there, for fifty-five a month, and no future except keeping books the rest of my life. Well, I had a few itches that needed scratching, you know what I mean? So I joined this outfit. They needed me bad; I can read ledgers and I have a little skill they like: I spot errors they can make use of."

"Make use of?"

"If a claim's flawed, or describes the wrong property, or isn't signed right, or the date's haywire, or there's anything else cockeyed, then it's no good. That's what we're here for."

"You'll look for bad claims and claim them?"

Huckleberry grinned, ear to ear. "Look at those packs, my friend. How many shovels and picks do you see? Eleven of us, three shovels, two picks. Digging up rock, that's real hard work. A man gets sweated up, worn down, bruised, aching, and frustrated when the dust doesn't pop right up and bat an eye at you. There's better ways. This old earth, it's divided between suckers who toil away for a living, and fellers that got their wits about them. The suckers, well . . ." he shrugged. "The drudges, they'll spend their days droning away. And the rest of us make our pile and have a little fun. You want some fun, friend?"

"I guess I do. Beats shoveling."

"There's places in Deadwood a feller can have a lot of fun," Huck said. "You like a little female company?"

"I haven't seen a woman this whole trip. They're all back east."

"Not all, " Huck said. "Some of the wildest of the lot, they're up ahead."

"Well, isn't that something. Deadwood's looking better and better."

"What does your old man do?"

"I never figured it out. He's got a company and rakes it in."

"Mine's a horse trader. Only he got caught too many times and finally vamoosed to Argentina or some place. No one knows. He was on the lam from about every county in Missouri and Kansas. He could take a horse with cracked hooves, or splints, or fistulas, or bots, and fix it up good enough to sell, and it'd look good long enough for him to get outa there, and then they came after him. He always had class. He wrote out his bills of sale on engraved letterhead. His boots always shone; he blacked them before every deal. He used to tell me to dress real nice, and I did, and that's how I got to be a clerk. At the courthouse, they want people with their shoes shined up and a good haircut."

"I'd trade my old man for yours any day," Jay said.

"I got a card from him once, from Chile. He was in the plow horse business, was keeping two widows happy, and was hoping I'd come down there some day. But I never did figure out how to talk Spanish."

"I was all steamed up for the daughter of the

Spanish ambassador, but look at me now. Here I am."

Huck eyed him. "You got money, then?"

"I don't. The old man isn't sharing. It's a bad spot to be in."

"Well, friend, you've come to the right party. We're going to clean up, but there's not a miner in our company."

"How's this going to work?"

"I'm on the ledgers and claims, two guys are looking for good dirt that hasn't been claimed, several of us will look at claims that aren't being worked. The owners got two days off before they lose their rights. You'll look for new dirt and do some digging."

"But I don't know anything about it."

"That's why you'll be digging. Don't forget, the outfit's going to sell claims too. Dig a hole, file on it, and sell it to whoever's full of dreams and beer. You'll be our ace hole-digger."

"Is there an exchange in Deadwood? Where we can buy and sell?"

"Maybe we'll start one, right?"

"I didn't join the company to dig holes, Huck."

Huck grinned. "Well, you can always quit us. I guess you'll find a way to pay us back for the chow and those rags you're wearing, and the moccasins."

Jay didn't like that and clammed up. They were getting closer now, moving into hilly country, heavily forested with jack pine, the trail snaking around bends, following small creeks, fording little rivulets. And there was traffic, too, a snarl of horses, people leading mules, cursing miners, all trying to get rich fast.

Chapter Thirteen

Deadwood didn't impress Jay. The pack mule outfit strode into a town in the making, set in a forested bowl in the Black Hills just big enough for a pocket-sized city with no space left over. Swarms of carpenters, stonemasons, lumbermen and bricklayers were throwing up structures right and left made from any material at hand. There were log buildings with canvas roofs; plank board and batten buildings with false fronts; fieldstone buildings with timbered tops, and a few brick structures, though bricks were scarce.

What Jay didn't see was any miner. The pack mule outfit worked past freight wagons loaded with raw lumber still leaking sap, sledges loaded with field stone, carpenters sawing through poles and planks, and wagons loaded with hardware such as kegs of nails, sheet metal stoves, and stovepipe. Just outside of the business district was a sprawl of temporary houses, cobbled together from mud-chinked logs and canvas. He would have thought it the ugliest dump he'd ever seen but for the vaulting beauty of the surrounding cliffs, black with jack pine with bold outcrops of tan rock.

He passed one completed board and batten building that had a simple sign painted across its front: Mars Bros. Grocery. Freight wagons clustered there, including some with the familiar F-Diamond, signifying Fairweather Foley's ownership. Which reminded him that this city was being erected by fools who toiled for almost nothing from dawn to dusk, throwing up these buildings for little more than the food they ate. It puzzled him. Just outside of town, from what he'd heard, were the gold districts, now divided into hundreds, maybe thousands, of claims where a man could make some serious money fast without drudging through weary days driving nails into boards.

His outfit was composed of men who were a lot smarter, and who had large dreams, not miserable little ones. They threaded the town, seeing the sights, and there was plenty to see. Jay spotted the first women he'd seen in weeks. They weren't fancy ladies, more homespun, but they were female, and that heartened him. The outfit hiked past three saloons, all completed structures, no doubt doing a lively trade selling whatever spirits rolled in on the wagons. But who wanted to pour drinks and listen to drunks all night for a living? Those places didn't earn enough to interest anyone with ambition.

Jake Bones halted them when they'd reached the far side of town.

"All right, we've seen the sights," he said. "We'll make camp and get down to business."

122

"Monkey business," Huckleberry Jones said.

That brought Jake over to him in a moment.

"We're going to do it like we planned, and it's all business, and if you think it's a joke, then quit us right now, because if you don't do your work, what we agreed on, you're cut loose."

"Hey, this is a real town, and there's women around," Huck said.

"You heard me," Bones said.

He led them back the way they had come, looking for a place to camp, preferably with water and grass. There was neither anywhere nearby. But he found a stand of cottonwoods in a side gulch a mile below town. It would do except for watering the mules. The nearest water was a half mile distant.

"We'll sell the mules tomorrow anyway," Bones said.

"There'll be a hotel somewhere," Jay said.

"Sonny, there isn't, and won't be. We're staying here."

The company pulled the packs off the mules and set to work cutting limbs that would provide frameworks for canvas huts.

"You two," Bones said, "take the mules to water and after they get back put the feedbags to them."

Jay didn't argue. Leading a few mules to water was a lot easier than building shelters and stowing packs in them. But Huckleberry looked grim.

"Just watch. They'll all go into town tonight

except us," he said. "We get to guard the camp."

"I didn't sign on to do menial labor," Jay said.

"They'll sell these fast, and then we're free," Huck said.

They each led a string of docile mules down to a slough below town. The mules didn't like the water, nosed it, but finally drank it. There would be enough cracked corn left to give them one or two meals. Jay despised the mules. They took a lot of work. They took feeding and watering and brushing and picketing and loading and unloading. Compared to mules, oxen needed almost nothing. Maybe once the mules got sold, Bones would rent rooms for the company.

By the time the young men returned, the company had built a camp, of sorts. Bones's discipline paid off in four huts each set on a slight slope for drainage, a pile of firewood, and a rope corral. The place was isolated, distant from any of the gold-bearing gullies. Maybe that was how Bones wanted it.

Jay and Huckleberry put the four feedbags to use, a quart of corn for each mule. It would be a while before all of the animals were fed. Boggs and Cassidy were boiling up some gruel, poor doings but that was about all the food left in camp. The upland country grew chill as the sun settled behind the surrounding mountains, but soon they'd be in town, having a fine time. Jay could hardly wait. No one else could, either. The company spooned up its gruel as soon as it was cool enough to eat. The itch was upon them all, and the gaudy streets of Deadwood seemed so inviting that the whole crew was ready to bolt for the nearest saloon.

But the boss man had other ideas.

"All right," Bones said. "This is a business trip, and we'll find out what we need to know. Boggs, you find out where the claims are recorded and what the rules are. Louis, you find out where the assayers are. Ephraim, we want to know where to sell the mules. Cassidy and Tyler, you talk gold with everyone. What's producing, what's not, what's placer gold, where the quartz veins are, and who's got them. All of you, we want to know what gulches were duds, what claims are played out, and where the gold's being milled or refined. You're not in Deadwood to have a fine old time. That'll come later. We're in Deadwood to move hard and fast."

He turned to Jay and Huck. "You two stay here, guard the camp and keep the mules close. There's going to be trouble around here, and you stay ready. We'll call you by name when we come in tonight."

"But Jake," Jay said. "We've been on the road for a long time."

"No buts."

"We can take turns. I'll stay two hours, then send someone else for two hours. Like that."

Bones stepped close. "You joined up. You'll fit in. Or you can beat it right now."

"Hey, let the boys come along," said Louis.

Bones whirled. "You want to try me?" he asked.

No one wanted to try Bones. One didn't become a sergeant in anyone's army without using his fists.

"Hey, it's not fair to the boys," Ephraim said.

Bones grinned. "Not fair at all. Life ain't fair. Want to test me?"

No one did.

They soon whooped away toward town, leaving Jay and Huckleberry to clean up the supper, scrape the tin messware, dig a toilet trench, and then stand guard, keeping a sharp eye for any sort of intruders, including angry Sioux.

Huckleberry toiled until the dusk thickened to the point where no one could see a thing, while Jay mostly pretended to work. He felt robbed of his liberty, cheated out of his reward for joining this rotten outfit. So he pretended to shovel a sanitary trench, and then quit, returning to the welcome warmth of the fire.

"Hey, you keep an eye out for a couple of hours, and I'll go in there and take a gander," Huckleberry said. "Then it's your turn. No need for two of us. You got that repeater, the mules are quiet, the night's young."

"Yeah, you go, and then I'll go," Jay said. "Quick little visit, look around, come back."

"I'll say my name. Don't shoot."

"Get back quick."

Huck vanished into the gloom. Cold air eddied down from the towering slopes, and Jay pulled a borrowed blanket around him. He needed everything: boots, clothing, tools, hat, and a side-arm, but so far he'd not even gotten what he'd need when cold weather rolled in. And now he was stuck.

Tomorrow he'd quit. All they did was make a slave of him, like Fairweather Foley. They were even. He'd put in a lot of work for a few pieces of clothing and some food. There'd be lots of good deals around Deadwood. He only needed to have a look and see what was the most promising.

Clouds obscured the heavens, making the night black, so he added some dry cottonwood debris, and waited for Huck. It really ticked him; Bones didn't trust him to do anything right. Maybe he should tell Bones he had a college degree. But some instinct told him to keep his trap shut about that. Tomorrow would be a good day. Maybe he'd stick with the company, maybe not. Maybe they were a bunch of crooks. But that wasn't it. They were sharp men, and going to do some dirty work, but probably weren't going to get into trouble around there. Maybe he could find a way to make his own fortune without telling them about it. There were other gold diggings nearby.

It sure was slow, sitting there alone. The more

he thought about it, the more he seethed. But nothing floating through his head speeded up the night. It just got more and more chilly.

A sudden thrashing told him there was trouble in the rope corral holding the mules. The mules were stomping and running, and he heard something break, and the mules were out into the night, heading every which way. He leapt up, carrying his Winchester, knowing it would be useless in full dark, and set out to find the mules, and see what was bothering them. He heard them as they pushed through the cottonwood grove and stepped on debris, but he didn't see a one. In fact, he was getting so far from his faltering fire that he was afraid of losing the camp himself. The truth of it was that eleven mules were loose, and he was responsible for them.

And it wasn't his fault. He didn't let it happen. It just happened. He didn't know what he'd say to Jake Bones, but he knew if he didn't get those mules back, he'd be in trouble. He drifted back to the camp, found no one there, tossed some more dead cottonwood into the fire, which caught quickly, and then collected a lariat and halter and headed into the dark. He didn't know where he was going, but managed to make wide circles.

He'd worked with mules for a while; he'd learned a thing or two. He headed downslope. The mules would drift downward, where grass and water might be found. And then he got lucky, almost bumping into one of them.

"Ho, there," he said.

The mule didn't shy. Jay worked his hands along the spine and neck, and soon had the mule haltered. But then he didn't know what to do. "Come on now," he said, walking a tight circle in the gloom, and finding the rest of the mules were nearby. Or most of them. Who could say? There were patches of clear sky, and sometimes these let in a little light, and he could make out the dark forms of the mules, which were mostly standing around, waiting for him to show them what to do.

What else was there but to take his one captive mule back to the camp and hope for the best? He tried talking, keeping his voice low and steady, and to his relief the other mules fell in behind him. When he reached camp Huckleberry was there.

"I thought you skipped town," Huck said.

"The mules broke loose. I could have used some help," Jay said.

"Serves you right for sticking around," Huck said, leaving the task of the mules to Jay. "I got to see the sights, and there wasn't anyone stopping me."

Chapter Fourteen

The next day the company got its marching orders from Jake Bones. Apparently the night in the saloons fishing for information paid off.

"Ephraim, you and Frank take the mules and tack to Billy's Livery Barn. There's standing offers for mules there. Get the best you can, but no less than a hundred a mule, and two hundred for the pack saddles and the rest. Bring the cash to me. If it's gold dust, get it weighed and checked at the assay office before you close the deal, and bring the dust to me."

"I'll be glad to get rid of the ornery beasts," Frank said.

"They served us well, and never forget it," Bones said. "Huckleberry, you're going to look at the claim ledgers, real close, and make some notes, and report to me. Cassidy, you and me are going to look for claims that aren't being worked. If they aren't worked for two days, they can be jumped. Boggs, you're going to study how things are laid out. I want you up every gulch and side gulch, seeing who's working claims, who's not, who's finding gold, who's armed, who's friendly. By the end of this day I want a report on every placer and quartz area around here. Warren, you're going to dig holes and build cairns. We're going to claim any unclaimed ground in any gulch. I got some ideas last night. You take a shovel, and a pick, and a tape. Placer claims are twenty-five feet across the gulch. You're going to prove up claims for the company."

"What do I know about gold?"

"You dig a hole and put up corner cairns and quit worrying about gold."

"That's hard work."

"Claims sell, and we'll profit. So get busy."

"How about someone with me?"

"Boy, you joined us late, borrowed clothing and ate our food, and you're about to start paying it back."

"When am I paid off?"

"When I say so. Now, the rest of you, you're going to find the quartz lodes, see what's being dug and who's digging it, and whether they're guarded. We're not jumping anything today, not tomorrow, not the next day. This is going to be a clean deal, and we're going to stay out of trouble with lawmen and miners' courts, and we're going to do just ⎯⎯ ⎯⎯ ⎯⎯ is careful, and we get it right, and there's no one sloughing ⎯⎯." He stared not at Jay, but at Huckleberry, so intently that Jay wondered if Bones knew about Huck's little excursion through Deadwood.

"Hey, wait until I see them books," he said. "I'll make us all rich."

"How do I know if I've filed right?" Jay asked.

Bones stared. "You're the college man, right?"

"Who do I list as owners?"

"The Fort Leavenworth Company, followed by my name. I own the company."

"How do I know it'll be divided right?"

Bones loomed suddenly over Jay. "If you want to leave the outfit, now's a good time."

Jay smiled. "We're almost on Easy Street, right?"

"Tell me now. Get in or get out."

Bones, like Boggs, was a massive man, and now he loomed mountainously over Jay.

"I'll stay," Jay said.

"We're holding your Winchester as a guarantee. That'll pay us if you skip."

There went Jay's only hope of a clean exit. He was counting on the repeater to get out and get connected with some other outfit. He was now a slave, for all practical purposes.

That overcast summer's day they spread out through the Deadwood Two-Bit Mining District to look things over, while Huckleberry headed into town to study the claims ledgers. Huckleberry was whistling; the rest, facing harder work, kept their silence. Jay, armed with a shovel and a twenty-five foot tape measure, watched the rest disappear on their assigned tasks until he was alone. Everywhere around him men in dungarees and worn boots and battered hats toiled, ripping gold from gravel, tearing it out of veins running along slopes and cliffs. Most of the men worked in pairs, usually with a sluice box. One would dig up gravel and load the sluice box, the other would bucket water through the box, washing away lighter rock while the heavy flakes of gold settled behind baffles on the slope. The lucky ones had water at hand, but plenty of miners were located up dry gulches, and had to bucket in every drop needed to pan or sluice their gravel. Jay could hardly imagine a more grueling way to make a few dollars. The toilers were at work again, grinding away at their diggings from dawn to dusk, with barely a break to eat, and not much to show for herculean toil. They were bearded, sweating men, their shirts soaked even in the gloom of the overcast. Some worked without shirts, their flesh roasted into chestnut colors.

Jay at first couldn't make out the claim boundaries; the corners were often marked with a single boulder, and the discovery cairn nothing but a few rocks with a tin can containing the claim itself. He wondered why the claims weren't stolen from their tin cans, and realized that the miners themselves stood watch, the protection of their neighbors' claims as vital as the protection of their own.

But no one was on Easy Street. These wretches would work themselves down to skin and bones and walk away with less dust than his father could spend in two minutes. So this was what Bones expected him to do? Dig a hole in gravel all day? Measure out a claim and put rocks in the corners? It was idiocy. With a little cash he could buy and sell claims and let others do the digging and hauling. He walked up one gulch clear to the rocky slope of the mountain behind it, and found the entire gulch claimed. So much for that crazy notion.

He found a couple of worn-out miners sprawled on the earth, taking a break.

"Found any color?" he asked.

"We're cleaning an ounce a day, friend."

"Is it running out?"

"Naw, getting better. We're getting lower in the gravel beds. We may need to do some serious digging after we scrape the surface."

"Hire men?"

"Nah, but get us some wheelbarrows, or wagons, and we'll take the ore down to water."

"You making good money, then?"

"This dust's worth about sixteen the ounce. That's eight a day. But of course nothing's cheap around here."

"We clear maybe five a day, friend. That's good money," the other man said. "Year or two, we'll take a good sum away."

"What'll that come to?"

"Who knows? We're hoping to clean up. Hit a pocket, and you go from a few dollars a day to thousands. Hit a big pocket, and you can retire for life."

"What's a pocket?"

"Oh, say a mess of dust has settled in a crack between some of the rock under the gulch. That can be big. Hundreds of ounces of dust, right there, ready to spoon out, hardly needs washing, big, heavy heaps of clean gold."

"Anyone around here hit one?"

"All over. It's not the sluicing and panning that counts; it's digging to pay dirt. I knew a man, two weeks ago, cleaned up five thousand, sold his claim for six more, and went back East."

"Any ground here not claimed?"

The older of the two eyed him. "You must be green, right?" He didn't wait for a reply. "Fella, there's not an inch of any gulch in any direction that's not claimed and staked and recorded."

"Where do you find pockets?"

"You got to be a geologist. You got to know how the rock lies, and where the old streams went that worked the gold out of the quartz. You got to know how it all got laid down. You need a good eye, a good eye you can't get from studying geology in some college; a good eye for the way the land goes. You got to have an eye for the seams and strata, how they dip. Maybe, if you have a good eye, you know where to dig for a pocket, fella."

"Sounds easier to buy a good mine or lode instead of looking for one."

"That's what all suckers think," the man said. "The ones looking for a quick buck, they'll believe anything."

He eyed Jay. "Guess we'll get back to the grind," he said.

"Yeah, sure," Jay said.

Those two had a hopeless task. Every pail of water they used had to be carried a couple hundred yards. They were drudges, doing everything the hard way.

He worked his way to the head of the gulch, where it gave way to a rocky escarpment. Every inch was staked and claimed. And there were cairns at the rugged scarp where lode miners had located seams of quartz.

He studied all the toiling placer miners on his way back down, seeing only the ceaseless toil; shoveling, lifting, carrying water, emptying sluice boxes of wet worthless rock, all for a few flakes of gold to put into their leather pokes. Madness. The world was full of idiots.

That day he ascended two more gulches, and found conditions in them much the same, except that the last gulch, called Elk Creek, had running water and washing the gravel was a lot easier than in the dryer gulches. He thought that any claim worth having would have plenty of water at hand to ease the burden. That creek had more miners on it than the dry gulches; but they weren't getting much out of it. Some told him they were cleaning only half an ounce a day out of their pans. Seven or eight dollars, if their luck held. But it sure was easier where the water was flowing. He hiked to the top, where springs rose at the base of a tan cliff, and found the whole creek marked. And there were cairns above it. The miners knew the gold flakes came from somewhere above, and got washed down, and they hadn't neglected the seamed, craggy mountainside where the original quartz veins still lay.

He wondered what Bones was talking about, telling him to stake a claim wherever he could. Everything was staked; he didn't see any likely ground all that day of wandering.

The sun was dropping behind the high ridges, and he knew it was time to start back to camp. Wherever he hiked, he saw ceaseless toil, even toil by war-wounded men, struggling with missing hands or limbs, somehow pouring their life-blood into the quest for gold. Even as shadows crossed the gulches and climbed the far walls, he saw not one miner calling it quits for the day. They would dig and wrestle rock and wash and hammer boulders until the light gave out, and maybe not quit then, because gold dust needed further washing in a pan, the debris carefully separated from the shining metal.

Suckers, the whole lot, but he grudgingly allowed that a few who hit pockets made their ordeal worthwhile. But it sure wasn't the way to make money; not the magic gateway to Easy Street.

When he got in, he found most of the Leavenworth Company collected there. Louis was boiling up some oat gruel. They were mostly silent, and Jay wondered what they had achieved that day, and how much closer they were to hitting pay dirt.

Bones let Jay wash up and settle down before he came over.

"Well?" he asked.

"I went up three gulches and didn't find any ground unclaimed."

"So you wasted a whole day wandering around?"

"I learned a lot about how it's done."

"Warren, we don't care how it's done. We don't care whether the claim's in a gulch. Go find a piece of ground anywhere, put up markers, dig the hole, and get us on record. Hear me?"

"You mean just ground somewhere?"

"Anything that looks likely. We're not going to mine it; we're going to sell it to suckers. Get that?"

"You mean just pawn it off?"

"Make it look good, boy. Pick ground anywhere near water. Dig your glory hole. You've wasted a whole day. You're not getting it. You're not helping the outfit."

Jay didn't answer. He thought he'd done well

that day. And he wondered why no one was talking about what the rest found or got done that long day. And why Huckleberry was looking uncommonly cheerful.

Chapter Fifteen

The mules sold easily, as Bones knew they would, and went for a hundred ten dollars apiece, and another three hundred for the pack saddles and tack. Bones divided the take with the eleven members of the original company, holding some back for food and supplies.

"I don't get any? Aren't I in with you?" Jay asked.

"Boy, these weren't your mules. These men supplied their own mules and gear, and this goes back to them. Now they got something to live on for a while."

"Well, what about me? How'm I supposed to live?"

"Boy, you prove yourself, and pay your debts to us, and we'll cut you in for a twelfth."

Most of the others watched this silently, but old Louis didn't.

"Here, boy, here's a five dollar greenback. You go have yourself a time in town."

"Don't give it to him," said Bones.

"I'm gonna give it. A man joins up, works steady, he needs some good times. Take it, boy."

Jay took the crumpled greenback gratefully. This time, he'd go to town too. There were no mules to tend. He eyed Bones, wondering what went through the man's head. The leader of the outfit was simply using him every way he could. If things didn't change, Jay was determined to get out.

Five dollars bought a lot, and seemed pure gold to Jay. Maybe he could have a few drinks, and keep out enough to double it at a Faro table. Or see about other things, he thought, his thoughts drifting to women.

They all took off for Deadwood after they had eaten. It was safe to leave a camp untended. They learned that camp thieves were hanged on the spot, and a sort of mutual protection operated powerfully in the districts across the Black Hills. So this time, he and his pal Huckleberry drifted in, finding lots of lamps lit along the clay Main Street. Deadwood seemed even more alive than by day. There weren't a lot of horses on the street. Miners traveled on foot.

"How come you're so cheerful?" Jay asked Huck.

"Looked at them ledgers. Man, they're full of trouble, just waiting to happen. Wrong dates, wrong everything. We're all gonna get so rich so fast we can keep a hundred girls happy at the same time."

"You're the only one in the outfit that thinks like me," Jay said.

"Yeah, they're all muscle and no brains, but we're all brains," Huck said.

"What did you see in the ledgers that's got you itching?"

"I'm not fixing to tell you. Old Bones, he's gonna look into it. But claim twenty-eight, it don't exist, and we'll make it exist."

"That's what brains are for, Huck."

They swung into the Gem Saloon and Dance Hall, which was booming. Wagon wheel chandeliers threw bright light over the throng, revealing a whole array of diversions. A bar lined one wall. A small dance floor filled with miners pushing a dime-a-dance girl around to the whine of an old accordion; and some green baize tables at the rear, including a Faro layout. A gent could find pretty near everything right there, and that's exactly what the bearded miners were doing just as hard and fast as they could part with their dust.

"You want a drink?" Huck asked.

They elbowed their way to the bar and Huck ordered two whiskeys.

"Redeye. You sip real easy until you get a little used to it," he said. He handed a tumbler to Jay, who sipped, gasped, and sipped again, downing the liquid lava. It didn't take but a moment for the stuff to steal through Jay, putting him into a cheerful mood. He eyed the dance floor and its thumping and stomping couples, and thought he'd try it if he could ever corral a girl. They weren't pretty and they weren't young, but they were real live ladies and they were whirling along, getting a cut of every dime, probably making money faster than the miners could pan it from the unyielding earth.

Huck vanished, and Jay didn't mind that at all. He wanted to prowl the Gem, and the other places along Main. There was the Number Ten Saloon nearby, quieter than this gaudy place. He'd prowl them all before he settled into some real fun for the evening. He choked down the redeye and tried the Number Ten, which was darker and quieter, with some serious gambling at several green tables, each table presided over by a tinhorn of some sort.

The whiskey was better at the Number Ten, but the place was a bore. It didn't bounce on its foundations, like the Gem. But he saw piles of chips on the tables, and men with greased-down hair doing some enterprising at the tables. But that wasn't what he wanted. He wanted a good time this first big night in Deadwood. So he drifted up and down the street, eyeing saloons and dens of various sorts, and finally settled on the Gem.

He bought five dances for fifty cents and waited, because every girl was tied up, and there were lines waiting. But he had some redeye to sip and real live women to watch. They were homely, but female, and they were gotten up in gaudy skirts and blouses, and could smile with the best of them while the accordionist sawed away at his squeeze box.

He finally got his chance with a freckled stout brunette who was showing some gray hair, and seemed a little desperate. He didn't care. He just wanted the company, and soon enough they were hand in hand, stomping away, while they careened off other couples. She wore a mechanical smile that never sagged.

"How much do you make?" he asked.

"I get half. The boss, Al, gets half."

"What does he do for his half?"

"Runs the business. Gets the music."

"You do well?"

"What business is it of yours?"

"I'm always looking at ways people make money."

"I do forty, fifty dances before I wear out."

"Two dollars? Two-fifty?"

"I get tips sometimes."

"Is that good money?"

"I can't make like doing anything else."

"You save it?"

"No, it all goes. Everything's high here."

"What about barmaid?"

"Hey, am I pretty or something?"

"Al, the owner, he just rakes in half? For what?"

"His place."

"Why do this?"

"Beats running from a mean husband."

The accordion whined down, and he spent his other dances on other women, getting the same story more or less. If the owner, Al Swearingen, got half of every dance sold that evening, he probably was making twenty dollars with no costs except for the musician. Easy Street. A man could clean up with a dance hall, at least until the gold ran out. And hardly do a lick of work.

He decided to head back to camp, with three and a half dollars in his britches. But he paused at the Faro layout, and decided on a sure thing, or almost. Three even bets, each doubling the previous so he'd recoup with any win. He bought some chips and bet fifty cents on the seven to win. It didn't. He bet a dollar on the jack to win. It didn't. He bet two dollars on the ace to win. But the aces tied and the dealer collected. It all happened so fast Jay hardly knew what hit him. Well, there'd be a lot more as soon as the company started cashing in. So he made his way out to the camp in the cottonwoods, and awaited a better day.

The next morning Jay got his orders.

"Here's what you're gonna do, boy," Bones said. "Ephraim's going to take you over to Fountain City and show you a gulch that hasn't been proven up, and you're going to lay out a claim and put up the corners and dig a glory hole, and we'll put it into the ledgers."

So Jay found himself trekking some distance from Deadwood, carrying a heavy pick and shovel, and a fifty-foot tape. The country was lower there, gentler, but probably less mineralized. Not that it made any difference. Bones had his ideas, and having a few unlikely claims to sell was one of them.

"Jay, my boy, heah's the deal," Ephraim said. "This here's been panned to pieces, and no one's found a dime on it, so we'll go a little lower, half-way flat around about, and you set to work. Claim's fifty feet across the gulch. You're gonna skip lunch; the old boy wants you to finish this up by sundown. That's how he laid it out. He wants a claim by sundown."

Jay eyed Ephraim and nodded. Another slave driver, he thought, as the older man settled into a ragged stride that would take him back.

Jay stared at the dry, forbidding, rocky gulch. There was no forest nearby; no jack pine on the slopes. Just a lot of nothing but tan clay and weeds. A rush to quit the company flooded him, but he didn't have enough in his britches even to buy a day's food. He felt like a slave.

It didn't matter where the discovery hole went, so he settled for the center of the gully and began digging through sandy clay that was full of small rocks. He didn't get far. A foot down he discovered a solid bed of rock. His shovel bounced off of it. He lifted the heavy pick and drove it, but the pick barely made a dent. He lifted the iron and dropped it again, but the point twisted away, hurting his hands. He stared at the forlorn little dent in the earth, and abandoned it. He would try a hole near the side of the gulch next time. He chose ground a little higher, and jammed his spade into hard clay that refused to break up, almost trapping his shovel. He jammed the spade down a few times, but the surface there was as hard as concrete. He had exhausted himself on the two attempts, and sat down to rest. The place was far enough away from the mining districts that he saw no one. That annoyed him too.

He poked his shovel and pick into a few more likely places and then gave up. That ground required a Hercules. He moved up the dry gulch a way, and tried there. The soil was a little more yielding, and he managed to get a foot down before his spade struck rock. He pried and twisted, but he failed to move the rock. So he tried another spot, with no better results. He had wasted a good part of the morning, and had gotten nowhere.

He made one last stab at digging a discovery shaft, with no better success. It was barely noon, and he had yet to dig a hole, measure out a claim, and build rock cairns on the corners. He wondered what he was doing there. This was what he called drone work. He was a college man, and there was no point in doing it when there were drudges everywhere, who could be gotten for a pittance. He stared at the solemn, empty gulch, and surrendered to it. This wasn't mineral land, as far as he could tell, and no one in his right mind would buy it, even if Bones salted the hole with some real dust. Wearily, defeated, he collected his tools and started back to camp, wondering what his fate would be. He scarcely cared. The Fort Leavenworth outfit had simply turned him into a slave, and he would quit them and hunt for some other outfit.

The route took him past some active digs, where sweating men were piling up loose gravel, and other sweating men were shoveling it into sluice boxes. They worked almost frantically, their bodies shining with sweat.

"Any luck?" Jay asked.

"You blind or something?" one bearded one shouted back.

"The claims all taken up?"

"No, we found color just this morning. We've got ours claimed, but up the gulch, who knows?"

His heart racing, he hurried up the gulch, past four other sweating, fevered men, and got to ground that was unmarked. There he dug a little dimple in loose gravel, not knowing whether he was in pay dirt or not because he had no gold pan. Then he measured out the claim, three hundred feet across the gulch, and put up corner cairns from loose rock.

"What's the gulch?" he asked.

"Cleveland Gulch, and you'll be number five from the discovery marker, friend," one of the miners said.

And then Jay hurried to Deadwood, intending to register the claim—for himself. And then he thought he'd better include Huckleberry, the one who was studying the ledgers. Easy Street at last.

Chapter Sixteen

They rose out of the mists shrouding Deadwood Gulch, twelve armed men, converging on Claim 28, and found no one there. And so they took it. They found the ownership cairn, put their own company's name on the paper, and settled down to wait. The former owners would show up soon.

It wasn't long after first light that two bearded men appeared, each with a shovel and pick. They surveyed the dozen members of the Fort Leavenworth Company, and approached warily.

"You're on the wrong claim, gents," one said.

"It's ours now," Bones said.

"This is Claim Twenty-eight, and we own it," the man said.

"Sorry, fella. Twenty-eight belongs to us. Go to the ledgers and have a look."

"You're stealing this," the other said.

"Be careful what you say," Bones said. "A man doesn't like to be called a thief."

Huckleberry was grinning. "Hey, go look at the books. There was no twenty-eight until we filed. It went from twenty-seven to twenty-nine."

"You goddamn crooks! This'll go to the miner's court, and we'll be back here in an hour. Now get off our claim."

But it was nothing but a whisper in the mist. He was talking to a dozen armed men.

"What's the trouble here?" asked a miner from the next claim, striding in.

"Claim jumpers!"

"You jumping a claim, are you? We've got a verdict for that, and it's called the noose."

"Before you start hanging us, you'd better check the ledgers," Bones said. He spoke it with such assurance that it sounded like the voice of God.

"I don't care what your flimsy excuse is. You've jumped my claim," the miner yelled. "And you'll soon find out how it plays out."

"I guess we will," Bones said. "Now, you gents get your tools and sluice box off our property, or we'll confiscate them."

"You can't get away with this!" the other miner bellowed.

Bones just smiled.

"Gents, you didn't file on it. You or whoever claimed it. Nothing there. You didn't even go to the books to check. So you got nothing but thin air," Huckleberry said.

By then, other miners from neighboring claims were swarming in, but none were armed, and they heard the story over and over, sometimes shouted, sometimes whispered.

"It ain't right. Damned trick," yelled one. "We'll be back, with some rope."

"You two, you got any dust? It's ours. You've been washing our dust."

"You'll roast in hell, and soon," the miner said. "This isn't over."

Another, older man, materialized out of the fog. "I'm Stuart. This is my district, elected last month. Now what's the trouble?"

The shouting miners told him.

"You jumped this claim?"

"We claimed this claim. They never filed."

"You sir," Stuart said. "Come with me. And you, Falmouth and Grady, you come with me."

Jay watched all this with amusement, his Winchester in hand ready to use. But it wouldn't be used. It was easy. The company would soon be sole possessor of Claim 28, and he would own a twelfth.

The dawn was oddly quiet. Far from hearing the sounds of men talking or shoveling or pouring water into sluices, Jay heard only a great tense quiet. He had arrived in this place before light, thinking it was reckless. But now his mind was changed. It was easy. Eleven revolvers and his repeating carbine made it easy. It was a lesson. Boggs, former army noncom, was in charge of all that, and had his men deployed artfully.

They could work the claim or sell it. They might fob it off for a lot of money. They might be ten thousand dollars richer tomorrow. And best of all, they had proven up their system. There'd be more like this, or more they could simply scare off and take over the abandoned claim. There were hundreds of claims in the area, and more filed every day, and new gulches being prospected. And any sharp bunch of sharp men could profit. Finally, he was looking at Easy Street.

It didn't take long. Bones and Stuart and the two miners returned. Wordlessly, the miners collected their gear. Then Falmouth approached Bones.

"Watch your back," he said. "We have friends, and claim jumpers don't."

"I guess that's a threat," Bones said. "We got it fair and square, and that's it."

The sullen crowd watched. The company had no friends here, and only the hardware at their hips was keeping things quiet. But in time the crowd drifted apart, men staying silent for fear of a bullet.

"All right, get to work, Warren," Bones said.

"Work?"

"Dig. We work the claim or lose it, and you're elected."

"Why me?"

"Because you've done least for the company."

"I've worked hard."

"What did you do yesterday? Set up a claim, like I asked? Got a hole in, cairns on the corners? Sorry, you shot an entire day eating our chow and doing nothing. So now you dig. You and Cassidy, you dig. Boggs, he's going to stand guard for a while. You're going to dig up gravel, Cassidy's going to wash it, and Boggs is gonna keep your neighbors honest."

"How about me standing guard? I got the repeater. Get someone else to shovel."

Bones loomed over him again. "You want to stay in or not? If you go, leave your repeater to pay what you owe us."

"I'm not good at shoveling."

"Yeah, all your fancy life you didn't shovel. So now you learn how it is in the rest of the world. So, shovel or walk."

Jay thought of his other claim, knew he'd quit the company as soon as he could, but intended to sneak out at night, with his repeater in hand, and the cartridges with it, and maybe get a shovel and a gold pan too. Then he'd be free, and rich enough soon. He'd have to slip word to Huckleberry, and figure out how to do it. Maybe the best deal would be to sell the new claim fast.

It occurred to him that maybe Bones saw the claim. They were, after all, examining the ledgers, but Claim 28 was on an earlier page. No, he was safe. He and Huckleberry would do just fine, but not this day.

He shoveled. There were other miners, watching all this with hooded eyes, and it wasn't hard to guess what they were thinking. A couple of men had been robbed of their claim, and this business wasn't over. So they stood watching, memorizing, waiting for the hour when things were different, when they were the armed party.

He scraped up gravel load by load and carried it to the sluice box where Cassidy washed out the gold and discarded the rest. It didn't take Jay long to weary of the unfamiliar routine, and he took longer and longer to scrape gold-bearing gravel out of the broad pit left by the other miners. His blisters were causing real trouble, too. He had a big, puffy one along the base of his thumb; several others on the heel of his hand and the base of his fingers. They broke, stung, and finally bothered so much he couldn't work.

He showed his hands to Cassidy and Boggs, and silently headed back to camp. No one said a thing. Neither of the other men sympathized, and neither offered him encouragement. They just stared at the ruin of Jay's hands and returned to the mining.

There was no one in camp. Bones was already working on the company's next projects, and had his men deployed, looking for unworked claims that could be jumped with some pretense of legitimacy. So far, at least, the company had stuck with the mining district rules. If the miners who worked Claim 28 failed to register it properly, it was their tough luck, and if the Leavenworth company collected, it was the company's good luck, but not a criminal act. That was all that kept a mob of miners from stringing up the claim jumpers.

Jay saw no way to bandage his blisters. They would simply leak fluids and blood and heal over. He wasn't good for anything for a while, so he lay down and napped. He was awakened rudely by Bones some time later.

"Show me your hands," Bones said.

Jay did. Bones studied them.

"Rich boy. I never should have took you on. You're no good to us. I should have known better. You'll sit here and eat our food and live in our clothing and boots and give back nothing."

Jay had no answer to that. He didn't ask to be sent into the West; he didn't ask to do menial tasks. He was only trying to survive.

But then Bones softened. "All right, if you can't do a man's work, you'll do boys' work. Your task is to look for unworked claims. I'm putting you on the Two-Bit district. It's a big district, lots of claims. You find any not being mined, you make note of it in writing, and take your timepiece with you. No miner can leave a placer claim for more than forty-eight hours, or it can be jumped."

Jay grinned. "Now we're talking," he said.

Bones stared so hard that Jay felt uneasy.

"I'll start right in," Jay said.

"Start at the claims office. Do it right. Maybe you'll prove your worth. Or maybe not."

Jay caught the implication. A last chance.

Jay headed into a fine summer's day, a glorious day, not too hot, breezy, bustling with life and delight. He was free. He'd never lift a spade the rest of his life. He'd never do drudge work. He'd leave toil to toilers. He found Deadwood alive with commerce. Wagons lined the streets. Men were loading and unloading them.

The claims ledgers were located in a rude building that also contained a mining hardware store and an assayer. It was not an official government operation, but one established by the miners themselves, who had organized their district and adopted rules, mostly based on the rules in countless other mining areas. The miners paid to record their claims with a pinch of dust, enough to keep a clerk on hand.

The ledgers were open to inspection by anyone. There were also simple charts depicting each gulch and district, the discovery claim and numbered claims radiating from it. These were what Huck Jones had been studying, and how he had struck pay dirt when he found that Number 28 had not been recorded.

There were few people in the building. Only rarely did a miner walk in with a new claim to record. That gave Jay the chance to introduce himself to the clerk, a war-injured veteran with a bad right arm and a perpetual scowl.

"I'd like to look at the Two-Bit District," he said.

"Another claim jumper," the clerk said.

Jay smiled broadly. "Well, maybe something's for sale."

The clerk spat into a brass spittoon. "Horse-pucky," he said. But he handed the ledger to Jay, who found the entries neatly recorded, numbered in sequence, with the owner or owners listed by name. There were plenty of foreign names, he thought. People fresh off the boats, trying out their luck. Obviously more toilers and drudges.

Among the names was his own. His claim, hastily filed, was in the Two-Bit district, and unless he worked in this day, he could lose it. He hadn't any idea what to do. He had included Huckleberry's name, but he saw no sign of him. Huck could work it. Jay had blistered hands, no shovel, no gold pan, no pick, and no sluice box. His heart raced.

He needed to head that way fast. There was one option, and that was to sell it, sell it fast, and for whatever anyone would pay for it. Before it was jumped. He raced out the door, into the dazzling day, and headed toward the district, hoping it wouldn't be too late. He hiked for half an hour, confused about where the claim was, which side gulch was the one he had wandered into.

And when he did at last figure it out, and headed for his claim, he found two familiar people working it. Jake Bones and Boggs.

Chapter Seventeen

Jay stared. He curbed an instinct to run. They halted their digging and waited. He knew that this had been planned and he could not turn back the clock.

"Well, Warren, you got us a nice little claim after all, didn't you?" Bones said.

Jay had nothing to say.

"Huckleberry, he was pleased to find his name on it, and he was quick to switch it over to the Fort Leavenworth Company, seeing as how we're all tied together by agreement. Of course, when you couldn't dig, we came right over to make sure no one jumped the claim. Good dust here; we'll do fine if the dust doesn't peter out."

Jay learned something fast. Huckleberry Jones was first and foremost a part of the company, and had wasted no time at all transferring the property to the company. Jay thought he might still own half, but knew he didn't. There was no agreement between Huck and himself as to how it was to be divided up.

"Well, boy, you go study on the other claims in the district, and maybe you can find another for us," Bones said. "We got relief coming; Ephraim and Louis will be shoveling here right quick."

There was no way to fight it. No way to get his

claim back. Maybe he'd get one twelfth, though. So he just smiled. "It's a dandy," he said. "Those men below, they're clearing two or three ounces a day."

Bones nodded. "Better than that. They told us they're into real pay dirt. They're looking at a bonanza. And to think you nailed this one for the company," Bones said.

Jay wondered what Bones knew. Maybe Huckleberry had made a hero of Jay. But no; this had been set up. It was no accident that the two top men of the company, Bones and Boggs, were on the claim when Jay showed up. They were toying with him.

"Pay dirt, boy. The company's doing just fine."

Jay contained his bitterness. He was damned if he'd let them see through him.

"I'll find a dozen more for us," he said.

They laughed, and it wasn't a pleasant laugh.

He swallowed his rage. Sergeant Boggs well knew what to do with men who'd gone berserk. And Sergeant Bones did too. They'd kill him, or maim him so badly he'd be a living ruin. Maybe he'd kill them. His repeater would do the job from a distance. The grim thought burned in him, and wouldn't go away.

He headed for the main diggings while they watched his back. It all flooded cold through him as soon as he got away. That claim had grown in his mind through the restless night. That claim would put him on Easy Street. He'd sell it, or hire someone to dig it and pocket a fortune. He could get out of the West, a place he despised, and go back to civilization, and laugh at his old man and his sire's whole stupid idea of what makes a worthwhile man.

All gone, drained out of him like blood. He drifted through the claims, watched bare-chested men sweat and shovel and sometimes sink into sand for a five-minute break, which was their lot from sunrise to deep into twilight every day, without surcease. He knew now that most of them would hardly pay their way or have a thing left over after shelling out for costly groceries, with sky-high prices because they had been carried in freight wagons hundreds of miles.

Watching them, he felt a deep fear, something he had scarcely known before. He couldn't toil that way, day upon day. He wasn't sure whether he could even walk into the camp of the Fort Leavenworth Company after betraying them. They were still feeding and sheltering him but would that continue? His fate hung like a Damocles Sword, and he couldn't fathom what to do.

He spent the remainder of the day drifting from one digging to another, blotting up whatever there was to learn. He saw no claim that was not being worked. Quite the opposite; men were feverishly gouging and scraping and clawing up gravel from the bed of the gulch, chopping lower and lower in pursuit of the heavy gold. He found no opportunity for another claim-jump that afternoon, though he did improve his understanding of how things worked in the gold fields. It had been a dull day. There was nothing entertaining in the sight of hundreds of sweating men clawing at rock.

Late in the day, he hiked back to camp, still fearful and now wondering if he would be welcome there. He was hungry. He did not want to face hunger. He found all the company present, most of them resting while the cooks boiled up some stew for supper. No one shunned or condemned him. Perhaps his betrayal was known only to Bones and Boggs, and of course Huckleberry. Then, before supper, Bones collected them close and announced that he had sold Claim 28 for a thousand dollars in greenbacks and would divide the proceeds with the company, saving out forty dollars for food. Jay's mind raced. Nine hundred sixty dollars, divided by twelve, would be eighty apiece. If they cut him in. He waited anxiously. He wanted that eighty, along with a night in Deadwood, as badly as he had ever wanted anything in his life. But what would Bones do?

But the boss man made no reference to Jay. Instead, he did pay out eighty to each man, mostly in tens. When he came to Jay, he did not hesitate, but laid the cash in Jay's hand, and went on to the next man. It worked. Payday. This outfit knew how to get rich. Money in hand, just by having a sharp eye. Old Huckleberry looked at the books and they all made money. The company had struck gold just a few days into its sojourn in Deadwood.

The other men were grinning, and making a few jokes about spending the whole lot in one evening. Well, Jay thought, that was the drudges and toilers for you. He'd put seventy away, and squander ten. He was on his way to Easy Street. And he had been made a part of the company at last, and had gotten his twelfth. A few months, and he'd head back to civilization as a self-made man.

"You want to head into town, Jay?" Huck asked.

"Soon as we clean up the stew," Jay said.

They all ate fast. Louis had come up with some buffalo stew, flavored with whatever vegetables he could find in town, mostly turnips and cabbage. Often there was no choice. The food supply barely kept up with the exploding population.

But who cared? Jay didn't. Cash in his pockets, cash for anything at all. A dime a dance, a tumbler of redeye, what did it matter?

They cleaned up. Part of the camp discipline was that everyone cleaned his mess kit, and cleaning up the kitchen rotated among the crew.

Jay and Huck took off just as fast as they could

clean up, and that wasn't fast enough to suit either of them. Others were heading into town, determined to enjoy the payday.

They'd hardly gotten beyond the firelight before Huckleberry opened up the forbidden topic. "You sure came close to getting axed," he said.

"I wanted you to have half of the claim. I thought you'd like that."

"Jay, I'm not the only one reading the claims ledgers. Quick as I saw it, I added the rest, which I could do, seeing as how I was listed as one of the owners. So the whole company got put on there. It didn't fool Bones none. He can read handwriting. But neither could he do much against you, not with everyone's name scribbled out, and no way of knowing whether you'd tried to pull a fast one. So that'll pay off, too. It's got good gold on it, and they'll see if it's a claim to work, or sell off like Twenty-Eight."

Jay laughed. "I was wondering how it went. I was wondering if I'd even have a meal tonight. We're heading for Easy Street."

"Quit living on wishes," he said. "We hardly got ourselves going, and there's other outfits doing the same claim jumping, and not getting anywhere. We'll get a little rougher soon; Bones has ways he ain't talking about yet. But for now, we keep it all clean."

"What ways?" Jay asked.

"Wouldn't you like to know, pal. Just stick with

us, and don't pull anything fancy like you just did, and maybe you'll do."

Jay resented the tone of voice. He was still not a part of the outfit, just someone they picked up along the way.

Deadwood was bustling that night. Lamplight shown from the saloons and dance halls. Stores were open too. The evening had cooled down, and lured miners into town from all the outlying camps. They headed instinctively for the Gem, which seemed the place where the action was. It sure was humming this night, with a mob of miners eager to squander the dust they had painfully collected all day under the boiling sun. Let them, Jay thought. If they went broke, he could buy up their claims dirt cheap. He'd hold back some of his loot and plunge when he saw the chance.

They were all strangers in there. Deadwood was a new town, flooded with people from everywhere. And the only friends people had were those they came with. Huckleberry drifted off to the dime-a-dance girls, but Jay wanted to wet his whistle first, and elbowed his way to the bar.

"What have you got that's not redeye."

"Redeye," the pocked keep said.

"You got some good rye?"

"Redeye," the man said, and started pouring. That was the choice, take it or leave it.

Jay took it, paid, eyed the crowd, sipped, gasped at the month-old whiskey, and drifted through the place, ending up watching a Faro game. There was a different dealer this time, this one gaunt and cheerful, with eyes that glowed like hot coals. The table was surrounded by plungers, blowing their dust as fast as they could, while the dealer and case keeper tried to keep up with the bets, measuring powder for chips, and drawing the pairs.

"Suckers," someone next to him said.

"Even odds though," Jay said.

"You're a virgin," the sallow man said. "You're just itching to lose your poke."

"Done that," Jay said.

"But you didn't learn a thing," the man said.

That irked him. "I'll show you what I learned," he said. He pulled out fifty dollars in greenbacks, and was served immediately. The dealer was happy to get greenbacks. Dust wasted time. He studied the cases, saw that the sevens hadn't been played, and bet a dollar on seven to win. He saw that two jacks had been played, and placed another dollar on a jack and coppered it, meaning he was playing it to lose.

Wild night. The first card out of the box was a jack, so he collected. The second card was a seven, so he collected. And that's the way it went, for one fevered hour in which he could do no wrong, and when the luck finally turned, he had the sense to get out. He had made forty-three dollars.

"You were lucky. Next time you'll be confident it'll happen again, and lose a hundred," the same sour observer said.

"So, I didn't see you playing."

"I only play where the odds are in my favor," he said.

"There's no game in town like that."

"Of course there is. You can bet on claims. Anyone with some smarts can make a fortune. Mind you, with some smarts."

"Claims? Buying and selling?"

"Regular curb exchange."

"What's that?"

"Street exchange, curb, they meet on the street at a place, and bid and sell. It rips away most afternoons and some nights, all depending on how many show up."

"Where's that?"

"Now, every night, on Main Street down at the Bella Union."

"I didn't get your name," Jay said.

"I don't offer it," the man said. "It's better if you don't know who I am. Then when you lose you won't have anyone to shoot."

"Show me the place," Jay said.

"Well, I've roped in another sucker," the man said. "What do you know about mining?"

"I'm learning."

"Will you even know whether you're bidding on a place or lode claim?"

"What do you care?"

"I thought I might advise you, for a piece of the property if you collect on a bid."

"You can tell me what's a good prospect?"

"It's your task to reject my horsepucky," the man said.

Chapter Eighteen

Jay sniffed opportunity in the wind.

"I didn't catch your name," he said.

"Call me Deal. Jack Deal. Now I have you. I'll clean you out."

"I've got nothing to clean."

"Claims come cheap, my friend, and you'll have one before the night's over."

He started walking, and Jay followed, and soon found himself at the new Bella Union saloon, where a dozen men congregated on the walk, sometimes shouting a price, sometimes just waiting for action.

"This is the curb, the street exchange?"

"This is where you'll squander your loot," Deal said.

"How does it work?"

"You dumb or something? Figure it out."

"Lot forty-seven, Two-Bit, asking two and a half," one man shouted.

"Strawberry, quartz lode three, asking ten five," another man in a bowler barked.

But there were no takers.

"Bid one, claim eighty, Elk Creek," a man said.

"Claim eighty, Elk Creek, offering one and a half," someone responded.

"Claim eighty, Elk Creek, bid one and a quarter," the bidder said.

"Done," said the seller.

Both repaired to the saloon, where an accounting book rested at the end of the crowded bar, and the sale was transacted and payment made, and a deed to the claim given to the buyer.

Jay watched, fascinated. The bidding was in hundreds of dollars, and there was no information about the value or history of the claim. It was up to the speculators to find out those things. The curb exchange dealt with prices and nothing else, and the new owner could record his ownership in the mining district ledger.

All of this had transpired deep in the evening, with the last light of summer glowing over the western ridges.

"We're about to fold. You want a crack at one?" Jack Deal asked.

Jay had his Leavenworth seventy, and forty-some dollars he'd won. Why not? He nodded.

"Offering, Claim Two, Deadwood, one."

The second claim, next to the discovery claim, just up the road, going for a hundred dollars?

"Bid one," Jay said.

"Done, boy."

They walked into the Bella Union. Jack Deal wrote the transaction in the accounts book, wrote out a deed, accepted the greenbacks, and handed the deed to Jay.

"You got to register that worked out bunch of gravel tomorrow to make it stick," Jack Deal said.

"Worked out?"

"Gotcha, boy. That old heap of tailings had been scraped to death. I knew you'd bite. You're the type. Always looking for quick cash. Cheer up. Maybe you can find another sucker. That claim's turned over thirty times, already."

"I'll sell it back to you for half," Jay said.

Deal grinned. "It ain't worth the effort."

"You mind showing me this claim?"

"We'll have us a hike, boy, the curb's quit for the night."

Nothing but alpenglow lit the way, but Deal knew where he was going. They walked up the gulch a little, and then he cut down a grade that was nothing but worked-out gravel, into the gulch itself. It was forlorn. Heaps of worked over rock lay about, catching the glint of afterglow, and not a weed or a plant survived in that desolated place.

"Don't know where the corners are. Rock in them's probably been busted up and panned," Deal said.

"You don't even know the borders?"

"Nah, and no one cares. You could dig anywhere in a hundred yards of here and no one would care. No one would stop you. It's dead workings. Same's true of all these old claims. They're dead and gone to heaven, boy."

Light from somewhere, stars or town or a moon

below the horizon, threw the rock pile into relief. There was indeed a lot of gravel, heaps and pits, some of the pits loaded with foul water. That's what he had bought. That's what he would try to unload on the next sucker, if he could summon Jack Deal's skills.

"You got me good, Jack."

"Now I'm Jack am I? How'd I get elevated to first-name from a rube I just took?"

"You'll teach me, Jack."

"Teach you, you better teach yourself or go broke even faster. Maybe you should stick with Faro, boy. You made a few bucks there, and now I got it."

"I can go in there, to the curb, and sell it if I can?"

"Sure, if you got the right papers. You get caught selling something you don't own, you could end up in hock the rest of your short life if they don't hang you first."

"I mean, I can be a trader?"

"Nothing to stop you, boy, except common sense."

"I'll get rich," Jay said. "This is the easiest thing I've ever done."

Deal laughed. It was a nasty, knowing laugh. "If you're not shot in six months, buy me a drink," he said.

They hiked up the gravel grade, and Jay found himself in town again. The saloons were alive.

There were miners drifting from one joint to another. The new Bella Union swallowed some, while others drifted into Number Ten, and a few were clustered around the open doors of the Gem, drinking their beer or redeye out on the rutted street on a perfect summer's eve. Jay eyed them, thinking that every one of them was a mark, and he'd sell his empty pile of gravel just as easily as Deal sold it to him. He spotted Huckleberry, who seemed transfixed with the dime-a-dance girls. At the bar of the Gem he saw Louis and Ephraim, soaking their flesh in spirits. He supposed the rest of them were enjoying the fine night, their pockets full of loot, their appetites uncurbed.

"So long, sucker," Deal said, and took off into the busy night.

That rankled, but Jay knew he'd get even soon. He drifted into the Gem, discovered Huckleberry standing free between dances, and decided to try a whirl or two.

"You having a time?" he asked Huck.

"Nah, I'm quitting this. Big time now."

"What do you mean by that?"

"Follow me, boy."

Huckleberry led Jay out of the Gem, across Main Street, down a cross street, and into a low area, ill-lit except for two or three red lanterns bobbing in the night breeze.

"Dora DuFran's," Huck said. "You're in for a fine old time, boy."

Why did they call him boy? It ticked Jay off. But he followed, his pulse quickening.

They were met by the rattle of an untuned piano, and discovered half a dozen gents and a few ladies in gauze around it. Someone with handlebar mustachios was banging on it, and Jay concluded it was a miner. No pianist would play that badly. But that didn't hold his attention for more than half a second. There they were, the first public women he had ever seen, and one could see a large amount of them under the gauze, which shifted subtly over them with every movement, and forcing his imagination to fill in what was not quite there in the warm lamplight.

They came in all sizes, lean, short, chubby, and a broad-shouldered one probably off a farm, and they weren't shy, not one bit.

"Oh, some new sweethearts," one said, meeting them with open arms and opened everything else. Jay got himself soundly kissed. They seemed genuinely delighted, and Jay couldn't decide whether it was all theater, or whether they really, truly, happily enjoyed male company. If they were acting, they were very good at it.

"Serve 'em a little warmer upper," said an attractive brunette lady in her middle years, who he guessed was madame. And that proved to be correct. At her beck, a nymph headed for a small bar, poured, added a splash, and returned with two drinks.

Jay didn't mind a bit that the stuff was rotgut. It warmed him up, just where he wanted to get warm, in the pit of his stomach. He tried to join in the singing of Sweet Adeline, but he was much too rattled. He just stood there and stared at one girl after another.

The truth of it was that he was almost virgin. A little hanky-panky with Consuela, the ambassador's daughter, in a rose garden was as far as he had gotten. But he considered himself a worldly man. Everyone at Harvard soon became worldly men, knowing all there was to know about such things. Only now he was rattled, and the more he tried to focus on the mustachioed piano banger, the more he was glancing at the merchandise.

Madame DuFran eyed him knowingly, and waited.

It didn't take Huckleberry long. A small, whispered consultation, and he vanished with a vast blonde Viking, looking pretty flustered himself. Huckleberry wasn't as smooth as a Harvard man, Jay thought. No, not at all. The blonde led Huck through wine-colored velvet drapes into some dimly lit paradise just beyond, which was mostly silent except for a giggle or squeal now and then. Jay eyed the drapes as if they were the entry into some mysterious heaven.

There were, at the moment, four nymphs to choose from, and he began examining them, as one does nude statuary, weighing the strong suits against the weaker ones. But then he reminded himself that it wasn't the package, it was the performance, or so the brothers at the university had said, and one ought to look for someone loose-lipped, smiling, and with good white teeth.

The most likely candidate was Clara, who smiled back, shrugged herself a little looser from her gauzy kimono, and offered him further examination. She was luscious, wanton, inviting, with alabaster flesh and fiery eyes. He wasn't sure about her teeth, but the rest of her would do in a pinch.

The pianist was playing Roaming in the Gloaming, and singing, too. But Jay had eyes only for Clara, who ceased singing and licked her lips.

"I see you have made a fine choice," said Madame DuFran. "Clara is our most popular, most sought-after, and most notable lady, the queen of our little establishment. Men across the whole world remember her and pine for her. And now she's yours. Of course, good taste has its price, but that is only a trifle compared to what awaits your eager lips."

"Ah," said Jay.

"A simple donation of five dollars, and she will be yours to enjoy and remember. I do believe it's your first experience? That always makes it better."

"Ah," said Jay.

"The thing is to go slow, my dear. Don't speed up if you can help it. Some poor wretches, why the whole trip to paradise lasts thirty seconds. No, you're much too much a man to succumb to that. You'll wander through the little moments of joy as you become acquainted in utter privacy, of course, and then everything will be simply beyond words."

Ah . . ." Jay croaked.

"Dear boy, dig into your britches, if you can still get a hand in there, and extract a small gratuity, and go enjoy her."

He did plunge a hand in, found only a single bill there, and desperately hoped it would be a five-spot. But no, it was a crumpled single, forlorn.

She looked at it, and at him, and sighed. "Maybe next time," she said, running a hand along his overheated shoulder and arm.

"Would you take a claim?" he asked.

She was suddenly all business. "Which?" she asked.

He pulled it from a pocket and handed it to her. "Deadwood, Claim Two," he said. "I'll trade it for Clara."

She sighed, not unkindly. "I'm sorry, dear. I've already owned it several times, and can't get rid of it for any price. Claim Number Two has seen its day. The first time I got it, I sold it for twenty dollars, but it's gone down hill ever since. I'm afraid it's nothing but gravel. And I don't offer my beautiful girls for free. But it'll pay me for your drinks," she said.

Jay took one last look at Clara, who was smirking, and plunged into the night.

Chapter Nineteen

Jay's mood was as black as the night surrounding him as he headed back to camp. But then Huckleberry caught up with him.

"Hey, that was fine," he said. "What happened to you?"

"I didn't have enough money."

"But you had your whole stake."

"I got suckered into a buying a bad claim."

He spilled out the whole thing to Huck.

"So there went my stake and my winnings at Faro. All to a confidence man called Jack Deal. It's a made-up name. No one gets named Jack Deal."

"Can you rattle his teeth and get it back?"

"Nah, but it's a way to get rich fast if you know what you're doing. I'm thinking how I'm going to work it."

"I don't get what you're saying."

"Jack Deal cleaned me out without half trying. It's the deal I've been looking for. I'm going to find dead claims and pawn them off for good money at the curb exchange."

"You? But you know nothing about that."

"That's the whole deal. No one else does either."

"Someone'll come after you with a loaded revolver."

"If they ever find me. I'll change my name to Jay Profit."

Huckleberry laughed. "I always knew there was something I liked about you, pal."

"Trouble is, I won't have a stake for a while, the way Bones is moving. Day after day, and nothing happens."

"Maybe he'll give you a stake and you'll trade for the whole company."

"This is my deal, and I won't share it, and I'll get into it with what the company pays out."

"They won't like that."

"Too bad," Jay said.

The camp was quiet. Most of the company was still in town, spending their piles as fast as they could. Huckleberry vanished, leaving Jay to his own devices. He'd gotten the best lesson of his life this evening, and he intended to use it, and use it hard. Newcomers were so eager to get a bona fide claim, any sort of claim, that they'd cough up real money and not bother to see if the ground was worth anything at all. What could be better? If there is a sucker born every minute, as the saying went, then he'd invite the suckers into his parlor and clean them out. So, even though he lost his stake this evening, he had gained a future. He climbed into his bedroll feeling comfortable, knowing soon he wouldn't be sleeping on hard ground, but in a fine room in town.

The next days dragged. He wanted the next

payout quick, so he could start picking up dead claims. The company was working the Two-Bit claim, and finding some gold, and that would be all it took to auction the claim off for a good price. No one wanted to work the gravel; why toil all day and half the night to collect an ounce of gold dust? That was the sucker way to get rich. Cassidy and Ephraim, who did most of the digging and sluicing, complained loudly about being stuck with the muscle work, so Bones compensated them with extra large servings from the cook pot.

Meanwhile, the outfit was hunting for more claims to jump. Jay had a small pocket notebook that he used to keep track of each claim in his area, and whether or not it was worked each day. An unworked claim was fair game. But each sunny day, and some rainy ones, too, he watched the drudges sweat away amid piles of gravel, all for a tiny pinch of gold dust.

But he was also seeing what claims had been abandoned, studying the heaped gravel and noting the location. Little by little, he collected an inventory of unworked claims he would try to pick up cheap. Once in a while he saw Chinese working the dead claims, patiently hunting for anything that had been overlooked by the original owners. Mostly other miners left them alone.

Jumping claims was proving to be slower and harder than anyone in the Leavenworth company had imagined, and there were half a dozen other outfits prowling for easy pickings. Bones and Boggs were turning sour, and took it out in explosions against the rest of them, usually at supper.

"What a bunch of pansies," Boggs complained. "If you don't come up with something soon, we'll be doing things a little different here."

Jay didn't know what that meant.

Then Rags Tyler came up with the next one. Tyler was one of the quietest in the company, mostly keeping to himself. Jay hadn't ever talked with him long enough to know his story.

"Fella I been watching on the Strawberry," Tyler said. "He's got dysentery real bad, and stays in a tent in the shade of a tree. His neighbors are feeding him, but the gossip is, he's not long for the world. The two miners in the claim below make a show of working the sick man's claim for a few minutes each day, but it's all for show. I say, we jump it. The man's croaking, so no one's gonna get mad."

"How many days has he been sick?" Bones asked.

"Three, four."

"It's ours then. And we'll move right now. There's a few other outfits around here that might be waiting."

This was at supper. Bones intended to jump the claim at dusk, and get settled in, taking advantage of darkness.

He named six men, including Jay, and told them arm themselves and to bring bedrolls. They set out for the strawberry diggings, kept out of sight, and crawled into the Strawberry District along the jack pine slopes.

It worked just fine. The claim didn't have a miner on it, and at dusk the Leavenworth men took it over, wrote an ownership claim and put it in a bottle there. And then a dozen miners, none armed, descended on them.

"You trying to jump this?" one asked.

"Beat it. It's ours, and if you want a fight you'll get it," Boggs said.

"Happy Parsons died this afternoon. It was his claim. He willed it to me. I've just recorded the transfer in the district ledgers. So, beat it. Not yours."

"Try to take it, if you can," Boggs said.

Jay could see that none of these miners were armed, and that whoever occupied the claim was likely to keep it, so long as they stayed armed.

The miner, a big man with a full brown beard, eyed the Leavenworth company, not missing that the claim jumpers were well armed. His gaze settled on Jay, and his repeating Winchester.

"The barrels of guns speak loudly," he said, "but a noose speaks louder."

Boggs grinned. "Where have I heard that before?"

The miners were keeping their feelings under

wraps. Guns ready to use against them did that. But Jay could sense the cold white rage boiling through them.

"I'll require you to abandon this claim, and right now," the man said.

"And who'm I speaking to?" Boggs asked.

"Storm Foley," the miner said.

Jay wondered if he was a brother of Fairweather. It seemed likely. Foley could muster a lot of support, including the army, which was policing the district. If the miner was from that family, there could be serious trouble.

"Sorry, Foley. We're here, and we're claiming it," Boggs said.

Foley simply stood for a moment. "We'll see," he said.

That chilled Jay. An innocuous sentiment, but one laden with menace as far as Jay could fathom. But then he remembered an aphorism: Faint heart never won fair maid, and he laughed. This would be easy. Life would soon be easy.

The unarmed miners drifted into the night. Jay could feel their heat, and no doubt it would be voiced just out of earshot. But muzzles of guns did speak loudly. The Winchester cradled in his arm didn't comfort him. And he didn't want to use it. And he feared that before the night had passed, he might. There were plenty of armed men among the miners, veterans of the war, who knew all that they needed to know.

And there was the threat that hung over them now, the loop of rope that dangled from a good hanging tree, and was an instrument of summary justice without appeal. The miners were many; the Leavenworth outfit a dozen. Their campsite was well known now. It wasn't exactly a fortress, a collection of tents on the edge of jack pine forest below town. It could be jumped just as easily as they had jumped a dying man's claim. Jay suddenly wanted out, wanted out so badly he was ready to walk away and head anywhere but back at the camp.

But Boggs, almost as if reading Jay's thoughts, had other ideas. "That gravel mound. Get behind it. That's your post for the night. I'll be next to you, over at that gravel pile there. Bones will get supplies to us in the morning. We dig in here until they give up, and then we've got it."

"They're more likely to show up with the army," Jay said. "And a coil of rope."

"You yellow?"

"This isn't a good idea."

"I knew it. You've got no balls. You want to quit? Go ahead. Walk away. Get out of the company. Who needs you?"

"I'll stick."

"I'd be a hell of a lot happier if you'd walk."

"Look, some people are good at some things, and other people have other talents. I can make money for the company easier than this. This isn't very bright."

"You accusing me of something, Warren?"

Jay shut up. He settled into the hard gravel, knowing he'd have a bad night. It grew dark, and the district quieted, and cook fires flickered out. About midnight, by Jay's reckoning, Huckleberry and Louis showed up with canteens of water and some hardtack of a sort the miners kept on hand. That helped, but it was still the worst night of his life, and he wondered what sort of hell would shine when the sun rose. He half expected to see a lynch mob, along with a few bluecoats from the army. He thought of slipping away, but he didn't. He tried to find some place comfortable, but couldn't, and finally just drifted through a terrible darkness until a little gray cracked the eastern horizon.

The day brightened, and nothing happened. The neighboring miners kept a good distance away. Bones arrived, sent the night crew back to camp, and put some others on the claim, with shovels and picks and a couple of gold pans. They would work it. They would prove it up. Boggs was right. The miners might gripe, but they didn't want to face down a group of armed men, especially over a claim that wasn't theirs.

Jay hiked wearily back to camp, which was far away. There was some oat gruel in the pot, which he ate and tumbled into his bedroll. He thought he knew what the company was up to now. If jumping claims required armed force, the company was ready for action. He didn't know how he felt about that. He wasn't sure this was over. He wasn't sure but what a whole army of miners and officials might show up and haul them away.

He dozed in the morning light, awakened, dozed again, and nothing happened. The Leavenworth company had a good claim going in the Two-Bit District, and now a working claim in the Strawberry District. And he had a piece of both. There was one thing about all this that tickled him. The man who'd gotten beaten out of the claim, Storm Foley, had to be related to Fairweather, and that made it all the more fun. Storm might rage, but the Leavenworth company sat on the Strawberry Claim, and Storm could go back to loading freight wagons for a living.

That late summer Thursday got better and better as time passed and no one troubled them. Foley didn't put the night crew to work that day, and Jay decided to head into Deadwood and watch the curb exchange in front of the Bella Union. Pretty soon he'd be in the middle of it, making easy money, and fast.

He wandered into town on a glorious afternoon, the benevolent sun stirring up cool breezes. The air was so good it brought out shoppers. A few women in bonnets were loading up their arm-baskets. Teamsters were, as usual, unloading freight wagons.

"It's you, is it?" Ike, the Foley wagon boss said. "Storm Foley's looking for you. You're getting quite a reputation, boy. It'll likely survive you."

Chapter Twenty

Angry thundershowers each afternoon made Jay miserable. He did four-hour shifts on the disputed claim, where there was no shelter and no recourse but to endure the lashing of icy late-summer downpours.

The storms made havoc of the Leavenworth camp, too, and forced the men to trench their tents to keep from sleeping in pools of muddy water. They'd spent weeks living in rough ways, barely sheltered, devoid of comforts, unable even to wash clothing or scrape the grime off their bodies.

There were other sorts of thunderclouds, too. Bones kept two men posted on the claim, and warned that anyone who approached it would be shot on sight. And neighboring miners had better be mining, because any trespass on the disputed claim would be fatal.

It didn't go well at the claims office, either. Storm Foley showed his bill of sale, given as an inheritance, and was duly recorded as the owner of the claim. But Bones had hotly disputed that, saying his outfit had moved in after two days of not working the claim, and owned it proper, according to the mining district's own rules. He'd taken over before the owner died and left it to

Storm Foley. And he was damned if he'd give up a valid claim.

But the miners didn't like that. A man dying of dysentery had an excuse not to be working his claim, no matter what the rules were. And then things got worse. Foley showed up at the camp with more news. The Leavenworth outfit hadn't worked the claim for over two days, and he had filed and recorded a new claim.

Bones was thunderstruck. They'd been so busy guarding the property that no one among them had worked it. Storm Foley had a valid right to the property.

That's when Bones abandoned the law.

"It's ours, and we're keeping it, and we'll be damned if we'll give up what we own. You want it? We'll sell it."

"That's your decision, then?" Storm asked.

"Go ahead, try," Bones said. "See what it gets you."

Jay didn't like it. Whatever they'd done so far had at least the color of legality. Not that a miner's district court was the law. It was simply a make-shift government intended to enforce the rules and keep peace among thousands of miners. The real law, and real courts, were far away and weak.

Meanwhile, the outfit was going broke. It was expending manpower guarding the disputed claim, and also mining the Two-Bit claim that Jay had located, which yielded about an ounce of dust a day, nowhere near enough to feed a dozen men. Claim-jumping wasn't exactly paying off, and the restless outfit knew it.

Huckleberry Jones spent days poring through the district ledgers, looking for another property to jump, without success. And nothing else was paying off.

Then the miners called a trial.

The elected mining district judge, H. P. Dickinson, set a date the next morning for a proceedings that would determine whether the Leavenworth outfit were illegally holding a claim. He sent a messenger to give the word to Bones: Miners Court would meet in the morning. Show up and face the verdict, which would be rendered by the miners attending the trial, acting as jury. Show up or face the music.

Which was probably some hemp.

There would be a lot of miners, and they would be in a hanging mood. And probably the army would be on hand.

Bones and Boggs consulted, and decided to quit the disputed claim. The whole outfit, Jay included, hiked over to Dickinson's cabin, which stood close to his placer claim in Deadwood Gulch, one of the original ones.

"All right, we're quitting the claim," Bones said. "Call off the trial."

"I don't think so," Dickinson said. "There'll be a trial. Show up for it."

"But we've quit the claim. Tell Foley it's his. I'll write it out."

"That's not enough. The trial will determine whether you've committed crimes against the mining district," Dickinson said. "The jury will decide. They may want to make sure your claim-jumping comes to an end."

"We won't be there," Bones said.

The judge smiled. "Your choice, and your fate."

A crowd had collected around Dickinson, and more were arriving by the minute in the last light of the evening. They were bearded miners with icy stares, men ready to nab the Leavenworth outfit then and there, even though there was no jail. They could do it, too. There were plenty of buildings around that would serve. There were twice as many bitter miners than of the Leavenworth men, and they were well armed themselves. They listened quietly, not missing a word, and not missing anything about Bones and Boggs and the rest. The silent crowd had a brooding quality, and Jay sensed that the slightest offense could result in a rush, and that a few revolvers wouldn't go far against this staring, seething mob of gold miners, all of whom were looking for an excuse to wade in. An image of a noose dangling from a stout limb flickered across Jay's mind, and fear gripped him as it never had in his young life.

Bones studied the mob, and retreated. "All right," he said. "We're through."

"I think you could avoid the trial if you agree here and now to leave the district."

Bones nodded, and signaled the outfit to retreat, which it did, sliding into the night. No one stopped them. The night cloaked them, and Jay had never been so grateful for darkness.

He found himself trembling. That was a hanging mob.

Back at camp, Bones wasted not a moment.

"Pack up," he said.

"We have no mules," Louis said.

"Carry what you can on your backs. The rest, cache. Maybe we can slide back and get it."

"Where are we going?"

"The Black Hills are full of little corners. And little mining gulches. We're not done; we're heading out into the hills. We'll have better luck jumping claims where no one's around and no one knows. So get cracking. We're going to be in a safe place before night's over, and we'll do better out there," he waved at the blackness, "than here."

That made sense to Jay, but he knew he'd miss the bright lamps and life of Deadwood. Any port in a storm, he said to himself.

"What about the Two-Bit claim?" Ephraim asked.

"Jay here says he knows how the curb exchange works. He can sell it."

"Yeah, I'll get the bidding up," Jay said, worrying about being in Deadwood at all tomorrow.

So he'd be back when the exchange started up, usually early afternoon. He alone. And he'd have to sell the claim, record the sale, get cash, and get out, all before the miners got wind of it. The thought scared him. On the other hand, maybe there was some opportunity in it.

They started out, each man heavily burdened with makeshift packs, tracing a trail that Boggs knew about even if no one else did. Their goal that first night, it turned out, was Strawberry Gulch, about four miles southeast of Deadwood. But Boggs planned to move again after they had gotten all their stuff transferred. So they repeated the whole operation, finally getting their gear out of Deadwood's grip about the time when dawn edged the eastern ridges.

No one pursued. They rested in a jack pine bower scented by sagebrush along its edges.

"Warren, here's the bill of sale. Go auction off the Cleveland Gulch claim," Bones said. He sounded almost kind. Jay alone would be wandering around Deadwood. He washed at a spring, scraped away some beard, thinking to change his appearance, and set out for the curb exchange at the Bella Union. He would do his first trading, and the outfit was depending on him.

He hiked the long trail into town, reaching the business district late in the afternoon, just at the height of the day's bidding. But he was not noticed. Sure enough, there were a dozen men, mostly in battered suit coats, braving the fresh air, an easel with numbers on it, and the usual singsong bidding, punctuated by sudden silences, especially when something sold, and everyone wanted to see the numbers.

He spotted Jack Deal, who was enjoying himself peddling something or other.

"I'm gonna trade," Jay said.

"You registered? You go in to the bar and write your name and address in the ledger, and then try the game, boy."

Jay headed in, found a pen and ink bottle, and supplied the information, listing his address as outside of Deadwood. He drifted out, watched a claim price drop from a thousand to seven hundred, and studied the way it changed hands. After some of that, he was ready.

"Offering Cleveland Gulch Claim Five, twenty," he said. He was offering the claim for two thousand dollars, and got no takers. He tried again, and got no response.

"Boy, that claim's been jumped. No one showed up over there for two, three days, and that cooked the goose. You got nothing to sell."

Jay was shaken. "Where do I find out who got it?" he asked.

"Don't know that it's registered in the district yet. I'm just telling you what I heard, is all."

"I've got to see!" Jay said.

"Well, move your feet toward the mining district office and have a peek."

"How do you know this?"

Jack Deal shrugged. "Beats me. I pick up stuff all the time."

"Who got it? I have to know!"

"Solve your own problems, boy. I got rubes to fleece."

He wondered whether he dared walk into the mining district office, where the clerk might well recognize him. Or maybe Dickinson himself. No, he couldn't walk in there. And now he was standing on the curb with a blank sales receipt for a worthless claim.

Well, there were suckers around; maybe he could get a price after all. He had a signed sales receipt. All he had to do was fill in the name of the buyer, collect, and beat it out of there.

"Offering, Cleveland Gulch Claim Five, twenty," he bellowed.

One trader eyed him and laughed.

"Offering Cleveland Gulch, five, nineteen," he yelled.

No one paid him serious attention. A claim on Elk Creek sold for eight hundred, and the traders duly noted it.

Jay eyed the street, half expecting some burly miners, accompanied by Dickinson, to show up and clap him in whatever makeshift jail they used in Deadwood. But in fact the sunny afternoon drifted by with nothing like that. Traders came and went. Few stayed more than an hour, but other ones replaced those who departed. The prices chalked on the easel changed slightly. But there was little happening of interest. No high-priced claims sold. Just a few penny-ante ones moved at all.

"Offering Cleveland Gulch Five, fifteen," he bellowed.

"Not very bright, boy," Deal said. "Who wants it? Claim like that. If your outfit's selling it, and the outfit was chased out of town, who wants it?"

"I've got a signed bill of sale, same as the ledgers," Jay said.

"Sure you do, boy, and it's waste paper. Anyone buying from you would have to take the paper into miners court, and then what? What good is a signed bill of sale from claim jumpers? So no one wants it, boy."

"There's new people coming along all the time," Jay said. "I'll get it sold."

"Sure you will," Deal said.

Jay hung on through the slow afternoon, trying new offerings whenever anyone new drifted to the curb, but he couldn't move his outfit's claim. Word must have gotten out that the claim had been jumped. He wondered who jumped it, and whether Bones would have a score to settle. But not only did no one express interest in his offer, there were no lower bids either. He was down to an offer of ten, a thousand dollars, by the time the evening rolled around. Jack Deal had disappeared, and the curb exchange was winding down the day's business.

Then Deal reappeared.

"Say, boy, if no one wants the Cleveland Five, I'll pay one for it. It's worth a fight. Maybe I can beat the claim jumpers and get something for my hundred."

"Sold for one," said Jay.

They recorded that in the Bella Union, Deal got the signed bill of sale, and Jay collected a hundred dollars in greenbacks, wondering why Jack Deal looked so cheerful.

Chapter Twenty-One

He'd been suckered again. He knew it. Jack Deal
had cleaned him out. He had a hundred in his
pocket. He'd have to take that back to the outfit.
They were expecting a thousand for a good claim,
maybe more. They'd kill him.

He stood in the middle of the rutted street,
feeling as desperate as he ever had. He couldn't
think. He spotted an eatery across the way, and
fled to it, ordering a two-bit bowl of deer meat
stew, which came gray and grim. He ate sparingly,
wondering if the contents of the bowl were lethal.
Eating didn't help him. He couldn't imagine
returning to the new camp near the Strawberry
Gulch digs with only a hundred dollars. What
would he say? A hundred would hardly keep
twelve men in chow for a few days. He dawdled
over his stew, afraid to face life outside the door.

The curb traders were still at it as evening
settled, so he headed for the Bella Union, slid
inside for a look at the sales recorded there, and
sure enough, Jack Deal had sold Cleveland Gulch
Claim Five for fourteen hundred dollars only ten
minutes after he had suckered Jay out of it. The
sight of it, nearly recorded in black script,
sickened him. He headed into the night air
heavily, scarcely knowing whether to head back

to camp. He could flee, in which case the Leavenworth outfit would likely hunt him down and kill him, believing he made off with the proceeds. He could take the hundred to them, tell them the claim had been jumped but he had fobbed the bill of sale off on a sucker, or he could take the next stagecoach out and spend the rest of his life as a store clerk.

The curb traders had largely vanished. The traders seemed to clot together at times, vanish at times, almost as if they knew when to be there for hot deals.

"Hey, you a trader?" a man asked. Jay found himself staring at a man in a pearl gray suit, a man with soft baggy eyes and profound sadness about him.

"Maybe," Jay said.

"I made some bad trades, sir, being an innocent here, and now I am facing hunger and grief. I wonder if you could do me a favor. I have a package of six worthless claims no one wants. They're mostly piles of gravel, worked over and discarded. I thought they might still yield a little, but no, they're not worth the price of a postage stamp. A gold rush passes quickly, sir. The good dirt in any claim is swiftly worked down to bedrock, and then the claim's little more than a rectangular bit of a gulch. Does any of that interest you?"

"What are you asking, sir?"

"For the package of six, one."

"And where are the claims?"

"Four are right here, Deadwood gulch. Numbers seven, eight, ten, and fourteen. Two others are in the Two-Bit workings."

"How do I know the paperwork's in good order?"

"The district office remains open, sir."

It was only a block away. Jay and the gent with the baggy eyes walked in, and Jay swiftly determined that the man, Dolomite Dan Dimsdale, was indeed the owner and proprietor of several beds of old gravel.

"Mr. Dimsdale, I'll offer fifty dollars for the lot."

"Young man, poor as the pickings are, that's a little light. Would you go ten dollars apiece, sixty for the lot?"

"I'll take it."

Since they were at the mining district office, the transfer was duly recorded, and Jay walked out with bills of sale for the six gold claims. Now everything would depend on whether he was as skilled as Jack Deal at unloading them on newcomers. He still had forty in greenbacks and a trade to talk about when he reached camp.

He wondered what they would think. Six worthless claims were worth nothing at all.

Deadwood beckoned. He itched to down some whiskey, maybe visit Madam's parlor with enough cash in his britches. Instead, he started the long hike back, noting that the darkness was settling sooner, and the evenings were getting chillier.

He reached the Strawberry district around midnight, and couldn't find the camp. That was big, steep country, with views blocked by jack pine forest, and no way to fathom directions. He wandered up the side-gulch he thought would take him there, and found nothing, not even the smoke of a dying fire. He would have to wait for daylight.

He drifted down to the diggings, noted a few huts and tents by the light of a quarter moon, and knew he'd spend the night unsheltered, cold, and alone. At least there were no clouds—for the moment—and he didn't face a cold drizzle, and trying to keep his papers dry. There was naught to do but find a south-facing gulch wall that had absorbed heat the long day and would radiate it now. That wasn't easy, nor did he know whether he was trespassing, but in time he pushed his back into a clay bank, and settled in for a long, grim night.

Oddly, it wasn't grim. In all of his young life he had never paid heed to the sky, and now a great bowl of stars hung over him. He made out the Big Dipper and the North Star, and he rummaged his mind for the names of the galaxies, without much luck. He saw a shooting star, and another. He wondered what it would be like to be this far down in the Southern Hemisphere, guided by the Southern Cross. He thought of the bills of sale, of six titles safely recorded in the district ledgers, all in his name because the Leavenworth Company was anathema, and he didn't dare alert the bookkeeper. He thought of infinity, and how vast the heavens were, and how vast human life was for anyone who dared to live it. He didn't doze, but he rested, and at last the murky dark began to lift, and shapes began to appear, and the eastern heavens grew gray and then blue.

He heard commotion up the gulch; miners wasted not a second of daylight, determined to extract as much dust as they could before the sun set. Most of the dust in these gulches was flake, and much gold was in the form of tiny pebbles, the gold amalgamated with other minerals, laid down not by water and erosion, but by geologic forces he didn't fathom. But it was there, no matter how unusual the formations, and people were getting rich. At least a few were. Which depressed rather than brightened him. Up the gulch cook fires were flaring, and miners were stirring. He studied them, wondering whether to ask for breakfast, and decided against it. As the day quickened he discovered where he was, and headed down the gulch a half a mile, and turned onto the trail to camp, walking quietly through dense jack pine forest, a carpet of brown needles softening his tread.

The camp wasn't there. The company had moved. He had an odd feeling about the place. There were trees with splintered bark. Scrapes of sticks or boots in the needle-carpeted floor. But only deep silence, broken not even by a crow's caw. Well, he needed to find a trail. But there were a dozen trails, boot-scuffed passage in all directions. And none led anywhere except back down to the Strawberry diggings. He didn't know where Boggs had taken them. Nothing had been said. Only they would slip deeper into the wilderness, set up camp, and see what could be squeezed out of isolated prospectors far from Deadwood.

Well, if he couldn't find them, they could find him.

He had the uneasy feeling that he should get out of there, so he quietly hiked away as the day brightened. By mid-morning he was back in Deadwood, with forty dollars in his britches, six worthless placer mining claims, and the clothes on his back. He never really came to a decision; he simply knew what he had to do. At the general store he purchased a readymade flannel shirt for a dollar and a quarter. He headed for the only barber in town. There he had himself shaved and shorn, and had himself a bath in lukewarm water, and his borrowed boots blacked too.

He listened closely to the gossip in the tonsorial parlor, thinking maybe to profit from whatever news was floating between the barber and his customers. But it was only about new claims, mostly quartz lode discoveries, and the swift decline of placer mining in the gulches. Maybe that was useful too. But the thing he listened most intently for, he did not hear. If something had happened to his outfit, he wanted to know about it, and fast. The silence left him uneasy. But they would know where to look for him. He would be lingering among the curb traders at the Bella Union.

The lodging in Deadwood was jammed, but he found a widow lady's rooming house where he could double rent a room, from midnight to noon, for fifty cents a night. He paid the old gray woman for a week and thought himself lucky. He wondered what the other renter would be like, and whether he'd try to cop more than his twelve hours.

He was presentable, sheltered, fed, and ready, so he headed for the Bella Union. This would be the hard part. He had six claims to fob off on whoever wanted one, at whatever price he could get. He'd have to find chumps, not just this day but every day, and he'd have to figure out how to part them from their cash. Jack Deal seemed to have his ways, and he used candor mixed with his own brand of hokum. The candor was disarming. Start in by saying the claim's been worked hard, and you win some trust. Suggest that maybe there's plenty of dust not yet dug out because the miner didn't know how to get at it, and you add lust. And lust, a lust for gold, for wealth, for ease, sells most anything.

He knew the game; he just had to find the right birds. They wouldn't be other traders. They'd be people off the road, looking for a chance. This curb exchange didn't offer any information about any claim, but the experienced traders all knew what claims might have value, and what ones never did yield a nickel. It mystified Jay. How did they know? Who told them what was good? They couldn't possibly find time to talk to the thousands of miners operating claims in the area. But somehow they knew, or guessed well.

He spotted Jack Deal trying to unload some claim or another, without success, even though he was steadily lowering the price. Eventually Jack quit, and drifted toward Jay.

"Whatcha looking for, boy? I might have it."

"I'm offering. I don't have enough to buy lunch."

"Whatcha offering, boy?"

"Six dead placer claims, mostly from Deadwood Gulch."

"Must be ones I unloaded a few days ago. Feller in a pearly gray suit?"

"That's it."

"He was looking for a fiftieth anniversary present for his ma and pa, so I sold him the lot. He thought they could retire on it." Deal sounded sorrowful. "Oh, the woes, the tribulations, that life deals us."

"I've a question. Where do you find out if a claim's worth something? There's nothing here on the curb that tells anyone anything."

"Don't trade until you know, boy. How do you know your claims are worthless? Did you go look at them? Talk to miners?"

Jay shook his head.

"You'll be cleaned out, boy. You might be sitting on thousands of dollars of claims, but all you're doing is trying to unload them for chump change. Here's how it works, boy. Offer them for big money and don't give in. Feller sees you asking twenty for a piece of gulch gravel, he thinks maybe you're selling something, and he bites your bait."

"So, you want to buy any of mine for twenty?"

Deal laughed. "If I do, boy, you'll be mad at me, because it'll be worth a lot more."

"But you'd buy it sight unseen?"

"You bet. It doesn't matter what the claim is. All that matters is what I can sell it for. Tell me, boy, what are your little offerings, eh?"

"Let's see, Deadwood Gulch claims twenty-seven, twenty-nine, thirty-four, forty-five . . ."

"Stop right there, boy. You're sitting on a winner. Don't let Deadwood forty-five loose for less than twenty."

"How do you know there's gold in it?"

"I don't. But it has a reputation. What you've got to do, boy, is give each property a reputation."

"How do I do that?"

"You went to college; you figure it out, boy. You need a line for all occasions."

"A line?"

"You're not going to make a trader, boy. You'd better give up and go back to Peoria."

"All right, if you know so much, bid twenty on Deadwood Claim forty-five."

"You don't get it, boy. It's not the value that counts, it's the horsepucky."

Chapter Twenty-Two

Making some cash by trading mining claims proved to be harder and duller and slower than Jay had imagined. The old hands trading on the curb hadn't the faintest interest in his claims at any price.

"Deadwood Gulch, forty-five, asking eleven," he'd shout, and find himself ignored. He never even got a counter bid at a lower price. The hours ticked by, the whirl of offering and selling spun around him, but he found himself isolated, holding a handful of junk. Occasionally there were hot claims, some miner working a good piece of turf was ready to sell out. It remained a mystery to Jay how traders seemed to know good ground from bad, but they did. They must have had all sorts of sources. Maybe the assayers in town were feeding information to traders. Assayers would know more about the claims than anyone else except the miners and their immediate neighbors.

Occasionally Jay would spot newcomers drifting in to trade, and he'd start his sales pitches all over, and sometimes one or another man eyed him carefully before turning away. At least some of them paid attention. The regulars at the curb gave him less consideration than they would a horsefly.

He didn't hear from the outfit that day, either, and was puzzled about it. Where had they gone? Why didn't they contact him? At the Beanery he listened to gossip, and it yielded him nothing. Wherever Boggs and Bones took their men, it was nowhere near Deadwood, or they would not have abandoned him.

Resolutely he stuck through the afternoon at the Bella Union, but finally surrendered and retreated to the Gem for a bit to eat and maybe a drink. He couldn't have the room until midnight and had to be out at noon. Midnight seemed a long ways away. He felt oddly lonely. He was in a bad mood and it was getting worse by the minute.

The Gem seemed to leak cheer and optimism. He found a corner of the bar and ordered a whiskey from the aproned barkeep. That would be another two bits, but he didn't care. He sipped, wondering why he was there, angry with his father for throwing him to the wolves, and bitter toward Bones, who'd abandoned him, along with that whole rotten crew.

One miner, a hawk-faced man with slick jet hair, kept staring at Jay, his eyes boring into him. He wore worn gray britches held in place by leather suspenders, and had square-toed boots useful for kicking anyone who was down. The rest of the customers ignored Jay. Over on the plank floor, dime-a-dance girls were getting set for the next dance, and the accordion player was trying out a few chords from his squeeze-box. Maybe Jay would try a few dances, but they weren't going to make him feel any better.

The hawk-faced man wouldn't quit staring, so Jay moved to the corner of the bar, but that did no good. The man's gaze bored into him there, just as it had before. That was too much for Jay. He finished his whiskey, intending to go to the Bella Union, and have another. But then, impulsively, he headed toward the man.

"Do I know you?" he asked.

"I know you," the man replied.

"I'm Jay Warren. I'm a claims trader. And you?"

"It doesn't matter. You're the one got away from Strawberry."

"Got away, sir?"

"Leavenworth bunch. Claim jumpers. You're the missing one."

"You're from the Strawberry District?"

"I'm the president of the district."

Jay was feeling witless, but he managed to babble something. "You got any claims to sell? I can make a good sale for you."

"You've been hanging around with that outfit. I seen you looking at the ledgers, looking to euchre some good miner out of his diggings."

"I've barely seen your district, sir."

"I think you're the one got away. You come in with that bunch a few weeks ago."

"Got away? You've said something I don't understand, sir. And what did you say your name is?"

"I didn't. Call me whatever you want. Your outfit came wandering over to Strawberry after being told to get out of the country and never come back. That was you, all right, your bunch. So you come on over to our gulch, and we saw it, and crashed your party, fella. Crashed it good. We put a noose around two, three necks, Bones was one, Boggs was another, and that rat who sat in the district office, looking for any little problem in the records. Jones, smart punk, he got a noose too. Strung 'em up, and the rest wet their britches and left for Mexico or some place like that. But we missed you."

Jay felt his knees buckle under him. He gripped the bar.

Hawk-nose grinned. "Knew you was it," he said. "You get out too. If I see you around Deadwood next time I'm over here, I'll start measuring rope."

Jay was dumfounded, unable to think. His only friend, Huckleberry, dead? Why him? What good did it do? He was just trying to get ahead, like everyone else. Gone.

"You look like you could use another drink," Hawk-nose said.

Jay wanted to flee, but nodded.

"I always think someone about to be strung up should have a good drink and a good meal on the way out the door," the man said.

Jay could barely control the tremors that shot through him.

The man summoned the barkeep, and moments later Jay had a refill.

"How'd you join that outfit?" the man said, lifting his glass.

"I was freighting for the Foley company. They overtook us, needed another man, said they'd strike it rich in the goldfields, and I joined them."

"Left your employer with a short crew, did you?"

"Yes sir."

"You need hanging."

"Now, sir, or later?"

"Drink up, boy, and we'll proceed. I know a few fine old trees that'd fit."

"You'll have to wait until I sell off some worthless mining claims."

"How'd you get them?"

"Ten dollars apiece, from a gent who bought them to give to his parents. Golden wedding anniversary."

"Oh, Duncan Dinwiddie. He's madder than a hatter."

"He got took by a sharper named Jack Deal."

"No, the other way around. Duncan Dinwiddie's the biggest crook in Deadwood."

"He is? In his gray suit and cravat?"

"Boy, you've got a lot to learn. You're just an

apprentice crook. There's sharpers here who'd fleece you, peel your skin off, and toss you to the wolves."

"The only one I know's Jack Deal. He's cleaned me out once or twice."

"Small potatoes, boy. You should aspire to greatness. Deadwood needs better crooks."

"Try the Faro tables. Check out any tinhorn gambler."

"You're amateur, boy. I'm going to take pity on you. You're too small potatoes to hang. Now if you were Dinwiddie, whose parents have been dead for forty years since he's an orphan, now he's worth hanging. But you're not. You've hardly got your toes wet. I'm herewith, forthwith, declaring you not worth the rope."

Jay quieted. "I just lost the only friend I have, sir. And you make sport of it."

"I have a peculiar humor, boy. You're small potatoes. Maybe if you're worthy of hanging some day, I'll come after you. I've hanged five, and aspire to hang a dozen."

"I think I'm exempt. I don't follow the laws of gravity."

"Well, it's like this boy, when you slaughter a steer, you want a big, meaty, fat one with lots of meat, so you get a good carcass and plenty to eat and tasty meat. That's what I want, boy. I want a good, fat, meaty crook in my noose."

Jay was suddenly more tired than he remembered ever being. "I've lost a friend. I'll go outside a while and think about him. I'm staying at the Bancroft Boarding House, midnight to noon, if you want me. Thanks for the drink."

Hawk-nose grinned, baring two black gaps between incisors. "Fatten up, boy, fatten up."

But Jay didn't laugh. "You killed my friend," he said. "You strung him up for nothing more than playing a sharp game. Sure, he studied the ledgers. He found entries that weren't valid. He used that knowledge. If people were careless, they paid the price. That may be tough to take, but it wasn't illegal. Murder's illegal. You strung up men who weren't breaking the law. If there's any man who deserves a noose, it's you, and the gang that you run. You're no miner; no real miner would have anything to do with you."

The outburst ended as abruptly as it started. This time Hawk-nose wasn't smiling.

The man stretched, polished off his drink, and eyed Jay.

"Guess we'll meet at the end of a rope some day," he said. "It'll be plain interesting to see which end you've got, and which end I've got."

The nameless man walked into the soft night. He seemed to be surrounded by night.

Jay watched him go. A few patrons were staring. He didn't know what they had heard, and didn't care. He felt bad. Huck dead, buried who knew where? Bones, not such a bad man. Boggs, a tough sergeant who held the outfit together. Jumped some claims, and did it proper, and now dead for it. There were rules to follow when claiming mineral ground, and if you didn't follow them, tough luck. That's all the Leavenworth company was about.

Why hadn't this lynching found its way around Deadwood? The thought arrested him in his tracks. If there'd been hangings anywhere in the area it would have been all over Deadwood. The man was talking about three hangings that no one knew about, and that struck Jay as very strange. An odd optimism began to infiltrate his thoughts. Why wasn't a triple hanging on everyone's lips? Why had he heard nothing about it until this hour? Maybe it never happened.

He thought about the disturbing man who wouldn't own to a name, and who enjoyed toying with Jay. Maybe the man was a sadist. Maybe just cruel. The cruelest people in the world are cloaked in virtue. If you want hard men, try anyone who oozes righteousness. Jay knew he was not far into his adult life, but he also knew that he preferred the company of people who were flawed, knew it, and laughed it off.

He would wait and see. And if one or another of the dead suddenly appeared on his doorstep, he wouldn't be surprised.

Jay glared at the men down the bar, who stared back. Then he slid into the night, taking care that he was safe. The night air was cleaner than the saloon air, and he sucked it into his lungs, grateful that air could still enter his nostrils, pass through an undamaged neck, and into his lungs.

It was far from midnight, when he could claim his room, a closet with a cot, shared with someone unknown. At least the boardinghouse had a parlor of sorts, intended as a place where men could wait out the hours until they could fall into a cot.

He found a skinny, worn man in the parlor, his gaunt face lit by a single kerosene lamp.

"I'm guessing you're the man I'm sharing with," he said. "You look like what she said."

"Room six?"

"The same. I'm Addison Crowe, and I've got all sorts of bad habits, but at least I know how to get to the outhouse."

"Jay Warren," he said. "I'm a trader."

"A trader are you? Well, we'll see about that. Right now, I'm night man at the Foley Freight Terminal. Pay's not much, but it keeps me going while I find something better."

"Freight terminal?"

"Freight coming in all hours, this town's eating everything up. They need a night man, put the oxen away, help unload, transfer cargo to light wagons, you name it. A dollar a day. This place costs fifty a night, so you can see how it goes with me."

"Foley's supplying the whole district. That'll keep you busy."

"Well, Warren, the room's yours. I start work at ten each eve. Six days a week. So I'm not around last two hours, except Sunday evenings. So most nights you've got her at ten."

"We'll get along just fine," Jay said. "Maybe I can trade for you."

"Maybe you can, boy. We'll see."

Chapter Twenty-Three

The only thing Jay learned the next day was that he wasn't ever going to sell his six lousy claims to professional traders. He made offers at all sorts of prices, and never got a bid. They treated his claims as if they were in quarantine, and were openly amused.

"You're not listening to me, boy," Jack Deal said. "You've got to give each claim a story. Like this: Jones had this claim, but he died just before he reached the good gravel. Or this: Smith had this claim, but he had a theory that the good gravel was over at this far end, and he never bothered with the other side of the claim. You give each claim a story, boy, and you'll get rich."

"Thanks, Deal."

"It ain't easy. It's hard work, selling claims. Your mind's too lazy to make up stories. If you had a hard-working mind, you might make yourself a trader. But your thinker ain't thinking."

"That's not how you operate."

"You're dead right, boy. I'm a pigeon hunter. I look for the bird. There's fresh clean birds flying into Deadwood most every day, and I go scouting for them. Like you. You were one of my best pigeons, boy."

Jay resented the advice. So his thinker wasn't

thinking, was it? Who went to college and who didn't? The problem was, he couldn't come up with a story that would hold water. He itched for a good story for Deadwood Gulch Claim 45, but he couldn't manage a story, and it irritated him.

Meanwhile, his tiny stake, if it even was his, was shrinking by the hour. He had two weeks at best to make his fortune. If the Leavenworth outfit returned, they'd claim what he had left. It was odd. Another day had passed without any word of a lynching.

He found Addison Crowe waiting for him in the cramped lobby of the makeshift rooming house.

"Hoped to catch you," Crowe said. "I want to hear more about how you make your living. It interests me."

"I'm a trader. There's a curb exchange in front of the Bella Union Saloon. You can market your own properties, or act as someone's agent, and you can buy on the same basis. You familiar with securities exchanges?"

"All too familiar," Crowe said. "I had a bit of money, enough to support me, but not in style. I studied the markets, decided I could profit from a few shrewd investments, and," he shrugged gently, "the markets decided I wasn't shrewd after all. That explains a great deal, does it not?"

"You're here to remake your fortune?"

"I no longer think in terms of fortunes, I'm

afraid. But sometimes hard work, and being in the right place, gives a man an opening."

"What sort of opening?" Jay asked.

"I don't know that I'd be able to explain it. It's not wealth. It's not about the fiancée I lost when my money gave way. It's not about my position in the world. It's something I can't convey to a stranger, but it has to do with coming into myself, or doing what I was destined to do before I made poor choices." He paused. "Now I've embarrassed us both."

"You need a lucky strike," Jay said.

"If it was pure luck, it wouldn't lift my burdens from me, sir. Now, it's time to go to work. The room's yours."

"Well, if you're looking for gold claims that have an interesting history, I'll tell you about a few," Jay said.

"I guess I've been talking to the wall," he said.

He watched the gaunt man shuffle to his feet, nod, and head out the door. The man wasn't young. It probably had been a while since he lost his savings. He'd probably failed at a dozen things, and coming to Deadwood looking for a lucky break was a last resort. Some people came west brimming with hope for a future; other people came west out of desperation, a sort of broken people's frontier.

Maybe the man was going to be the bird after all, Jay thought.

The next day he woke to a drizzle and sharp air. He spent a little of his dwindling cash in the Beanery, ordering a costly platter of steak and eggs, to change his luck. But no one was out in the rain in front of the Bella Union, and no one was trading inside, either. He didn't mind. Traders weren't his birds any more.

The drizzle matched his mood. He peered dourly down Main, seeing very little of the bustle of a sunny day. The rain chased shoppers inside. There were no women in the butcher shop or at the greengrocer. Even the barbers were sitting in their chairs, staring through the streaked glass. The rain made him mad. There were no pigeons out on the street.

Far down the street were two giant Foley freight wagons, and teamsters were dragging stoves and stovepipe and other heavy items into the hardware store, ignoring the rain. Pigeons maybe. There they were, grinding away in the cold rain for their pittance, hardly knowing any better. But maybe there was someone in that outfit who wanted a better life. Maybe a pigeon or two dragging cast iron and casks of nails into the store.

Jay braved the rain, drifted that way, and watched two men ease a crate of window glass down to the muddy street, and then ease it inside. One was Ike.

"Well, boy, they haven't strung you up yet," Ike

said, while he and the other teamster rested just inside the door.

"I'm a trader, Ike, and doing just fine."

"Sure you are," Ike said.

"You done unloading? I'll buy you lunch and tell you about it," Jay said.

"We're hardly started, boy."

Jay peered into the first wagon, and discovered a dozen more items, including a zinc sink, small casks of horseshoes, an assortment of tools, and a kitchen range.

Ike was grinning. "Want to help? Maybe I'll give you two bits."

"I make more than that in two minutes," Jay said.

"Sure you do, boy. You want to treat me to lunch, do you? All right, I'll be at the Beanery at noon. Mind if I bring Walter here?"

"The more the merrier," Jay said, hoping they would order beef stew off the bottom of the menu.

The oxen stood patiently in their yokes, having learned early in their brief lives that there wasn't anything they could do about the wooden prisons they lived in when working. Jay thought that the teamsters were wearing yokes too, even if they were invisible to the eye. A brief, miserable life, grunting and dragging, and then death. Some people were doomed from birth.

He rehearsed his stories while he waited for his pigeons, wanting to master Jack Deal's art and improve on it. Ike and Walter showed up at the Beanery not long after noon, and swiftly ordered bowls of beans, steaks, and beers. Jay blanched, but hid his dismay behind a big toothy smile. He ordered a couple of slices of toast.

"Well, boy, you're doing just fine trading, you say?" Ike asked, between shoveling beans into his cavernous mouth.

"I'm doing so well I can hardly believe it. There's lots of traders with more experience, but I got lucky, and slid into a sweet corner."

"How so?" asked Walter, who was downing his beans even faster than Ike.

"I've got six claims in hand, ready to sell. They're all mine, too. They range in quality; one or two are risky, but the rest, oh, how shall I say it—they're like owning the United States Mint."

"You got takers?" Ike asked, piling through beans as if he hadn't eaten for a week.

"It's a funny thing. I've got takers for the risky claims, but not for the real classy ones."

"How's that?"

"Lots of people looking for claims want to pay low prices, and take their chances. So they're sniffing around at claims I'm offering for six— that's six hundred. But they're not interested in the three proven claims I've got listed for twelve—that's one thousand two hundred. I've got one, Deadwood Gulch forty-five, where the miner died of dysentery suddenly, after pulling out about three ounces a day, a true gold mine, but buyers are superstitious, and don't want anything to do with a sick man's claim, so there it sits in my inventory, waiting for the right person."

"Well, ain't that something," Ike said. "You get a commission on these?"

"No, they're mine, and I'm trading them, and whoever buys gets a bill of sale and a deed to the claim, and it's registered in the ledgers of the district."

"What are you worth, boy?" Ike asked.

"On paper, about ten thousand. It'll vary a little when I get this batch sold. I've found what I was looking for, a good, steady, clean way to make money fast."

"I'll bet," said Ike.

"It beats a lot of shoveling," Jay said. "People get ahold of these claims, and they still got work ahead of them, enough to bust their backs. But I'm doing it my way, and I'm right at the beginning of Easy Street."

"Sure you are, boy."

Jay sensed a certain skepticism in Ike, but what did it matter? Ike would tell the rest of the Foley teamsters about all this, and there was a good chance one or another had the itch and the cash to buy a claim.

"If I was buying, I'd go for one of the riskier ones that can be got for less," Jay said. "There's one, the miner had worked only half the claim,

224

one side of the gulch, and then got called east, his pa was dying and his wife was sick, so he traded it out, cheap, and I've got it, and only one half is proven up. The other half, it's not yet seen a shovel. Now there's a deal for you. I could let that go a little cheaper, because the ground's never been disturbed on half of it. You want a chance to hit it big, and not pay a pile of money, that's the one I'd go for."

"What claim's that?" Walter asked.

"That's Elk Creek Seven," Jay said. "You can go look it up in the books if you want to know who owned it, and who to talk to. One way is to go talk to the miners next door, and see what they say. You want a crack at it, you go talk to the men scratching gravel in the next claim."

"How'd you come to own these wonders?" Ike asked.

"I spent time studying the whole district, and what I was looking for was men in trouble. They're the ones that sell cheap because they need to go somewhere, or they're too sick to work the diggings."

"Don't you have to work the diggings to keep the claims going?"

"All you need is to make a show of it. Turn over a few shovelfuls and that's it. Easy enough to hang on."

"Well, ain't that sumpin," Walter said. He took a slice of bread and slopped it around his stew bowl and made room in his vast mouth for this dripping morsel.

"If you would like to see the claims, I'd be glad to show them to you," Jay said. "The Deadwood Gulch claims are just up the way a bit."

"No, we got teams to look after, and then we head for Cheyenne," Ike said.

"Just remember, I've got a whole portfolio of first-rate properties," Jay said. "I got lucky, and now I'm making a market for them."

"Thanks, boy. Good stew," Walter said.

"I'll have good ground to show you next time. You spread the word. I'll make a deal for Foley men," Jay said. "Just for old times' sake."

"Sure, boy," Ike said.

Jay watched them head into the noonday sun while he unhappily dug into his britches for a dollar and a half's worth of chow. He figured it had been a good investment. It would take a while for them to figure it all out and tell others in the Foley company, but in a few days he'd have teamsters knocking at his door. And one or another would plunge. There were plenty of teamsters arriving in Deadwood each day. And one or another would have money, along with the itch. He had his stories lined out, and he'd put them all to good use.

Meanwhile his purse was lighter.

Chapter Twenty-Four

Neighbors. Why hadn't he thought of that? Two more days had slid by without the slightest progress. He was down to seven dollars. He was on the brink of starvation.

He headed up Deadwood Gulch, looking for whoever was working claims next to his. He got to Claims thirteen and fourteen, both his, and found desolate heaps of gravel, and no one in sight. Obviously, the gulch had been mined out. He hiked further up and found his thirty-seven forlorn and empty, with no neighbors working gravel. He hiked a couple hundred yards more, into a narrowing canyon, and located Claim forty-five, which seemed less disturbed than the ones below. The place was idyllic, forested and comfortable, the narrow creek rushing down the long grade. He saw no one.

But at forty-six two burly miners were shoveling gravel into a sluice box.

"Having any luck?" Jay asked.

"Played out," one said. "We're mostly wasting time. Yesterday we scraped two dollars of dust out of the box. Less than that today."

"That the way it is here?"

"Placer diggings, they're done for. There's quartz lode around, and that's where everyone's gone."

"I own forty-five, below you. It's for sale reasonable," Jay said.

"No price is reasonable on that one. That's a heart-breaker."

"Jay Warren here. I'm a trader."

"Mitch Mount. And he's Cyrus Dance."

"What's wrong with forty-five?"

"It's the way the bedrock lies. You can see it from here. There's no gravel. Sloping bedrock on one side, and a shelf of bedrock on the other. No gravel. The water just carried the gold off. Nothing caught it there. I'll show you if you want a look-see."

Jay shrugged. The miner, a muscular man with thick arms, led the way, and was soon pointing to a pitiful pile of gravel, and smooth-surface underlying rock.

"Anyone mined the cracks?"

"Ain't any."

Jay felt his last hopes drifting away. "I'll sell four claims in this gulch for a hundred dollars," he said.

Mount smiled. "Nice try," he said.

"What are you going to do next?" Jay asked.

"We've saved a little. Look for a quartz claim, and start digging."

"There's some gold over at a place called Lead," Dance said. "That's the word."

"Lead?"

"Not in this district. Not the metal. Like the prayer, Lead me not into temptation."

"Guess I'll have to go there," Jay said.

"It's all staked out already," Dance said. "But there's quartz, and a man that can swing a pick and shovel can get three dollars a day wage."

"I'll sell you the four Deadwood claims for fifty," Jay said.

Mount laughed. "Nice try, fella," he said.

Jay left them and they were soon back to their brutal toil. They'd hardly get enough to pay for their food this day. Unless their luck changed. That was the thing about mining. Nature was never orderly. One day you're down; the next day you're rich.

They sure were working in a pleasant place. Far upslope, some aspen formed a lime-green clump amid the black pine slopes. It wouldn't be long before the aspen turned gold.

The other two claims were in Two-Bit Gulch, some distance away. But it was a mild day, good for a hike, and he made good time. He realized that the claim was high up the gulch, and headed upslope, past working miners, which was a good sign. He had not visited this one because it was a good hike from Deadwood. Well, it was time to see what sort of rock heap he was fobbing off. It never did a trader any harm to know his inventory.

He found the first claim easily enough. Sixty-two, corners marked, the claim in a bottle in a cairn. It lay in a dished valley with steep forested sides, the trees stretching clear down to the narrow gulch, crowding it. To get at gold, you had to clear forest away, which the previous owners had done half-heartedly. Ah, there was a good story. There's what he needed to peddle the claim. There's gold under there, but bring an ax and a buck saw first. Lots of gold, gold by the bucket, but hard to pry away from the forested slopes.

He was ecstatic. This was the story that would sell this one for a fortune.

But even as he studied the odd claim, a man approached, and it proved to be the last man he wanted to meet. Hawk-face, his eyes coals, his jet hair loose, was closing in on him. The man ought to be in the Strawberry diggings, but there he was, so Jay braced himself.

"You is it?"

"I'm checking on my claim, sir."

"Your claim, is it?"

"It's for sale. Are you interested? I'm offering it cheap for a quick sale."

The miner smiled, baring gaping holes where teeth once lived. "Not in buying it, that's God's truth. Not from some scum claim jumper, some pest trying to cheat honest men out of their property. You're parasites, boll weevils eating our cotton. I should've driven you out, like the rest, long ago."

"Ah, driven out, sir?"

"We jumped your bunch at supper, cleaned them out of every weapon in their possession, and told them they'd hang if they ever returned to the

Deadwood area, boy, and that includes you. You're the only one we never laid our paws on."

"You'd said you'd hanged them."

The man grinned. "We did. Put hemp around their throats, drew it tight until they was wetting their britches, and told them never come back, and they never did. That was a sight to behold. They's all taken off for the new digs near Lead. All except you."

Alive. They were alive. Maybe he could find his way there. Huckleberry would help him.

"Now then, you sapsucker, what're we gonna do about you? You got this claim, do you?"

"I do. I bought it fair and square."

"You mind showing me the papers?"

"It's for sale, sir. There's money to be made here. There's going to be gold under that forest. Especially that old watercourse."

"You know, for a cockroach, you got your thinking cap on, boy. There's gold under the pines, and it takes a man to get it. But you ain't going to sell it. I'm going to take it. Serves you right, jumping claims like that."

"Take it?"

"By force, boy. It's called six-gun action."

Hawk-face smoothly drew a revolver and jammed it into Jay's chest. "Don't move, boy, don't move, don't twitch, and don't start blubbering, or you'll get most of an ounce of lead through your heart."

The cold muzzle terrified Jay. He cried out.

"Boy, here's what you're gonna do. You're going to give me this piece of Dakota country. You're gonna draw me up a bill of sale, and you're going to deed Two-Bit Claim Sixty-Two to Newton Dogg. And then you're going to get your skinny ass out of here, and out of the district, and out of Dakota."

"But that's . . ."

"That's what, boy? You calling me a thief?"

Dogg lifted the revolver, shot a ball just past Jay's ear, and then jammed it back into Jay's chest, the big bore pressed hard against him.

The blast shattered Jay's hearing. He quaked. "I'll sign," he said.

Dogg smiled, and returned his weapon to its holster.

Jay trembled so badly he could scarcely write. "It'll have to be in pencil," he said.

"Don't make a whit of difference."

He scribbled out the paperwork and handed it to Dogg, who lip-read it, and finally decided it was fine. Dogg folded the sheets, stuffed them into his shirt pocket, and grinned.

"Gotcha," he said. "And better than a hanging."

That was one thing Jay could agree to.

"Gulch used to flow over there, covered with jack pine now. I'll hack them suckers down and sell the lumber and start digging. Boy, I'm on millionaires' row."

"It seems a hard way to get rich," Jay said.

"Boy, the hard way to get rich is doing what you're doing. You do what you do, and end up flat on your fanny."

Jay had enough. "Where's Two-Bit Claim twelve?"

"Oh, that dog. Just head downhill, boy, and when you reach hell, that's where it is."

Jay shrugged, collected his papers, which he kept wrapped in oilcloth, and started down the gulch, his back prickling.

"Wait'll I tell 'em at the Gem how I took a crook," Dogg said.

But all Jay wanted was to get out of there.

He had trouble finding claim twelve; its corners were not marked, and nothing tangible marked it. But he found thirteen, which had been abandoned, so he knew he was on twelve. But it was an obvious dud. The gravel ran only a couple of feet and had been scraped away from bedrock, and except for a little gold in the fissures, the claim had plainly yielded nothing. He would have trouble unloading it for ten cents.

He sat down on a heap of gravel, examining the ruin of his dreams. What had his father done to him? He was disinherited, and his worldly wealth consisted of a few heaps of broken rock. A flash of anger roiled him. He'd nearly been killed this morning, and had a claim stolen, and owned nothing more than gravel.

Bitterly, he trudged back to Deadwood. Maybe he should try to find the Leavenworth bunch, He had no idea where the Lead district was, or whether he had enough left to go there, or whether they'd want him. If they had wanted him, they would have gotten word to him somehow. But at least his friend Huck was alive—probably. Who could say what Dogg had done?

The world never seemed so cold, though it was a warm enough day. Deadwood seemed a place populated by people from some other land, people different from any he had ever known. But they were toilers, and he still intended never to toil away his life.

It was still afternoon, but he entered the Gem Saloon, and buttonholed the first miner he saw at the bar, a young fellow with yellow eyes and a wedding ring on his hand.

"I've got some bad claims. But who knows? You can have them for a dollar apiece."

The man sighed. "The world's full of those. I'll buy you a beer, and you can sign them over. How's that?"

Jay decided that would not do. He fished a crumbling dollar bill out of his pants, headed for the Faro table, put the crumpled bill on number seven, lucky seven, and three minutes later watched it vanish into the dealer's purse. The oily-haired dealer was smirking.

He bought a ten-cent loaf of bread. That would

have to do for his dinner. There wasn't much that was cheaper. When he got to the boardinghouse he found Addison Crowe.

"Thought I'd wait a bit to see if you came in. I'm going to work early, so the room's yours," Crowe said.

Jay nodded. He didn't feel like visiting with the other boarder.

"You had a bad day?"

"It's just bad luck. I've run into trouble. Can't trade anything."

"Well, I'm looking, you know."

"For gold property? But how, I mean, night man at the terminal?"

"I'm looking for a quartz property, not placer. I'll buy into something that has a future."

"But how?"

"Oh, I don't have any cash, and have to earn my bread, but I have my father's farm. A hundred-sixty acres of good, black, rich bottomland in Illinois. House and barn and shade trees and corn crib. I wasn't cut out to be a farmer, and I don't like being tied down so much, especially out where it's lonely. But it's a good farm, productive, and worth plenty. I'd say twenty-five hundred, but maybe more if it catches someone's fancy. And I'm looking for a way to trade it even-steven for something that'd win me some money."

Chapter Twenty-Five

Jay had his bird. All he had to do was feed it. After Addison Crowe headed to the Foley freight yard, Jay leapt into action. The man wanted a quartz claim, ore still in the native rock, a mother lode that could be mined by tunneling into the ancient rock that underlay the Black Hills. None of Jay's placer claims, segments of streambed containing flakes of gold washed out of the surrounding mountains, would do.

A first-rate farm for a gold claim. He didn't know anyone in Deadwood with the slightest interest in an Illinois farm, but that didn't matter. He'd go back there and sell it, once he had the deed, and put the cash into more lucrative ventures. A farm was as good as gold, he thought. He'd get the farm.

Then reality set in. He wasn't at all ready for bed, so he hurried over to the Gem, laid out two bits for some redeye, gasped his way through the first sip, and then hunted for someone who would know something about lode mining. It took only a moment to discover Jack Deal, blandly working on a prospect, some youth with a bobbing adam's apple, new in town and looking for a way to get rich. But Deal had other plans for the fellow. Jay waited, watched Deal yawn, as if disinterested, smile, shake hands, and the young one headed out the door.

"Putting your ducks in a row, Jack?"

"He's a fine fellow, with money to invest. I thought to help him."

"What do you know about quartz mining?"

"You got a pigeon, do you?"

Jay grinned. He wasn't going to reveal anything at all.

"Well, boy, a placer claim's anything you want to invent. But the details aren't important."

Jack Deal was toying with him, but eventually he'd cough up what he knew.

"If you want to sell a good quartz gold claim, boy, you've got to have a lot of paper. Assayer's reports, how much gold per ton, and how pure. And a good estimate of reserves. How much gold's in there. Is it easily milled, or refractory. That's the word for ore that's hard to work. Is the quartz seam thickening as you go farther in, or playing out? That sort of thing. Then you've got to have a good patented claim, usually fifteen hundred feet by six hundred feet, with a hundred dollars a year of improvements on it. Without all that, boy, you're not likely to get Uncle Sam to cough up a patent on the claim, and he can take it back."

That wasn't encouraging at all.

"But there's always ways and means. Now, then, boy, who's your pigeon?"

"He's a friend."

"Well, there's little pathways, boy. You've got to come up with a registered claim, and come up with the paperwork, and come up with ore samples, and come up with an engineer's estimate of reserves, and all that can be gotten, boy, for a little cut of the profits."

"How do you do that?"

"Boy, leave it to an old pro. It takes work. It can't be done overnight. Things have to be put in shape."

"Put in shape?"

"Leave it to me, boy. Who's the pigeon?"

"He's come out here looking for an opportunity. He's got no cash, but he's got a first-rate farm in Illinois, black soil, good land, house and barn, he says would sell for twenty-five."

"A farm, boy, are you mad? Who'd want a farm around here. Farming is what all these people here quit doing as fast as their skinny legs could walk them west."

"I'd go back there and sell it. That's money in the bank, but not here."

"Who's the pigeon, boy? I keep my eye on this place, and there's no one like that I've heard about."

"I'll tell you when we work out a deal. I'd even cut you a quarter."

"Not interested. A farm? You can be a hayseed, not me."

"That cuts both ways, Jack. Show me a patented claim, quartz ore of good quality, and all the paperwork, and then we'll talk."

"You drive a hard bargain, boy."

"And do it fast. I'll want it all together in a day or two, and you're going to take me to the claim and show me the ore, and show me the papers."

Deal shrugged. "Guess that's going to put the kibosh in it, boy. See you around town."

Jay had a notion that it didn't end matters at all. He spent the rest of the evening nursing his fiery redeye, trying to find out more about quartz gold mining, and finally heading back to the shared room. He noted that Addison Crowe left no presence there, nothing but a small cloth duffel sitting in a corner. But the man had more wealth than most everyone in Deadwood, save for a few gold kings who were heaping up a fortune.

He couldn't sleep, couldn't even think of it, with a mind fevered with possibility. So he quit the cloistered room, headed into the night, and found his way to the Foley Freight Terminal. Crowe was unyoking an ox team.

"Well, I have company," he said.

Jay watched him pull yokes off each pair, and let them drift to a hay-filled manger or a water tank, where the lumbering cattle licked water, nosed around in it, and then drank. The sweat stains and harness marks covered their long bodies. Crowe seemed to enjoy the work, and handled them with ease. He had been born to agriculture, and was comfortable doing this sort of work.

"I'll put four teams together around dawn," Crowe said. "They'll roll out for Cheyenne by sun-up."

"Do they go back empty?" Jay asked.

"Nothing to ship out of Deadwood," Crowe said.

"Except gold."

"That goes out on the stagecoaches, with armed guards. This is different. Here's where nearly all of the food, tools, hardware, clothing, cloth, and animal feed pours in. Foley's usually got a hundred wagons on the trail any time, coming and going. It'll all quit when they build a railroad, but that's a couple of years off."

"This is a little like farming."

Crowe smiled. "That's why I hope not to be here long."

"You had your fill of it?"

"A hundred sixty of prime land in Illinois takes more than one to work it. My injured brother can't help. His arm's withered up. My mother can't. Bad heart. I've worried this thing around, thought it, wrestled it, figured it, and there's no out for me back there. I'm not a good farmer anyway. I should be proud of my corn, proud of plowing straight furrows, but I'm not. If I can trade for a good gold claim, I'll tear the gold out of the rock myself. I'll blast it, stamp it, cart it, refine it, and provide for my mother, who's getting on and needs help, and my brother, who needs help too. That's my hope, my friend."

"Who around here would want a farm back there? Seems to me that's the flaw in your plan," Jay said.

"No, it can be sold back there, not here. I've an agent there. If I can find a good, proven gold claim, I'd wire my agent to sell. There's plenty would buy a farm that fine, six feet of black topsoil. I've got the deed here, and I'd do the papers here, and send it express there, and use the gain to buy the gold mine."

"What are you willing to invest? Maybe I can scout something for you."

"Farm will go for two and a half thousand, at the least, but I'll be asking three."

"Good gold mines here go for more than that. But maybe I can find something that'd suit you."

"Sure, fella, you just hunt around. I'm a born skeptic so you'll need to do a lot of showing. I should have been born in Missouri, the Show Me state."

"I have important connections," Jay said.

"Well, they don't seem to be doing ye much good, fella."

"Oh, a few reverses. I have some prime

properties to trade, first-rate, but their history gets in the way, so people back off."

"History?"

"You betcha. When the claim-owner dies of typhus, no one wants that property. I've got three properties, all of them bought from estates. And they go begging. I'd do better out there digging instead of trying to sell them at the curbside market."

"Probably earn faster, too," Crowe said.

"Well, I'll find someone who's not afraid to dig for gold, and he'll get rich, and I'll get out from under those claims."

"You dug for gold at all, boy?"

"I have, but it's faster to trade for my living."

"What's your aim? We're all aiming for something."

"I'll tell you straight off. Money, as much as I can get, as fast as I can get. I want it to come easy, by the bucket. You can call it what you want. Greenbacks, shinplasters, coin, gold, gelt, moolah, dollars, doubloons, or capital. If I wanted to go slow, I wouldn't be in Deadwood, surrounded by good prospects. I'd be wrestling freight or plowing a row, but that's not who I am, sir. I'm ambitious, and determined, and I'm going to get where I'm going."

Crowe smiled faintly. "That makes us distant cousins," he said. "Tired of waiting for corn to push through the ground and green up. Only I don't mind hard work. I'll show the world what a determined man with a pick and shovel and wheelbarrow can do if he tries."

"Well, we're alike then," Jay said.

They weren't, but that didn't matter. Jay knew he had a bird, and he knew he'd find a way, and he knew he'd soon be on Easy Street.

"Well, boy, I got to shuffle things around here, some. Feed the oxen, yoke up some pairs. But I enjoyed the visit."

"It'll take me a few days, but I'll have your property for you," he said. "A good quartz vein, ready to be worked."

He headed into the night, heartened. Now he had a clear picture. The man had the papers right here, not in Illinois, and he'd go for the right property. He abandoned the freight terminal, headed into a moonlit night, and made his way along Main Street, delighting in Deadwood's sleepless nights. Deadwood was a happy place. He heard laughter spill from the saloons. He saw yellow light spill from their doors. Everything was his, or soon would be. He could hardly contain the itch to celebrate. Instead, he veered into the Gem, and laid out some precious coin for some redeye, and smiled broadly at the rough men in their brogans and flannels and untrimmed beards lined up like piglets at the teats.

He engaged the gent next to him, who it turned out was cross-eyed.

"Say, you got any idea where a man could pick up a working quartz mine, with good prospects?" Jay asked.

"If I knew, I wouldn't tell you," the man said. "But I could show you a few played out pocket mines, good prospects that went sour soon as someone got to the back side of the quartz. Mess of those everywhere. Good for a month, then dead as a doornail."

Jay was delighted. "Could you lead me to them? And put me in touch with the owners?"

"Jaysas, you're one of those," the man said.

"Actually, I specialize in reviving exhausted mines. Thanks to extensive training I'm able to go in, evaluate, and sometimes revive mines. It's a knack I have, and I'm able to put new life into about a quarter of my properties."

"One of those," the miner said.

"You show me some mines tomorrow, and I'll cut you in on the profits."

"Yeah, one of those. Gonna salt a few before peddling them?"

"I'm sure I don't know what you're talking about."

The man was grinning. He downed his drink, dug into his britches, and withdrew a card that read, Joe Josephson, Ph.D., Mining Engineer, Geologist, Evaluator.

"You're the man I want to talk to," Jay said. "You're the man who'll lead me to Easy Street.

You're the man guarding the Pearly Gates."

The man grinned. "Meet me here at nine. Wear your hiking boots. We'll hike about ten miles, and I'll show you every played out pocket mine around, so you can pick one to fob off on a sucker. And I don't want a dime. It amuses me."

Chapter Twenty-Six

Josephson was as good as his word. A long hike straight up Deadwood Gulch brought them to a cluster of defunct quartz workings. The small heaps of tailings were barely visible against the vaulting slopes and dun rock of the surrounding high country.

They had hiked in silence, while all the while Jay was wondering what was in it for the geologist and mining engineer. It turned out to be nothing.

"Why am I doing this? Part of me wants to see fools and their money parted. Another part of me wants to review the reasons these properties are worthless."

"I have a client interested in a good quartz mine, is all."

"Why hasn't he come to see a reputable geologist?"

"He's full of dreams."

Josephson laughed. "That explains it."

They climbed a steep slope littered with talus, and came to a cramped cavity that had been clawed into the face of the outcropped rock there. Jay peered in, discovering the hole penetrated only fifteen or twenty feet. At its far end was blank rock.

This is the Honeysuckle Mine, though it might

better be called the Heartbreak," Josephson said. "See that rear wall? That's where a good and promising quartz lode stopped dead. That's a fault there. Massive segments of rock ground past one another there, and no one knows where the gold seam went. It could have gone any direction, up or down, sideways. It could be inches away or miles away. It tempts miners to claw in all directions, looking for the lost gold seam. My guess is that it picks up miles from here, maybe straight down, and no one will ever find it. But who's to say it's not a foot this way or that?"

"It can't go far; the earth doesn't shift that much," Jay said.

"Who says? Are you the geologist?"

"It's probably close."

"You sure of that, or is it wishful thinking?"

"People get lucky; they read the rock, and know where to dig."

"I own it; I'll sell it to you. I own all the claims in this group. Actually, they're claims, not patented mines. I have to do a hundred dollars a year of improvements on each one to keep the claim valid, and that goes toward proving them up. I mostly keep them to sell to people like you."

"I'm not buying."

"Yes you are. And the more I tell you about the bad prospects for each of these pocket mines, the more you'll itch to own them. You've already talked yourself into thinking the gold seam here's only a few blows of the pick from sight. It could be a mile from here, and straight down, but you'll ignore the reality and itch to scratch your dream."

"I'm simply representing a buyer. I don't want the thing."

"Of course you do. This one and the rest. They're all the usual fifteen hundred by six hundred feet prescribed by the mining codes, and none are patented yet, and they're all for sale, and you'll scratch your itch and buy one from me."

"Fifteen hundred's a lot of land. There might be gold elsewhere on it."

"Let's walk this one. Or climb it, since it's uphill mostly. You can tell me where the other quartz gold is."

Jay did scramble up ragged rock and talus, dodging scree, hanging on to pine trees whose roots pierced into cracks in the slope. He was looking for the shine of quartz, sensing it had to be somewhere, anywhere.

Josephson was close behind. "That's the northwest corner cairn," he said. Over there's the northeast cairn. Six hundred feet on the level, but more than that if you count slopes. It's all yours for two thousand dollars."

"What do I get for the two thousand?"

"The claim, mineral rights to whatever's under our feet."

"It's a good prospect. It's been mined. How much gold was taken out?"

"Ran six months, two-man operation, about three hundred ounces, good quartz, until they reached the fault."

"It made money?"

"Depends on how you look at it. Quartz had to be milled and refined, and there were all sorts of expenses. They sold it to me for a dollar; I'll peddle it for two thousand just because there's lots of people like you, and the more I try to discourage them, the more they secretly think they'll find what others missed. That's gold for you. I've been offering this one for sale for months, and listening to people talk themselves into it. I can't even discourage you, not even if I tell you the seam resumes some vast distance away, and on someone else's land."

"Let's look at another one."

Josephson led Jay down the treacherous slope to the main wagon trail, and headed uphill, turning off at a grass-choked two-rut road. This one was almost on level ground, some of it swampy. The geologist stopped at the upper end of the swamp.

"There used to be a strong spring here, and prospectors found a lot of gold just below it, and it was plain that the spring was eroding gold out of some sort of lode back in that slope, so they claimed the place, and dug back, following the spring into the strata inside the hill here, and found more evidence of gold deposited by the water in every crack, but not the mother lode, not the original source of the gold. So they tunneled in, letting the water flow along the bottom of the tunnel, and went in about fifty yards and found that the water actually welled upward there, some sort of artesian pressure, and that the water wasn't carrying gold uphill, so they began hunting for the lode they'd missed following the water back into the rock, and never did find it. Somewhere, if they figured it right, the stream cut through a vein, and washed out the gold."

"You own this too?"

"Got it for a dollar. Sell it for two thousand to someone who's smarter than I am and knows how gold gets washed out of the rock by that spring."

"Many buyers?"

"The more I discourage them, the more they study the rock, trying to find the magical place where the water washed out gold. They come here with lanterns and spyglasses, and pick hammers so they can go outside, in sunlight, and see what they've knocked off a wall of this tunnel. And the more I tell them it's not worth pursuing, the more determined they get. Gold does that, and it's doing it to you."

"Not me," Jay said. "I would never fall for that stuff."

Josephson smiled. "What are you bidding?"

"Show me the other properties," Jay said. "I don't have time to waste."

They were in rough country, high above

Deadwood. The resinous scent of the jack pines perfumed the air. Some sagebrush was clumped in drainages. The rock varied from tan to red hues, with the tan higher than the red. Some giant geological force had upended ancient strata, and water had cut through the softer rock, leaving the bitter bedrock behind. And most of the quartz was there, lying on the most ancient beds.

Josephson was gazing at Jay, the geologist's thoughts deeply hidden. Jay felt himself being examined. It was as though the geologist had a conception of Jay, and was testing it to see if there was truth in it. Jay decided to ignore that. He wanted every scrap of information, the sort of thing he could put to use on Addison Crowe.

"Two more, neither of them patented, both requiring annual development work of at least a hundred dollars," Josephson said. "Follow me. I should add that the remaining claims are for sale for three thousand. They offer grim prospects."

They ascended a rock-strewn trail that had seen little traffic, finally topping out on a narrow green plateau surrounded by black walls of pines. A dun layer of rock tilted upward, atop ancient granite. A tiny black rectangle, a minehead, was obscured by the low-hanging limbs of pines.

"This is the Heartbreak Mine," Josephson said. "A fitting name. The mine's squarely in the middle of a standard claim, fifteen by six hundred. It's the worst prospect of all. There's a thin quartz seam that outcropped there, about as wide as a thumb. And it had a little gold in it. The farther in they went, the thicker the seam, but only a little. It was maybe two inches, and angling toward the west side of the claim. And it had a little gold. In thirty feet of hard tunneling, they extracted only five ounces of gold, and had the task of wheel-barrowing the quartz down slope to the nearest wagon road. Three sets of owners tackled it, inspired by the fact that the seam thickens as it goes in, but none ever made a nickel of it. There might be a little gold in there, or maybe tomorrow someone will work it and the seam will suddenly be a foot thick and loaded with free-milling gold."

Jay studied the aperture, which was barely three feet high and three wide. The miners didn't waste energy cutting a full bore. The seam wasn't visible at the mine head, nor could he see it when he gingerly penetrated a dozen feet.

"Quartz has all been shoveled away," Josephson said. "You can see it on the face, if you want to crawl back that far. Three thousand, and not a penny less. And whoever buys it will end up just as discouraged as the rest."

"Why the higher price?"

"Because it's a heartbreaker. People love to have their heart broken."

That seemed odd to Jay, but he thought he understood the attraction. The lure of a fortune hidden behind all that rock was more alluring than a proven and assayed claim.

"More than my client has," Jay said. "Let's see the other one."

Josephson led him up a long feeder canyon, past some marker cairns, to an overhang that had trapped a pocket of quartz, now gone.

"This is a pocket mine, simply worked out. A couple of miners cleaned about six hundred dollars of gold out of it, and probably spent more getting the quartz to a mill. It's got no future. It's not worth doing improvements to keep Uncle Sam happy. So I've jacked up the price. Some people figure a higher asking price means it offers more chances."

"You've got it all figured out," Jay said.

"The geology, no. Human nature, maybe."

"Which gets the most attention?"

"Heartbreak. Even the name draws lookers. Most of them stand there, in front of that rabbit hole of a shaft, thinking that just behind that wall of rock is a Golconda, and they're going to snatch it." He paused. "And that's the one you'll show your client."

He was right. Jay knew exactly what he'd say to Addison Crowe, and exactly what Crowe would do when he got the history.

"Yeah, these are good properties," he said.

Josephson said nothing, merely smiled, and led Jay down the steep gulch, into the main canyon, and back to Deadwood. They didn't talk. Jay was preoccupied with turning one of these into a personal bonanza. So far, he hadn't figured a way, but he would.

"You'd take a farm in Illinois of comparable value?"

"What would I do with a farm a thousand miles away?"

"It's a hundred sixty, prime land, good producer."

"I milk rock, not cows."

"Mind if I bring my client up there for a look?"

"Show him all of them. Give him a candle and let him crawl into that rabbit hole and see the little seam of quartz. Let him chip off some quartz and hand it to an assayer. Let him pay the assayer and pocket a few cents of gold that he dug himself. And maybe he'll figure out how to sell his farm and lay cash on the line. I make more selling dead mines than I make from my geology, and the thing is, the more I talk a mine down, and point out its weaknesses, the more they itch to buy it."

That did seem like a plan, though Jay had yet to figure how to benefit from it all. He'd come up with something, and fast.

Chapter Twenty-Seven

Crowe was fascinated. He agreed to forgo sleep and see the mines the next morning after work.

Jay met him at the freight terminal, equipped with a pick, hammer, bag, and candle. He led Crowe straight up the gulch, past the placer mines, into a canyon with vaulting slopes, past great outcrops of hard rock, climbing all the while.

"I should get out more," Crowe said. "I spend my life in a dark wagon yard."

"Well, today you get to see a real gold mine, for sale cheap. You can take your own samples of quartz, have them assayed, and draw your own conclusions."

"There's no such thing as a cheap mine if it's any good," Crowe said. The man was taller than Jay, had a longer stride, and seemed to speed his way past rocky outcrops and downed timber.

"Well, that's the thing. The gold's there but it's hard to get out. The seam thickens as you go in, but it'll take digging. It was only an inch at the outcrop, and now it's two inches, thirty feet in."

"And there's a tunnel?"

"A small one, narrow and low, what prospectors call a glory hole. You'd need to enlarge it when you get to the serious gold mining."

"What's the name of this place?"

"It's called Heartbreak Mine, and for good reason."

"I'll need a good assay," Crowe said.

He seemed to go even faster, propelling himself up the winding, treacherous trail into the high country.

"I'll need enough to support my mother. She doesn't have a dime. She's good at cooking up chickens, or corn, but she's got nothing. And my brother Bart, he's got half an arm missing, so I've got to find something here that'll fix them up, and me too. He's a good man, and would work if he could, and he can do a few things, like gathering the eggs. But it's up to me. If I trade the farm or sell it, I've got to get us all fixed up. I'm a man for hard work, and I'm a man for sweat, if that's what it takes."

"Well, the owner's a geologist named Josephson, and he's got it up for sale, all right. He's got some others here, but I'm your friend, and I wanted to get you something that would work well for you, fix you up, prove out."

But Crowe wasn't listening, He had worked ahead, his eagerness to reach the little mine inspiring a pace so fast that Jay couldn't keep up. They topped a slope and stood in a hanging valley where the little mine lay against a far slope.

"I can see it," Crowe said, beelining toward the workings.

There was no one in sight. Nothing but blank,

solemn forest, and a narrow grassy valley rimmed with talus. A man working a mine so remote would have to get used to being all alone for long hours.

Crowe raced across the flat, and was soon standing at the works.

"That's an awful small rabbit hole," he said.

"It's an exploratory hole. It can be widened. That's how they follow a seam, to see if it'll pan out."

"That isn't very high. I couldn't stand in there."

"Three feet or so. About that wide, too."

"So I got to crawl in?"

"You've got a candle and a bag and a pick hammer."

"This better be good," Crowe said.

"Think of your ma," Jay said.

Crowe seemed changed. He was no longer in a hurry. He knelt before the descending shaft, which sank at a mild angle, uncomfortable with the hole. He tried to work rock loose from the roof, but it was tight and hard. He slid into deep silence, while Jay sat in the grass nearby, enjoying he show.

"All right," Crowe said. He put the candle and a few kitchen matches in his shirt pocket, took hold of the hammer, and eased in, pausing just inside, while Jay watched in the sunlight. It was only midmorning, and still cool in the shadowed valley. Later, and briefly, the sun would reach the floor, and brighten the crease in the mountains. It took Crowe a long time to go a few more feet in, but at last Crowe's boot heels vanished, and Crowe was inching his way into that choking aperture.

Jay waited, watching a hawk circle, and then he heard an eerie moan, that slowly ebbed into silence. And then another, some sort of ungodly cry of horror.

Jay knelt at the face of the shaft.

"You all right?"

He heard another sound, this like a sob. Then, faintly, "I can't."

"You can't what?"

"Help me. I can't."

"What's the trouble."

"I'm perishing."

"Well, come on out."

He heard only silence, but perhaps a sob too.

He waited a bit, but whatever was afflicting Addison Crowe seemed to have mastered him. There was no movement toward the bright daylight just outside of the hole. Jay hated the thought of crawling in there, and thought to abandon the man, but knew he couldn't.

"All right, hold your horses," he said.

He crawled slowly, suddenly realizing that crawling backward was the only way out. He eased forward, and then tried the backward crawl, crabbing toward daylight. He could manage it, but thirty feet in was a vast distance. He saw no candle ahead, only darkness that descended swiftly each additional foot.

He heard another low wail, the sound of a man paralyzed with dread or worse, with terror. The man had crawled into his own grave, or so it seemed.

"Addison, I'm coming behind you. We'll back out together. You're in there too tight, and you'll have to lift each knee back, slowly, one at a time."

"Can't breathe," Crowe whispered.

"There's air. It's just that you're all stiffed up and can't make things work."

Jay hated it, hated inching his way down that soft grade, knowing he couldn't turn around either. But he kept on.

"I'm behind you. I sense you're just ahead, Addison."

"Help me."

"Are you stuck? Rock on you?"

"I can't move."

"Try it. Move your legs, then your arms and hands, nod your head, lift your feet."

"I can't."

Jay felt around, determining that the roof of the shaft was a foot or so above him, and would be for Crowe, too.

"I'm going to back up a foot, and you do it too," Jay said. "We'll just do this one foot a time, and pretty soon we'll be right back in sunlight."

That got him only silence.

"If you don't do it yourself, I'll have to do it for you," Jay said. "I'm going to pull each foot back. We're going to back out."

He reached for Crowe's boot, and started to tug, but Crowe jammed his foot forward, breaking Jay's grip. Jay grabbed the other boot and pulled steadily, gaining a little ground but also lowering Crowe from his crouch to flat on his belly. The thought of trying to drag Crowe out without his cooperation weighed heavily on Jay, but he saw no choice. The air was thick and foul and hot, and Jay felt sweat building under his shirt.

He grabbed Crowe's boots only to have him flail violently. Jay got mad. He caught the boots and yanked hard, pulling Crowe along about a foot. Crowe howled and flailed.

"If you don't quiet down, I'll quiet you down," Jay said.

Crowe sounded like he was sobbing. The dead air was heating up fast, and Jay was sucking air hard. He backed himself up a couple of feet, caught Crowe's legs, and pulled steadily, finally dragging Crowe up the grade another bit. Dragging a man along a rough rock surface was the hardest thing he'd ever done. He again backed up, pulled quietly, got another foot out of it, and lay down, worn out. He was tempted just to back out to fresh air and leave Crowe. Especially because Crowe was clinging to any rock that gave him purchase, and was ready to crawl down again. That's what worried Jay the most.

"I'm getting you out of here, and you're going to help me. Get up on your hands and knees and start backing up. If you go forward I'll knock you down."

Crowe did nothing, but at least he wasn't moaning. Maybe getting three feet closer to sunlight was helping the man return to his senses. But the air was terrible, mixed now with sweat and body odors. Then, oddly, the man got to his hands and knees, and Jay hung on to keep Crowe from working downhill again. Crowe tentatively pushed one leg back, and the other, and again, gaining two more feet. Jay could dimly see the head of the shaft behind him. But it seemed a vast distance away.

He rested, mostly because Crowe let him. The man was still mute, except for incoherent sobs, but things were a little different. A little less hysterical.

"All right, we're going to back up six feet now," Jay said. "One leg at a time, foot by foot. Just keep on going, one at a time, and we'll be out of here."

Crowe responded slowly, trembling, but working his way backward and upward.

There was some daylight now, dim and seductive, and Crowe must have seen it. The man's breathing steadied. They made a few more feet backing out. The air was a little better. Jay backed, and Crowe backed, and Jay backed, and the light got fuller and the air sweeter.

At about ten feet, Crowe finally talked. "I can back up now," he said.

Jay let him. Crowe came along five feet, and quit, worn down to nothing. Jay let him rest.

"One last push," he said, easing into sunlight.

Crowe labored backward, and then his feet emerged from the mine head, and then the rest of him. Addison Crowe was soaked in his own sweat and urine and saliva. His shirt was black, his trousers stained and dark.

Crowe sat outside the mine, not looking at Jay, staring at the natural world as if he had never seen it before. A sweet serenity permeated the quiet valley.

"We're a way from water," Jay said. "I can bring you a little."

He knew a teamster's trick. Go soak a flannel shirt in fresh water, and bring it back, and twist the water into a thirsty man or animal's mouth. There was a creek a quarter of a mile down.

Crowe didn't respond. But then wordlessly, he clawed his way to his feet and began staggering down the long slope, not looking at Jay, not thanking him, not acknowledging Jay's presence or help. Crowe stumbled a few times, but never paused until he reached the cheerful creek, plunged straight into it, and wallowed in it, blotting up water, washing everything he wore in cold water. Jay was sweaty as well, and splashed the water over his face, and then he soaked his shirt in the fresh water, wrung it out, and put it on wet and cold. It felt good.

The pick hammer and bag and candle were up there in the shaft, and Jay knew he was liable for them. He no longer had enough to pay for them. And he wouldn't get anything out of this deal. Crowe was terrified of underground mines and the dark world where gold was torn from rock. He was paralyzed down there, frozen into uselessness. And that wasn't going to change. And Addison Crowe would never again dream of mining quartz gold.

The water gradually revived the Illinois farmer, but now there was something new. Crowe never looked at Jay or acknowledged him. The man finally rose, and started quietly down the long slope, through a serene and bright valley, glistening with grass, flanked by black pines. Jay walked behind, ready to help, but Crowe drew upon his years behind a two-bottom plow. The man continued straight to the boardinghouse, and into the room they shared, and closed the door behind him. He could still get a few hours of rest before he reported once again for night duty at the freight terminal. Jay stood, staring at the closed, blank door.

Then he headed for the curb exchange, where traders eyed him, his soaked shirt, his wild demeanor, and avoided talk. He was all but broke, with no prospects, and no hope. He hadn't gotten to Easy Street.

Chapter Twenty-Eight

The hard rap on the flimsy door yanked Jay out of a restless sleep. Morning light hurt his eyes.

He rolled out of the tumbled bed. The room somehow stank of Crowe's terror, which even a dip in the creek failed to scrub away. He pulled the door open and faced a big man with a star.

"This Addison Crowe's room?" the lawman asked.

"He has half-time."

"And you are?"

"Jay Warren."

"And you do what?"

"Trader."

"That's Crowe's stuff there?"

He pointed to a worn carpetbag jammed with Crowe's meager possessions. Jay nodded.

"Where's your stuff?" the lawman asked.

"I don't have any."

"A transient, then?"

"Trying to make my way. I've got some claims I'm selling."

"I can imagine," the lawman said. "Crowe's dead. Killed himself last night at the freight terminal. Used the shotgun they keep there. Found him, what's left of him, when the day men came in. I've come for his stuff."

"Dead? Dead?"

"Do you know any reason?"

Jay sat, reaching for words. "He dreamed of working a small gold mine and yesterday he discovered he couldn't stand to be in any cave."

"How do you know that?"

Jay told him. The officer listened intently. "All right, I might talk to you some more."

The man departed, carrying Crowe's gear, and Jay settled into the narrow cot, absorbing the reality of death.

Dead. He wondered why he had wrestled Crowe out of the shaft. If the man couldn't cope, that was his problem. Jay knew he should be horrified, but it wasn't in him. Crowe was his pigeon, and if death meant anything, it meant that Jay's last chance at making a killing had blown away with a shotgun blast. It was odd, not sharing the cramped room any more. Not that it made any difference. He owed a week's rent, due this day, and didn't have it. In fact, he had a dime or so, maybe enough for a bun or a roll. So there was no point in lamenting the death of a man who dreamed of operating a gold mine when he couldn't go underground.

But in spite of that train of thought, he felt bad about Addison Crowe, whose desperate dreams came to nothing. Maybe Crowe had weaknesses, but so did everyone else. Jay kept trying to push his concerns aside. He had more important things to do this bad day than worry about a dead man and his mother and brother. The man would have bet the farm, and Jay had intended to pocket it. And now, bright daylight, a hard city, and a belly he could not fill this morning.

Try as he might, he couldn't shake Crowe from his mind, and spent the next hour reliving the brutal effort to drag the farmer out of the shaft. What a damned fool he had been, trying to rescue a crazy man. Jay dressed and headed out, the thin dime his only weapon against hunger. He bought a roll from the bakery, and wolfed it, and then had nothing. He had nothing in the room, so he simply abandoned it. He was on the street, and Deadwood was a hard blank wall.

He studied the town, bustling with mid-morning life; its few women toting shopping baskets, the men loading wagons. He spotted Jack Deal hurrying toward the Bella Union to do some trading, and caught up with him.

Deal eyed him askance, noting the battered clothing.

"I got five claims, Jack. You want them for five dollars?"

Jack heehawed. "You're broke. It's a great teacher."

"Could I borrow a dollar?"

"Borrow's not the word, boy, since you're not borrowing. You're begging. No. If you starve to death, then you haven't solved your little troubles."

"How can I make money?"

"This town's begging for labor. Everyone wants to dig for gold, and no one wants to lime outhouses or carpenter buildings."

"But that's for drudges."

"The answer, boy, is no. And I'll warn the rest of the traders to follow suit. Work or starve. Your pigeon croaked this morning, and now it's your turn."

Jay stared. The man he thought was his ally was nothing of the sort, just another heartless bastard trying to wring cash out of anyone he could steal it from.

"I saved his life and no one cares. He got hysterical in there, and I dragged him out."

"He sure didn't care, and proved it. I'm busy, boy, go starve. Or get a job."

"I need to find some friends of mine near Lead. Can you stake me?"

"Your pals got chased outa Dakota, boy. They're out of the Territory. Dumb bunch, if you ask me. They couldn't skin a potato. Now don't bother me unless you've got a pigeon for me."

He drifted toward the Beanery, and waited until the old proprietor had a moment. The smells made him dizzy.

"I'll wash dishes for a meal," he said.

The old boy looked him up and down. "We don't wash dishes here, boy. We just serve the next on top of the old."

"I'll work in the kitchen."

"Nothing to do for the likes of you. You been a cook?"

Jay shook his head.

"Slop bucket out back," the old goat said.

Jay hastened to the rear, and found a stinking barrel of slop, alive with worms. The worms had more to eat than he did.

He spotted a woman, her wicker basket laden, and hailed her.

"Ma'am, I'm desperate for food. I'd do chores for you for a meal."

"Not the way you smell," she said.

Jay raged. He couldn't help how he looked or smelled.

He drifted toward the Foley Freight Terminal, finding it quiet and in the hands of the day crew. He corralled a teamster who was strapping a feedbag on a horse.

"You lost a friend of mine last night," Jay said.

"If you're the man took him to that hole in the hill, you weren't any friend of Addison Crowe," the man said. The horse dug into the oats and chewed noisily. "We've just collected a little to bury the man. He was our friend, and we were his friends. We wanted to see him put to rest proper."

"I was his friend."

"Naw, you don't have friends. We know a thing or two here. You had pigeons and schemes. A man needs friends to get along, and you ain't one.

Looks to us like you put out the lights of Crowe, and for keeps."

It was true. Jay hadn't made a friend since the Leavenworth days, and he had never given a thought to a friendship with the man who shared his room.

"I'm looking for his job as night man."

"You check with the devil first, and if the devil says so, I'll talk you up for it."

"I was a teamster; I can do it."

"You were a deserter. You gave the boss your word, and skipped the first chance you got. A man's got to be good as his word to get ahead. You left that wagon short of men and guns, just when the Sioux were running loose through here. Ike says he was lucky to get back to Cheyenne."

"Is there any way I can start over?"

The teamster eyed Jay for a long time, and Jay saw a gentling of his gaze.

"We all were young once, and full of wild oats. I was. I got a few chances I didn't deserve. I'll think on it."

"I'd like to start now."

"I said I'd think on it."

He plucked up a pitchfork and headed for a hay pile and began forking hay into long mangers for the oxen. He also shut out Jay, somehow keeping his back toward Jay.

The day was waning. He had no friends. If he had made some friends he might have shelter and food. He hadn't thought to befriend anyone; everyone was a pigeon, someone to sucker into buying a worthless claim. Not since Huckleberry Jones had he possessed a friend, and maybe that wasn't friendship either, since they were mostly scheming to cheat people one way or another. Nor had anyone attempted to befriend him. He stopped in the middle of Main, suddenly aware that he was a loner and not one soul cared whether he lived or died.

All around him, busy people were advancing their lives, raising families, working toward their dreams, forming business partnerships, meeting in saloons for a social hour at the bars, offering labor and skill for wages and security. It made him envious and angry.

The sun was heading toward rosy clouds off toward the western ridges. Deadwood was a good place, alive and warm and mostly happy. He didn't have the slightest idea where to turn, and found himself drifting toward the Gem, the big enterprise that had something for every appetite. But it was mostly a giant saloon, which somehow drew crowds of males each evening. It was owned by a man named Al Swearingen, something of a genius at supplying relief for any itch.

He found the boss in a cubicle high up, where he was afforded a view of the whole saloon and dime-a-dance hall, as well as the gambling tables.

Swearingen eyed him. "You're looking for a

job, you're broke and hungry, and you stink. And you took that dead bastard to the mine."

"Yes sir."

"You're the one looking for easy money."

"Not any more, sir. I'll work hard at any job you offer me."

"You sick? You got consumption or something?"

"No, sir."

"All right, I can use a swamper. They usually last about three nights. You'll mop, clean the spittoons, lime the privies, clean up the girls' rooms upstairs, run errands, polish tables and woodwork, nonstop, but mostly when the crowd thins at night. I like clean privies. I've got six holes, and they're all in use all the time. You'll wipe them down and keep lime on the crap. It's for the women. Most of the males piss in the creek. You'll get to sleep in the storeroom on a cot, and get three meals the cooks will give you, and you won't get fat on them. That's it."

"No pay, sir?"

"You're being paid. You mean cash. Most swampers get two bits or fifty cents of gold dust out of the floor sweepings. They pan it. One made a dollar and went on a drunk and I never saw him again. There's always some dust being spilled. Bright swampers mine the cracks and get more. That's it. Oh, yes, you get to drink up what's left in glasses, if you're a drunk. Free booze, but not from the bar. You want it?"

"Yes, sir. I'm Jay Warren."

"I don't need a name. You'll last a few days and then I'll get another."

Swearingen eyed him. "Clothing in the store room. Find something that fits, and wash up; you smell. Tell the cook you're the new swamper, and you'll get a bowl of stew. Then get to work. You work from noon to midnight. And you get no time off. And leave the girls alone."

The boss turned back to his ledgers. Jay hastened down to the main floor, found the kitchen, got a small bowl of gray stew, full of things he couldn't identify. He wolfed it down, feeling something in his hollow stomach at last.

He found the storeroom, lit a lantern, eyed the grimy cot, found a heap of clothing, things customers had left, and got himself into pants and a shirt that were more or less clean and comfortable. He found a push broom and other supplies, and set to work, ignoring the revelers at the bar and tables, who in turn, ignored him. It was going to be a long night, and a longer week, and a longer month, and a life so long he wished it could end soon.

Chapter Twenty-Nine

All Jay wanted was another bowl of stew. He eyed the crowd, envious of them all, most of them with some money in their pockets, enjoying drinks and company. He, Jay Warren, rich man's son, had nothing.

He hardly knew where to start, so he tried the foulest task first. He found a sack of lime and a shaker device used to spread it, and a bucket and mop, and headed out the rear door where the outhouses stood in a row. Three were in use. Two men were pissing on a tree stump. The area stank, and no breeze lifted the odor away. He entered the first crapper, cranked lime into the pit, dipped his mop in water and swabbed the place down. Then he did the next one, and waited for someone to vacate the third, and did the fifth while he waited. In time he got them all, and the place stank less and was almost bearable when he finished.

He pitched the used water over the tree stump, and headed in. For some reason, he felt oddly satisfied by his labor. He noticed that the dance floor, where the dime-a-dance girls worked, was littered, so he waited for the tune to quit and swept it clean with a push broom, all in a few moments, and hauled the grit and rubbish away in a bucket. The girls ignored him. The customers didn't give a damn.

He found half a dozen spittoons lining the bar and tables, some of them choked with stuff he couldn't identify. But there were cigar butts in chewing tobacco mixed into the slime. He carried one out to the outhouse and dumped the contents down the hole. The spittoon stank of tobacco and other odors beyond his knowing. He set it under a pump and jacked the handle until a flow of cold water filled the spittoon. He poured it out, and did it again, and finally got the brass spittoon looking and smelling clean. Then he did that to the rest of them. No one noticed or cared. But he knew the spittoons were bright and clean and good for a while.

Table tops were grimy. He got some fresh water, found an ancient rag, and began scrubbing the table tops, rolling away gummy stuff that probably once was food or drink, or maybe spit or filth from dirty hands. Some of it didn't yield to scrubbing. But there was nothing else he could find. So he did what he could, dissatisfied, wondering how he could improve his task, and finally moved on to other things. No one noticed. Men with drinks sat down, and it didn't matter to them whether the table was polished or filthy.

One of the girls upstairs sent for him. He headed up there, into a mysterious world laden with heavy perfume and strange odors and a sickly light.

"He puked on my bed," the girl said.

He eyed the mess. It had penetrated through a cover over a stuffed cotton mattress. He eyed the girl, wrapped in pink, with varicose veins around her ankles and bad teeth.

He pulled the cover off, and with it most of the puke.

He found a water pitcher and hand bowl, and a grimy towel, and put the wet towel to work, soaking up most of the mess.

"Now I gotta sleep on that?" she asked, eyeing the dark patch. He tugged the mattress up and flipped it over. The bottom side was clean.

She smiled. "You're new," she said. "You'll last a day or two."

He carried the fouled cover downstairs, not knowing what to do with it. He dropped it in the storeroom and looked for other things to do. No one noticed. The dime-a-dance girls were whirling, their customers stomping.

He saw empty glasses on tables, many with an inch or so of booze in them. He collected them, found a place at one side of the bar where the glasses were dipped into water and set aside to dry. He did that after watching one of the barmen do it. The barmen eyed him as if he were a creature from under the seas.

The Gem didn't attract a late-night crowd, and when the place quieted down, Jay swept the floor, carefully stowing the debris and grit. Then he mopped. He thought he was doing a good job, but when it dried he realized all he had done was swirl the dirt around. No one noticed. The boss was nowhere in sight. The remaining barman yawned. The dime-a-dance girls quit, along with the accordion man. Jay found a pan in the storeroom, dropped some of the sweepings into it, along with water, and whirled the pan around, spilling off the lighter stuff until a few dark grains remained in the bottom. He spotted no gold, not a glint or shimmer. He tried again, worked his way through whatever he had swept up, and didn't see a flake of gold. He needed to learn how to do that.

He was starved. The kitchen was dark. He entered anyway, found some boiled potatoes, ate one with his fingers, and called it a supper. The storeroom was windowless and pitch dark, but he memorized where the door was, and turned down the lamp. The cot stank of misery, but he had a roof over him, clothing on him, and a little succor in his belly. The building creaked, and he heard occasional shifting above him, on the upper floor. He was too worn to feel sorry for himself, and swiftly fell into deep slumber.

He had earned his keep.

The next shifts were much the same. There was no payday. He never learned to pan the sweepings for spilled gold dust. One night he found two bits in the sawdust. Another night a dime-a-dance girl gave him a ten-cent tip. He had cleaned up a puddle of urine on the dance floor. It had run down a man's leg. No one noticed him. But he won an occasional smile from the women upstairs. They were mysterious and secretive, but they had errands for him to do. They were a sorry lot, worn and troubled and drunk, and by daylight they looked even sorrier. They rarely stirred anything in him. He was told not to mess with them, so he didn't.

The meals rarely varied, but he was fed. He suspected it was food that was destined for the garbage pile out back, for raccoons to haul away. He did his job thoroughly, kept the place clean and shining, and no one noticed. It was a dead-end job with nothing to look forward to, not even a pay envelope. But he began to feel better. He couldn't explain it.

He cleaned the storeroom, and washed his canvas cot, and turned it into a refuge. There was no privacy, but it didn't matter. He heard no praise from the boss, but neither did anyone rail at him. He began getting up earlier, and took to the streets, enjoying a little sunlight and autumnal breezes. He drifted one day over to the Foley Freight Terminal, found the day man forking hay. Jay found a pitchfork and joined the man, who looked surprised but said nothing.

"Railroad'll be here in a year or two, and then I'm out of work," the man said.

"Maybe not. It takes a lot of freighting to get goods out to smaller towns."

"It's progress," the man said. "Can't stop it."

"If you had your druthers, what would you do?" Jay asked.

"Just what I'm doing. I'm good with stock. If I ever got enough together, I'd ranch. Still a lot of good pasture if a man could find the beef to put on it."

He glanced sharply at Jay. "And you?"

"I swamp out the Gem. Maybe some day I can try for a job."

"You're man enough for one. Heard about you some."

"I didn't know anyone ever heard of me."

"Crowe, the day he died, he talked and talked. He told a dozen of us you pulled him out of that hole. He talked and we left the yard around dusk and when it was black as midnight he shot himself."

"He talked about me? I was trying to beat him out of his farm."

"You pulled him out when he was frozen up solid."

"It wasn't anything."

"You were man enough. You wouldn't quit. Stubborn about it."

Jay didn't like it. "I got to go to work."

The day man grinned. "Shine up them spittoons," he said.

Jay did that. He was amazed at what went into spittoons. He wondered why men spit. Why didn't women have spittoons? He never did master the art of scraping spilled gold dust off the plank floor, but for some reason, the spittoons sometimes had coins in them. All he had to do was reach in, through the foul contents, and pluck them out. Pluck dimes or nickels out of vomit and piss and spirits that had been emptied into them. If he dumped the contents into outhouse holes, the coins were lost. So he emptied them beside the nearest creek, extracted and washed the occasional dime, and then bucketed the slime into the creek. He could hardly imagine anything lower.

Neither could the crowds of males drinking, spending, dancing, and whoring, all with money they got from somewhere. Somehow they knew a swamper was at the bottom, probably a drunk, barely clinging to life, so he was invisible to them, and to all the staff in the Gem. Except the women upstairs. They noticed him. One or two even tipped a dime now and then. He ran their errands, brought them spirits, got them Dover's powder or opium from the town's doctors. He itched to explore their bodies, but feared it, both because they were mostly fevered and consumptive, but also because he had been warned off by the boss. If he didn't have bowls of gray stew, he would die of starvation.

He took to walking over to Foley's Freight Terminal for a couple of hours before he started his long shift, and there he simply helped the teamsters. There were oxen to yoke or unyoke or pin down while a farrier shoed them. There were horses and mules and bovines to hay, or sometimes grain. There were crates and casks and burlap sacks to pull out of wagon beds and store in the warehouse. No one gave him pay; no one interfered.

The freighters rolled in regularly, day after day. It took a dozen wagons a day, each loaded with necessaries, to keep a bustling town like Deadwood supplied. One day his old wagon boss, Ike, rolled in, with a train of eight burdened freight wagons, each drawn by an ox team. Ike's men swiftly unloaded the goods, while others unhooked each team and took care of the weary oxen. The big beasts were worked down to rib and bone, but continued to drag tons of freight across an empty land.

"So it's you, is it?" Ike asked.

"I just help out. I work at the Gem."

"Swamping, I heard."

"I keep the place clean," Jay said.

"That's what I heard."

The conversation wasn't going anywhere, so Jay returned to forking hay into mangers for the worn-out oxen.

"I heard you tried to peddle some bad mines to

Crowe, and maybe that's what killed him," Ike said, relentlessly.

"He was my last hope."

"For a life without toil. And you lost and he killed himself."

Jay set his pitchfork against a wall. "I've got to go to work," he said.

"Glad you're helping out here," Ike said.

But it was too late. Jay seethed. He strode away, hiked up to Main, and into the Gem, well before his shift began. To his surprise, he found Swearingen at the bar.

"You. Yes, you. I don't know your name. Give me a name."

"What did I do now?"

"Here's a dollar. Place looks half way clean. Even the crappers don't smell."

There, in his hand, was a grubby greenback. Jay took it.

"I'm Jay Warren."

"Well, maybe I'll make you a barman some day." And with that, the boss headed for his cubicle, where he could overlook his whole operation.

So Jay possessed one whole dollar. It only triggered a rage in him. He stuffed it into his britches and set to work. He'd developed a routine, and now, while the sun shown through the dreary little windows, he swept and polished, mopped and wiped down tables. He eyed the sole barman, who was mostly staring at the nude hanging above the bar, a little come-hither that probably added to the Gem's overall prosperity.

The next morning, he found Ike and his crew preparing for the return to Cheyenne, with six empty wagons and thirty-six oxen and only three teamsters.

"You want another man?" Jay asked.

"I could use one. I always lose a few to gold fever. I can hire you for the trip, but not full time. You'd have to deal with Fairweather Foley to stay on with the company." There was a certain question unstated.

"I'll be with you all the way to Cheyenne," Jay said.

"We'll be off soon as we're yoked up."

"I'll tell them at the Gem I'm gone," Jay said.

Chapter Thirty

Moving six ox teams and six freight wagons with only four men was tricky, but Ike was up to it. He created two massive trains, each consisting of three ox teams and three wagons, all hooked together. They were soon out of Deadwood, working through sloping country, always harder than out on the flats.

Jay knew the work. It was better than swamping out the Gem. He would have ample trail chow, some pay, and fresh air. The weather was milder now, at the end of summer, and most days would be little more than a pleasant hike.

They would return to Cheyenne in three weeks, load up, and begin another massive shipment of all sorts of merchandise and food to the hungry gold camp in the Black Hills. Ike put Jay on the forward train, along with himself; his two experienced teamsters worked the rear train. The wagons creaked along, sometimes needing grease from the bucket dangling at their rear, while the ribby oxen enjoyed an easy haul, and moved comfortably, even up steep grades.

Jay was ill-equipped for travel, but at least he could sleep in one of the three wagons with covers if it rained. He didn't know what he would do in Cheyenne. Teamstering was as dead-end as all the other drudge work he saw around him. Maybe Foley would let him manage the big depot in Cheyenne. He was born to supervise. Meanwhile, he was a prisoner of his stomach. He wouldn't be here, an ox whip in hand, supervising stupid bovines, were it not that he got hungry. He'd find some way out, and soon, and put this grinding labor behind him.

Freighting was slow and steady, and gave men a chance to talk along the way. He and Ike often walked together, especially on level ground. On downgrades Ike climbed up on the first wagon to brake the descent and keep it and the wagons behind it from rolling into the slobbering ox teams.

"Foley's operation's so big that he's got one outfit does nothing but haul feed to the stations. He's got two more stations now, which spares the oxen and spares the teamsters, too," he said.

"Foley's getting rich," Jay said.

"No, freighting's not like a railroad. The more you ship, the higher your costs. Now a railroad, they just add boxcars and there's more profit at the same cost, pretty near."

"If he's not getting rich, why does he do it?"

Ike eyed him sharply. "Same reason you're working for him, Warren."

They camped in woods the first night, and Jay discovered that the other teamsters, Sam and Josiah, were pretty quiet. The thirty-six oxen were unyoked and allowed to graze freely. They wouldn't go anywhere.

There was a sharp wind that night, so Jay slept in one of the covered wagons, listening to the wind flap the canvas. It wouldn't be long until cold weather set in, which was another reason not to be a teamster. Their winter trips were miserable.

They were up before dawn, and yoking oxen for an hour before they dipped into a bean pot for breakfast. It was a dull, boring, uncomfortable life, and not as interesting as swamping out the saloon. But there'd be pay at Cheyenne; two dollars a day, waiting for him.

They started south again, as the Black Hills began to subside into long ridges and gulches, and a cold wind harried them along.

"Whatever became of that Leavenworth outfit you joined last time?" Ike asked.

That was a touchy subject, so Jay chose his words carefully. "They were claim jumpers, or thought they were. Turned out jumping claims was less rewarding than they thought. And even if it was legal, the placer miners didn't like it."

"They? Not you?"

"I was part of it, and they ditched me."

"How'd that happen?"

"First they got chased out of Deadwood Gulch, and then they ran into trouble in the Strawberry diggings. By then they had cut me out. I heard they'd been hanged, but that was some old bird at a bar rail trying to scare me, since he figured I was one. After that, I lost track. They never contacted me. But I hear they're around."

"They're around, all right, Warren, and they might stop us. They're not jumping claims now; they're looking for gold shipments."

"Stop us? With empties?"

"Gold's carried in coaches, and with armed guards, but they sometimes check empties like ours to see if we're sneaking gold south."

"Where does the gold go?"

"Smelters and the mints. There's no way to refine it in Deadwood. It goes by rail, express, out of Cheyenne."

"What about northbound?"

"Not much gold going north, but we always carry valuables." He eyed Jay. "I think you're lucky they ditched you. You'd have your mug on a wanted poster now if you stuck with them."

"How do you know it's the same bunch, from Leavenworth?"

"Bones. It's the Jake Bones Gang now. With Boggs and Cassidy and Jones and Tyler, and some that's not the original gang. There's posters around; see for yourself. Wanted dead or alive. Seems to me, Warren, you got real lucky. Or maybe quit wanting something for nothing."

"Maybe so," Jay said. "Any been hanged?"

"Not yet. But sure as the sun rises, it's coming."

"I heard a few were strung up for claim jumping, but that was bar talk. The thing is, they had no use for me. So I'm lucky, like you say."

They met an enormous ox train heading for Deadwood, and it took some doing to make room on a narrow trail, with a drop-off at one side. The teamsters knew one another, and they made talk, mostly about the trail ahead, even as they worked their massive teams and wagons past the other wagons.

"Road's dry, no trouble south," their wagonmaster, Birkenwood, said. "And you got the wind on your tail. It gets cold our way."

The country was dryer as they left the hills, but no less convoluted. Massive stands of juniper crowded the slopes. In places the trail had been hacked through thickets of the aromatic bush that never quite reached tree status.

They rounded a broad bend, and discovered trouble ahead. A northbound Foley mudwagon, the lightest of coaches, stood canted to one side, its four-mule team slouched in harness. There were no signs of life. Bits of white paper lay scattered across the trail and some had blown down the slope into the dense juniper, so thick no man could push through it and come out untouched.

"That doesn't look good," Ike said. He reached into the first of the wagons, grabbed a shotgun, and hastened forward, past the plodding oxen, while Jay hurried the ox teams forward.

In a couple of minutes, all four teamsters were staring at the coach, and two dead men lying on the earth. The boot had been opened; a mail pouch had been rifled, and letters were blowing in the breeze.

"That's Olaf Olson, dammit to hell," Ike said of the coach driver. He had been shot dead, the ball passing through his chest.

The other, the shotgun messenger, they didn't know. A black-bearded man stared lifelessly toward the sky, shot in the neck. His shotgun lay nearby.

There was no one in the coach.

"Ambush, right out of the juniper, where a man's least likely to expect it," Ike said.

The front right wheel of the coach had been shattered by something, making the coach inoperable.

"Get yourself armed and spread out," Ike said bleakly. "I want to know where they were waiting, and if there's blood I want to know it."

They swiftly found a spot on the hilly side of the road, a place to ambush a passing wagon or coach that gave no hint of trouble. There were horse apples there, and nothing else. The teamsters stared bleakly. Some intelligence had gone into this one. It was not any sort of spot to expect trouble.

"All right," Ike said tautly. "We'll carry the men to my wagon. Josiah, unhook the mules and tie them behind your wagons. Dammit, dammit, dammit."

Ike and Sam rolled Olson onto a blanket, and then all of them carried Olson to the wagon and settled him gently inside. Then they carried the shotgun guard to the wagon, and settled the body next to Olson.

"I wonder why they hit a northbound coach," Ike said. "They must have known something. Whatever was in the boot, they got it."

"Who?" asked Jay.

"I can guess," Ike said. "Jay, you start collecting the mail. Get it all, and get it fast. There's letters blown down there." He waved toward the low wall of juniper descending the slope.

Jay collected the mail pouch and set to work. There were plenty of letters, and he caught them up, one by one, and stuffed them into the pouch until he had the wagon road cleared, and then he worked down the slope, into thick grass, brush, and juniper, chasing after bits of white wherever the wind had carried them. One lay deep in the juniper thickets, and he thought to abandon it, but pressed ahead.

That's when he saw the olive-colored canvas sack, its drawstrings tied tightly in an elaborate knot. He pushed into the juniper, reached the pouch, discovered it was heavy, and difficult to drag. He fumbled with the knot, his heart racing, and it finally yielded and he could pry open the pouch. Within were tan pasteboard boxes, some ajar, and each filled with packets of greenbacks, big bills, money beyond imagining. His heart raced. He gaped at it. Then he knew he was on Easy Street. And he had no time at all.

He tied the drawstring, dragged the heavy pouch down slope, shoving through impenetrable juniper that stabbed him and resisted him. Below the thicket he found a small animal hollow under a ledge, and stuffed the money pouch into it, and found some brush to conceal it. His heart raced. He took a moment to orient himself. He memorized his locale, the nearest big tree, the distance from the trail above.

No time! He jammed his way out, retrieved his mail bag, and reached the road.

Ike was smiling. "You must have chased some letters deep in there."

"I got them all," Jay said.

He memorized the place. It was so anonymous he could easily miss it when he came back. It was so obscure, in that vast wild, that he doubted he could ever find it. But there was the camp axe in the wagon. While the others were turning the mules around, and checking the mudwagon, he blazed two or three of the higher junipers, creamy white slashes he would not miss. And then he slid the axe back into the kitchen goods.

Then they were on their way, the lumbering ox teams once more dragging the wagons south. But Jay's mind wasn't on his task. It was on the money pouch, that would soon be all his, and would put him on Easy Street at last.

"You all right?" Ike asked.

"Sure, just a little afraid. Maybe there's bandits here."

"You look like you ain't quite with us."

"Well, I'm not," Jay said.

The northernmost of the Foley stations was only five miles down the road, and there the freighters pulled in, carrying their bodies and bad news. The station man, Cyrus Wilkes, was awaiting them with fresh teams all yoked and ready. The slouchy man was a loner, like most of the station men on the road, and he took the news desolately.

"They come through here, fit as a fiddle, carrying something in that boot that took some guarding, switched out the mules, and they were gone. Now look at them," Wilkes said, staring into the somber light of the lead wagon.

"Who's the big one?" Ike asked.

"Bugs Barber," Wilkes said. "He only rides with big payrolls. He's as tough as they come. Shoots first, asks questions after. The bushwackers must of made off with a fortune."

"What do we do? We're two weeks out of Cheyenne; we can't take the dead that far."

"Send for the sheriff. Deadwood, Dakota, not

Wyoming. He can get here in two days on a good horse."

"What do we do with the dead?"

"I've got a spring house that'll keep them a while. Cool in there, good for a week. But you fellers, you dig graves since you found 'em. Next northbound rider or coach, I'll send word, and they'll get the story."

The next northbound riders rode in even while the teamsters were carrying the bodies to the spring house. Swiftly, the riders agreed to notify the sheriff, and rode out again. They were four mounted prospectors with pack horses.

Jay hoped they didn't look too hard when they reached the broken down mudwagon. He wandered the livestock pens, seeing plenty of resting oxen and mules. The latter interested him. Some had Foley brands. Some had no brand. Some had the marks of pack saddles on them; some looked pretty green. And there were several sawbucks and a few panniers around, all of which helped him form a plan. He would return here some night; a mule and pack saddle would hardly be missed.

Ike and the teamsters scraped two shallow graves out of a corner of the yard, and left them open. Then they started south again, working long hours to make up for lost time. Jay went with them, working steadily, though his mind was elsewhere. A thousand times he thought of ditching Ike, but he resisted it. That was a sure way to get caught. So he kept to himself, walked the long walk to Cheyenne, and arrived with the train.

By then, word of the robbery was all over the city, arriving roundabout by wire.

The paper said that the gang, some called it the Bones gang, made off with upwards of fifty-eight thousand dollars, sent up to Deadwood business interests so the town wouldn't need to rely on gold dust for its commerce.

Fifty-eight, Jay thought. Enough for a lifetime, and he'd never toil again.

Chapter Thirty-One

He hadn't gone to college for four years for nothing. He had to examine every risk and prepare for it. The first thing was not to be in a hurry. There might well be people lingering around the ambush site for days, or even weeks. The broken wheel of the mudwagon needed to be fixed or replaced before anyone could move it.

In addition to the gawkers, the holdup men might be hanging about, using spy glasses to see who found the cash they somehow didn't find. And it would do no good for Jay to take his pay, forty dollars for twenty days on the road, and vanish. He needed to stick with the Foley company a while, even while subduing the fear that his hasty cache would be discovered and the money gone by the time he got there.

If he did it right, he'd collect. But even then it wouldn't be over. The serial numbers on the bills had no doubt been recorded. They appeared to be new, as best as he could recollect from his single hasty glance. And he couldn't spend new bills, big bills, and that meant he'd have to wear each one down, crumple it, age it. And he couldn't spend any of it in the immediate area. He would need to take it all to California or some place like that, and leak it away a little at a time, and only after a few months.

The Dakota sheriff tacked up wanted posters, with crude drawings of Jake Bones that looked nothing like him. Wanted Dead or Alive, which was stretching things some, since there was no hard evidence that the Bones bunch had robbed the coach and killed the jehu and shotgun messenger. But frontier justice didn't pause for niceties. Pretty quick, there were posters tacked up around Cheyenne offering a thousand dollars for the capture of Bones or any of his gang, and another reward for recovery of the missing cash, which totaled $58,000.

His forty dollars weren't enough to buy what he needed; a good saddle horse, tack, and an outfit that would enable him to camp far from city lights for weeks on end. That meant another trip with Ike, about twenty days each way, around eighty dollars in pay, and then he'd have what he needed.

Still, all these things were feasible if he kept his patience. So he signed on. Fairweather Foley eyed him sharply, but put him on, and a new train, this one carrying flour, oats, stovepipes, stoves, and drygoods, headed north up the trail to Deadwood.

It was a smaller outfit, four wagons, four ox teams, eight men. Before he left, Jay spent twenty dollars on a revolver, holster, and a box of cartridges. The Indians were quiet now, but there were other things to worry about. The freighters made good time, perhaps because the heat had lifted and the oxen enjoyed cool air and brisk breezes. Jay had become an experienced teamster, and rarely needed instruction from Ike. They rolled past Chugwater Station, and several more up the trail, arriving one evening at the uppermost station, where the graves of Olson and Barber occupied a corner of the yard, covered with yellow clay and no grass.

Jay and Ike went to visit them.

"They were good brave men," Ike said.

"Yes, and where did it take them? Here," Jay said.

"They'll be remembered. I'll never forget them."

"What good is honor?" Jay said. "They don't even know of it now."

"They knew it while they lived. They knew who they were, and it rode with them. They knew they were men, and good men, and men who could look any other man in the eye."

"That was their choice," Jay said. "Hardly worth living for."

"Warren, you sure are a loner," Ike said.

The wagon master turned abruptly away.

Jay strolled the station, seeing exactly where things were. There were mules, some branded, some not. He spotted a row of pack saddles, mostly sawbucks, and panniers, in an open-sided log shed. He noted the two gates in the stock pen, and where the mangers lay, and whether there were windows in the station cabin looking out on the pens. There weren't. The two windows faced the dirt road.

They switched ox teams and continued up the road to Deadwood. When they reached the ambush site, the mudwagon was gone, and the dried grasses were much trampled on, and the two blazes Jay had cut were visible, but just barely. He stared into the juniper thicket, and his heart raced.

It was all he could manage not to quit on the spot, but he contained his fevers and they rolled north, to Deadwood, and unloaded their cargo at the terminal, some of it directly into delivery wagons that would distribute vital goods to the booming town. Jay helped unload, doing the drudge work because he must. He must remain as invisible to these people as possible.

That evening he spent a few of the dollars in his pocket, mostly at the Gem. He avoided the Bella Union and the sharpers and traders, preferring his old haunts. No one recognized him. Swampers were not remembered. The girls upstairs would have welcomed him, and he had money enough, but all that could come later. He was about to make a killing, and he wanted no one at all to see him. He lost five dollars are Faro, and headed out to the terminal, and bedded down in the hayloft. The next morning the teamsters hooked ox teams to empty wagons, and headed out. Jay took one last look at Deadwood, glad to escape the barbaric place. Soon he'd be a gentleman of leisure in California, enjoying the favors of senoritas, which were more to his liking. Soon now.

The trip back to Cheyenne was uneventful, and he even managed to trod past the ambush site with little more than a sharp rise in anticipation. He would be back.

In Cheyenne, he collected his eighty dollars for forty days on the road, quietly left the company, not bothering to say good-bye to Ike, who was loading wagons for the next trip. But Ike found him.

"You sure are a loner, Warren, sneaking out without a good-bye."

"I didn't know anyone cared," he said.

"You might care about us, man."

He didn't. Weeks on the road with the teamsters hadn't resulted in any friendships. There was no point in befriending people he'd never see again and didn't care to know.

Ike's outfit would leave the following morning, and Jay planned to be ahead of them.

He headed for a horse trader who tried to sell him some lamed animals, a handsome sorrel in particular, but he had gotten enough knowledge on the trail to spot most trouble. Saddle horses usually harbored a few surprises, unexpected bucking, or panic, or a habit of busting out of pens. But he finally found one he trusted, bought an ancient saddle and pad and bridle and halter, filled a warbag with chow, mostly rolled oats for both horse and man, added a bedroll and a few more items, and quietly left town. He'd spent everything.

He knew that when trouble came, it usually arrived on the wings of poor planning, so he weighed what he would do once he recovered the cash. The best plan was simple enough. He'd return to Cheyenne, board the next westbound, buy a ticket from the conductor, and keep his panniers full of greenbacks in sight at all times.

A saddle horse could cover thirty or forty miles a day, which would put him far ahead of Ike's freight outfit, and could put him at the ambush site in maybe five days. The weather was turning, and he might face rain and cold, but he would deal with it. He rode easily, making Chugwater station the first day, but not bedding down there. The less anyone saw of him, the better.

The ride was a bore, the scenery dull, the occasional traveler not worth knowing. Things would heat up in California. He smiled at the thought.

He arrived at Beaver Creek Station, just south of the ambush site, with perfect ease, and hung back in the gulches until deep dark. So far, everything had gone just fine. He took his time, watched the station, saw a half-moon top the hills and cast pale light on the station. The lamp in the cabin went out early, but he waited a while more, and then eased his gelding down from the gulches and onto the flat at the creek. He tied up the gelding at the pen, took his halter and lead rope, slipped silently into the pen while all the stock watched him alertly. If there was to be trouble, now would be the moment. He studied the mules, which were watching him even as he selected one, and approached gently. It laid its ears back, but let him approach, accepted a halter, and allowed itself to be led to the open shed, where Jay soon fitted a blanket and pack saddle with empty panniers on.

Moments later he was outside of the pen, leading the mule, then letting his gelding and the mule sniff each other out. He rode north as silently as he had arrived, welcoming the dull moonlight on a clear night. He was lucky. He hadn't calculated what he would do on a cloudy, pitch-dark night. But he felt his luck was strong, and he deserved some luck, and the gods of justice were at last repaying him for all of his bad luck.

About two hours later, walking the lonely road up the creek valley, he reached the ambush site. He knew it even in that vast wilderness, even in the sickly light of a half moon, knew it because it had been scorched into his mind, scorched into his senses. It was utterly quiet. He did have some trouble locating the blazes he had cut, but he finally found the important one. He took his animals off the road, leading through the whipping limbs of juniper brush, which they didn't like, but soon he had them peacefully standing in a secluded patch of grass, where they stood peacefully.

He felt oddly serene, not anxious at all, just delighted with the night, with the moon, with his utter success. He knew approximately where the money pouch was hidden, and hoped to find it by moonlight, but was prepared to spend whatever daylight it took if he couldn't manage it at night. The key was a rock ledge and the drop off just below it.

So he had terrain to guide him. He calculated that he was below the ledge, and began working upward through scattered juniper. It took only a few minutes. And there it was. The pale light caught the smooth texture of the sack, just where it had been shoved weeks earlier. He freed it, felt its heaviness, pulled it back to the open glade, and quietly opened the drawstrings he had knotted. He felt not excitement but a vast peace, the world made right, an end to the ordeal his father had shoved him into. He found the money intact, packet after packet, clean, fresh greenbacks, multiple denominations, plainly intended to put Deadwood on a cash economy and reduce the cumbersome gold dust transactions.

All his. He fingered some packets of big bills, watching the hundreds slide by, and the fifties, and then the twenties. That was enough. He began loading the pasteboard cartons into his panniers, one by one, balancing the weight on either side of the mule, and when he was done he returned the bank bag to the place where he had hidden it. He did not want to be carrying it.

He loaded his gear atop the bills. His oats, his kitchen, his bedroll, his spare clothing, and when he was finished, he buckled the panniers tight, and made sure there was no weakness in them.

His gelding whickered, which seemed strange, but the night was full of movement.

He rode out, a rich man, a man who could enjoy all the rest of his days, secure and free. He headed south, circled wide around the Beaver Creek Station, and continued southward, his horse moving easily. Near dawn, he turned off the road entirely, heading into an open prairie to camp and rest his animals.

The riders materialized around him, coming quietly out of the gray pre-dawn, men in dungarees and flannel shirts, beards and slouch hats, and they all had drawn revolvers in hand, and were encircling him.

"Well, if it isn't our friend Jay," said Jake Bones.

Jay sagged deep into his saddle.

"Let go of the rope, boy, and keep riding, and you might live."

Jay saw how it was. Still he hesitated.

"Boy, do we have to take it out of your dead hand?"

Jay released the lead rope. It fell to the earth. Huckleberry swiftly took it, and led the pack mule away.

"Go on, boy, ride away, and don't look back," Bones said.

Jay kicked the ribs of his horse, and it jumped forward, and Jay rode away, his back prickling, until he was well away from the others. It was getting light, but he rode on into a rosy dawn.

Chapter Thirty-Two

He was alive. The more he rode through that rosy dawn, the more he focused on that simple fact. He lived. He had come within a few seconds of dying. Why had he been so reluctant to let go of the lead rope when his life was at stake? Did that bundle of cash mean more to him than life? Alive. It had been money versus his very life, and the money almost won.

As the day blossomed he saw the world around him as he never had before. Being alive meant seeing and hearing and smelling. Seeing the sun crawl up the flanks of the hills, hearing the cawing of angry crows, smelling the pungency of the sagebrush that crowded every draw. Suddenly these things meant something. What he had taken for granted, the glory of the world in which he traveled on a weary horse, was new and bright.

He rode through the morning, almost unaware of time, until around noon he struck a shallow valley with a creek parting brushy banks, and an occasional cottonwood. He was hungry and thirsty. What few things he possessed had been lost on the pack mule. Here was water; he didn't know what he would do for food, so far away from any settlement—and without any means to purchase some. He steered the weary horse down a game trail, through river brush, and finally to the shade of a stately bank-side cottonwood.

And there he discovered an older, weathered, graying man, resting at ease in hollow wrought by the roots of the tree.

Jay stared, startled. The man made no move to rise, but simply nodded.

"I didn't know you were here," Jay said, aware that the man had surveyed him thoroughly.

"That's how I prefer it," the man said. "I'm Tom; and you?"

"Jay, sir. Have you any food? I'm half-starved."

"You're a long way from anywhere," Tom said. "Without food."

It was probably a question.

"I had some, but—lost it," he said, not wishing to say more. "Bad luck," he added.

"Some raisins here in the cotton sack," Tom said. "Best trail food I know of. Light weight, and they stay good."

Jay dismounted, and took his horse to water, and let the old nag nose around in the creek a while. It was probably gyp water, and the horse was reluctant, but finally drank.

Tom watched closely.

Jay washed his hands in the creek, cupped them, lifted some water to his face, and lipped some down.

"It'll do," he said.

"If you don't get the trots," Tom added. He

gestured in the direction of the white cotton sack.

Jay tried a few dark, soft raisins and found them satisfying and even pleasant. He'd never given raisins a thought in his life, but now they were gold.

"Anything I can do to thank you?" he asked.

"Nope. It's thanks enough helping someone in need." He eyed Jay. "How far you going?"

"Cheyenne, I guess. My plans got changed."

"Take the raisins; they'll get you there."

"What'll you live on?"

"I have ways," Tom said.

There was a protocol at work here; neither would ask anything about the other. Whatever Jay might learn about Tom would be whatever Tom volunteered. And Tom was volunteering no more than Jay, who had plenty to hide.

Through the brush Jay spotted Tom's saddle horse and a pack mule.

"You know where there's work?" Jay asked.

"What kind?"

"I've been a teamster. I don't know much else. I tried mining a little."

"Then it's muscle you're offering. I thought maybe you wanted brain work."

Tom was reading him all too well. "I'm from the East," Jay said. "But that doesn't help me here."

"Out here, it's muscle and willpower that gets a living," Tom said.

The man rose, and dug into his shirt pocket. He

found a card there and handed it to Jay. "Look me up. I'm always looking around the country here," he said.

The card read Thomas Jumbo, Wyoming Stock Growers Association. There was no address.

A range detective.

Jay felt weak-kneed. What if he had walked in with the money-laden company-branded pack mule?

The older man collected his horse and pack mule, which had been picketed on grass. The saddle had a sheathed rifle. The pack mule was heavily loaded.

"Cheers," Tom said, and headed north.

Jay waited until he was alone, then tore off his ragged clothing. Piece by piece it fell away, and when he was naked he took the clothing into the creek and began scrubbing it furiously, slapping it on boulders, squeezing it and rubbing it: shirt, britches, underwear, stockings. He had no soap; it didn't matter. He would clean every scrap of clothing with creek water from the distant mountains, clean every scrap of grime away. He washed so furiously that time vanished. Finally, he draped the clothing over brush where the pleasant sun could dry it, and waited. There were raisins to eat, and soon clean clothing to wear. He liked the idea.

When the duds were half dry, he clawed them on, liking the damp clean cool. The shirt had busted sleeves and his britches were out at the knees. But they were clean. Then he collected his horse, climbed on, and began riding toward Cheyenne with no plan or purpose. His horse carried him across endless sere vistas. The land was as empty as his soul. The sun set and rose again. The raisins sustained him, and he finally rode into the dusty, bustling railroad town, still blank about his future.

A job, then.

He had run out of raisins.

He thought about applying to Fairweather Foley, but decided he had pushed the man's patience to the limit, and should look elsewhere. He hitched his horse at the railroad station, looked around, and settled on the American Express office there. A Help Wanted sign invited him in.

A wiry, close-shorn graying clerk eyed him from behind rimless spectacles. "You're an unlikely prospect," the man said, studying Jay's stubbled face. "All express personnel are snappy and clean."

"I'm interested in work, sir. I've had a bad spell, and you'll find me careful about my grooming as soon as I am able."

"Talk to me," the man said.

"I've been a teamster, and tried mining, and want to work for you now."

"I can well imagine," the man said. "You'll want a bath and a shave and a fresh set of duds before

I'd let you loose on the world. What makes you think I'll employ you?"

"I worked for Fairweather Foley; that's a start, sir. I am schooled, and that will help. And I'm willing to start at the ground level, and learn."

"Somehow I thought you wanted to start at the top, and work down," the man said, an odd smile on him. "Do you know what we do?"

"Express parcel delivery, sir."

"Well, that's a crude beginning. We deliver parcels fast and accurately. We handle trunks and baggage. If Mrs. Watson is sailing for England, her suitcase goes on the Pullman Car, and her steamer trunk goes with us, and we make sure that trunk is in her cabin when she boards the ship." He eyed Jay. "We transfer valuables and money. If a bank needs cash or gold, the Treasury sends it via American Express. We deal in credit. For that reason, sir, we require certain recommendations. Can you be recommended? By Foley?"

"Try him, sir."

"I intend to. You are?"

"Jay Warren, sir. I've teamstered for him on and off."

"That doesn't commend you."

"I will do my best, and will follow your direction. I don't know what else to say, sir."

"You'll be dealing pleasantly with people—that is, if I employ you. You'll be delivering promptly to our customers. You'll be diligent in finding them and getting parcels to them. We work closely with Western Union, and you may be delivering a telegram along with a parcel. You'll be muscling heavy items into our railroad express car. Sometimes it's the baggage car. You'll be carrying pouches to bankers. You will be required to make a good impression. You will be honest, faithful, and reliable. I'll talk to Foley."

The man eyed Jay. "I'll advance you a dollar. That will get you a shave, for starters. And we'll see about the job."

"Your name, sir?"

"Joseph Hightower." The man handed Jay a greenback. "Return when you're presentable."

Jay got a shave at Willis's Tonsorial Parlor, and waited while the barber filled a tin tub with tepid water in the back room. The shave was two-bits; the bath fifty cents. Jay would have two-bits to buy a bait of hay for his nag. An hour later he was as presentable as he could manage, with boots wiped free of grime. He left the horse at Boxcar Livery for a haying, and headed back to the express office.

Hightower was waiting. "I'd call it a qualified endorsement," the man said. "You have inflated notions about your worth, but worked steadily once you got on the road. You didn't stay long with the company. Your ambitions outpaced your skills. Is that a fair assessment?"

"Yes, sir. But I would like to add something. I'm

hoping you'll find me a better man now than I was then. I want to show you I'm more worthy now."

Hightower studied Jay. "I don't know why, but I'll give you a chance. Help is hard to find here. You're lucky that everyone else heads for the goldfields."

It wasn't a vote of confidence.

"We can't have you delivering in those duds, so I'm stuck with advancing you more cash. Get a white shirt, plain dark britches, and some boot polish and apply it, and report to me. Go to Porters Mercantile; I will have them charge it to the company. You will repay out of your salary, which will be a dollar a day for starters."

By three of that summer's day, Jay Warren was ready for work. Hightower looked him over, and nodded. "It'll do for the time being," he said.

"What are my hours, sir?"

"We have no regular hours, fella. We meet every train that has an express or baggage car. If it's late we wait. We unload what's destined here, and load what's going out. And we deliver as swiftly as possible. And that brings me to the next point. We offloaded half a dozen parcels just minutes ago. You'll deliver. The first is to Crawley's Pharmacy. That's an order of pills or something, and you'll walk it over there. Then you'll get the horse and dray and deliver an icebox to the Witherspoons, up in the north side. Oh, and get a signed receipt from each. After that, report to me."

Jay found the wrapped parcel addressed to Crawley, found the bill of lading, headed toward that place, which was two blocks distant, and delivered it to Crawley himself, who was unsmiling.

"Took long enough," the pill-pusher said.

"Please sign this delivery receipt," Jay said.

"I don't have a pencil. Just take it. Tell Hightower I got it."

Jay hadn't brought any writing instrument. "I'll take the package back, and deliver it when I have a pencil for you, sir."

He reached for the parcel, but Crowley snapped it away.

"Oh, all right," Crowley said. He found a nib pen and ink easily enough, and acknowledged receipt, and stuffed the paper in Jay's hands.

It was a lesson learned. Jay equipped himself with a sharpened pencil, located the small icebox, made of oak. It stood on the station platform. He discovered how to get the company's dray, and hunted for a dolly. It would be all he was worth to load the chest and deliver it. It turned out to be a struggle, but a friendly railroad baggage man helped him, a favor he knew he would return some day. He drove the icebox to its destination, and knocked.

"Oh, yes, right here," Mrs. Witherspoon said. "And of course you'll remove the packing, won't you?"

It took a while. There was shredded paper packing material keeping the innards in place, and all this he removed and carted out to the dray. Mr. Witherspoon arrived from wherever he had spent his day, and watched silently.

"Ma'am, if you're satisfied now, please sign the receipt," Jay said.

But it was Witherspoon himself who finally scribbled his signature on the line. And then he tipped Jay a dime.

Jay stared at the silvery dime in his palm, a flood of memories flowing through him. All through college he had flipped dimes to bootblacks, waitresses, barbers, bartenders, and whoever else happened to serve him.

And now he was staring at a dime in his sweaty hand.

Chapter Thirty-Three

One thin dime. Jay stared at it. Earlier in his life he would have been amused. Later, he would have been enraged. He thought momentarily of pitching it away, but something about that dime forbade it.

He left the Witherspoons, dime in hand, and returned to the Express office. Hightower had more work for him. There were parcels to load onto a hand truck and take to the next train, an eastbound due shortly.

"We meet all trains," he said. "When there's an expressman on board, he'll hand us what's coming here, and we'll hand him what we're shipping, east or west. But some trains haven't an expressman, and we unlock the baggage car, find what's due here, leave what we're shipping, and lock it up before the train pulls out. That takes some care. And speed."

Jay spent the rest of the waning day mastering all these things; far more things than he had imagined. There was more to it than delivering parcels.

Hightower watched amiably, peering from over his rimless spectacles as Jay performed one duty after another. There were procedures to follow. Accounting to be done, a complete bill of lading to be prepared for every outgoing parcel.

Jay grew weary. He had come a long way that day, found a job waiting, and stepped into it, but now he was dragging, and wondering when he would be released, and where he could spend the night, and how he would pay for a dinner. He was determined not to spend his tip, his lucky dime, if he could help it.

"All right," Hightower said, "the eight o'clock eastbound's the last train for the night. After that you're free."

"When do I report, sir?"

"We're always open, you know. We meet every train, day and night. You're on duty day and night."

Jay stared.

"Young fella, you're pretty tired, I imagine." Hightower found a key and opened a door at the rear of the depot office, and invited Jay in. There, in deep dusk, was a small bunk room. A narrow cot, desk, chair, and coat rack. Barren of all amenities but comfort.

"Yours if you want it," the expressman said. "Train comes, you'll hear it and meet the express car, day or night, asleep or awake. You can't miss the bell, and the screech of brakes."

Jay stared at the room as if it were heaven.

"I'll give you the key. It'll also unlock express car doors. I'm going to trust you to use it properly and do what is needed. We're responsible for everything placed in our care, so guard it faithfully." The older man stared at the youth. "And here's two-bits for a supper. There's a beanery up a block. Go eat. I'll meet the eight o'clock and leave the rest to you."

The sudden kindness shattered Jay. He had not known kindness existed.

"Mr. Hightower—I will try . . . thank you."

The older man smiled, settled into the wooden swivel chair, and set to work on a stack of bills of lading.

Slowly, for he was far more weary than he could remember ever being, he walked along the street fronting the rails, and found the beanery readily enough. It was lit by two lamps, and offered quick, plentiful food, most of it ladled from a bean pot. It was literally a beanery. The price was twenty cents a bowl. He ordered a bowl, and received plain, satisfying stew, with a dash of onion for flavor. He left a nickel tip.

When he returned to the station, the eight o'clock eastbound had come and gone, and the office was locked. His key fit the door. It fit the interior door to the bunk room. He found several parcels to be delivered in the morning. He would do that, first thing.

In short order, he made use of the station's facilities, locked himself into the office, and settled in the bunk room, so worn that he could barely pull off his boots. He lay on the cot, marveling at the kindness he had encountered in this place, by a man who had little reason to trust him or care about him. Jay thought he had done little to win Hightower's confidence, and the kindness was little more than charity. And trust. Jay wondered whether he could call himself trustworthy, but instead of dwelling on the past, he chose to think of the future. From that moment on, he would be as trustworthy as he knew how to be.

The last thing he remembered was the dime. And the next thing he knew, a train was screeching to a halt, its bell clanging. Jay hastened up, pulled on his boots, and headed into the chill night. But it was a freight, without an express car. He waited to see if there was anything he should be doing, and watched the engineer tug the whistle, and pull the throttle, and bring the train to life. Then Jay locked himself into the express office, and slept like a drugged man deep into the dawn.

He was disoriented at first. Where was he? The room wasn't much larger than a closet in his parents' New Haven home. Still, he was lying in a safe place, and the thin army blanket over him kept the chill at bay, and outside, the sun was stirring the breezes.

He realized that acts of kindness had brought him to that spot. The range detective had fed him, and hadn't looked too closely at a desperate young man. And his new employer, Hightower, had taken a chance on him, lent him money, saw to his needs, and—the kindest thing of all—entrusted him with responsibilities.

He stuffed his odorous feet into his boots, performed his ablutions in the station's facilities, and decided to forgo breakfast. His dime tip would buy a bun, but he preferred the dime to the bun. It was a lucky dime, and he intended to keep it all of his days.

Hightower was there when Jay returned, an odd inquiring gaze emanating from him.

"You found the company's accommodations suitable, I trust, and now you're ready to begin."

Jay spent the morning delivering parcels, mostly to businesses close to the station. He got no tip and no thanks, and one merchant complained about slow service.

"These canning jars, they should have been here two days ago," the man said. "Season's half over."

"I will see about a refund or a discount, sir," Jay said.

"Yeah, I'll bet," the man said, as he pried pasteboard away and began setting the jars on a shelf. "Express, that's a joke."

Jay hastened back to the express office and passed along the complaint. Hightower examined a few papers. "So old Wally Pike didn't like our service? Well, he's a hard man to please. We delivered on time."

"I'll tell him that, sir."

"No, boy, give him this. It's a ten percent discount he can apply to the next shipment."

The expressman scribbled a note and handed it to Jay. "See what that does," he said.

Jay hastened back to the Pike Hardware Company, and handed the discount note to Pike.

"Well, that won't help much," the man said, but then he brightened. "Better than nothing, boy. Here."

Another dime dropped into Jay's hands. Jay's stomach was growling from the lack of breakfast, and this dime would buy him a bun. He hurried to the bakery, bought his bun, and wolfed it down, feeling some better. He had placated an unhappy man, and gotten a tip for it. Somehow, a door had opened in his mind, and he was beginning to see possibilities.

Time flew. He learned how to meet trains, locate the express car, load and unload, deliver, check bills of lading, keep a running account, and console people who came in for a parcel that had not yet arrived. And all the while, Hightower was keeping a casual eye on him, rendering an occasional verdict, sometimes offering advice, sometimes showing him a better way to get something done.

"We pay a man on Saturdays," the expressman said. "You've put a day in. Here's a dollar."

One greenback. It would keep him going for a while.

Jay discovered he was the agency's sole employee, apart from Hightower. He had no idea who he replaced, or why, or when the man had left. But the Black Hills goldfields drew men away, and steady, faithful workers were hard to find in Cheyenne. Only a short time earlier, Jay realized, he had been among those who quit a job abruptly and took off.

He learned fast. In the space of a few weeks he had mastered the business, and was capable of performing any duty that his boss required of him. He worked long hours, and barely had time to think about the direction life had taken him, or what his future might be, or even who he was. It wasn't always easy, being an express company clerk and delivery man.

Hightower raised Jay's pay by two-bits a day, which gave the young man a little leeway. He wasn't earning much, but he was startled to realize he usually had more greenbacks in his pocket than he did during those long, desperate forays into mining camps looking for easy money. His pay, delivered in a brown envelope on Saturdays, sufficed.

But it was far from a good life, and he was often bored. Drudgery was the fountainhead of his income now, long hours, lack of friendships, not a woman in sight. But not a sheriff or a jail cell was in sight either. And no one was trying to euchre him out of those few things he possessed. He called it resignation. He was resigned to this new life as a clerk, and knew of no way to better his condition other than to do his work well and faithfully, and look after the needs of his customers. The dime tips continued, and that at least suggested that his efforts were pleasing people.

He sold his horse, having no need for it, and invested the proceeds in a wardrobe. For the first time in years, he was presentable.

Hightower watched closely, rarely complimenting or criticizing, but well aware of whatever Jay's mood and energy might be. And every once in a while, the agency head surprised him.

"Take the day off, Jay. You need some fresh air," he would say. "I'll cover, and you can call it a paid vacation."

That kindness again. Jay marveled at it; he was still unfamiliar with kindness, with people reaching out to him, offering him something, seeing a need in him. Hightower's kindness had evoked something in Jay; not a wish to return the kindness, but to pass it on, and be aware of others' troubles.

Sometimes he yearned to return to the privileged life he had enjoyed as a boy. But he was no longer a boy, and no longer privileged, and no longer able to scratch every itch, buy whatever he wanted, or go where the girls were. He had an odd thought about that. He supposed that if he were still that privileged boy, he'd be bored, or jaded, or seeking more and more risky adventures. And maybe even unhappy.

It dawned on him one day that his father had done him a favor, booting him out, and sending him West. It wasn't a favor he enjoyed much, not yet anyway, but a favor it was, and Jay was at last coming to understand the why of it. And he began to forgive his father, a little, around the corners anyway, for the sudden ejection from a life of luxury. But not entirely. There were times, when he was alone in the dark, when it all hurt anew.

Then, only a few months into Jay's new life, Hightower sat him down and told him what the future would be. "I'm being transferred to Denver," he said. "There's trouble there, and they think I can fix it. I recommended you as the agency man here, and they've accepted it. The job is yours if you want it. A hundred a month. You'll want to hire a promising young man to replace you."

"Me?" Jay was astonished.

"You. I've been watching. You're ready. You're faithful. You work hard. You care about the company and its customers. You often go out of your way to help people who have problems. You're young, but ready. I've watched your progress; I have no doubts. Do you want to think about it, or shall I arrange it?"

"There's nothing to think about," Jay said. "I accept."

Chapter Thirty-Four

Jay swiftly discovered that he might know the express business, but he didn't know people. His Help Wanted sign brought in one person after another—but not the sort of man he wanted. Cletus Draper, a middle-aged gent with a red nose showed up, delivered parcels for a day, asked for the day's wage, and then vanished into a saloon never to be seen again.

The next hire was a kid from Iowa who wrestled parcels for a week, got paid, and headed for the Dakota goldfields. The one after that, Mack McCormick, didn't wish to be bothered meeting night trains, slept through two arrivals, which resulted in packages failing to reach their destinations, and Jay had to let him go.

Until the right man came along, Jay would have to wrestle with the agency himself. He was doing a twenty-four-hour-a-day job, and it wearied him. He marveled that Mr. Hightower had been able to hire competent help, at least most of the time. So far, Jay had no success.

He realized how valuable a good man could be. A thoughtful, industrious, eager clerk or deliveryman would make his express business run smoothly, help meet his customers' needs, and bring sales to the business. In all his years, Jay had never given any thought to that. But suddenly he was aware of what businesses required, and why they snapped up promising people. His father had found the right people, and built a coastal shipping company upon their character. Jay thought that if he could find the right man, he would promote the man just as fast as the company permitted. Reward a good man.

Then one day Huckleberry Jones walked in, surveyed the small office, and grinned.

Jay was not glad to see the Missourian. Jones had changed in his brief sojourn in the West. Where once there had been a cheerful, cynical carrot-top clerk, now there was a subdued, unsmiling, man who looked twenty years older.

"Huckleberry?" Jay asked.

"Found you. We've been keeping an eye on you, Warren."

"Who's we?"

"Your old pals in the claim business."

"Are you looking for work?"

"Holy cats, Jay, you think I'm nuts?"

"It's hard to find a good delivery man," Jay said.

"Sucker work. Dollar a day, slavery. How come you're doing it?"

Jay smiled thinly. "It suits me." He started to tell Jones he was earning much more managing an express agency than he ever had jumping claims and trying to sell worthless mining claims to pigeons. But that wasn't Jones's business. And he sensed that it would bounce off Jones anyway.

"Must be dull, hanging in here all day, for nothing," Huckleberry said.

"I'm too busy to notice it," Jay said. He was wishing Jones would leave. His presence there in the express office was unwelcome. But Huckleberry was not about to leave, and seemed to be heading somewhere with his palaver.

"Drudge work. That's what you used to call it," Huckleberry said.

"Look, I've got a train coming in. I've got to get some things on a handcart and get out there."

"Need help?"

"No, only employees of the express company handle parcels."

"Big deal," Huckleberry said, looking amused.

Jay loaded parcels onto a four-wheel handcart, checked bills of lading and inventory, and wheeled the cart out to the station platform, choosing the place most likely for the express car to halt. That was always guesswork.

Huckleberry watched silently, and tagged along, saying nothing while Jay checked his handcart.

The train was only a few minutes late, but eventually wheezed in, its diamond stack pouring coal smoke over the station, its great drive rods turning high wheels and then slowing down as the engine slid past the platform.

Jay had pegged it right. The express car, usually

immediately following the coal tender, screeched to a halt directly in front of Jay's cart.

It remained locked. Jay, annoyed that Huckleberry was watching, jammed a key into the lock and slid the door open. Within, an expressman stood ready to collect the parcels, and hand down the ones he was carrying. Jay moved swiftly, handing up the parcels, and barely noticed that Huckleberry had edged down the track where he could peer directly into the express car and survey the contents. Jay was suddenly aware that Huck could see the express safe, note that it had a combination lock rather than a key lock, and note that there was a shotgun cradled on the coach wall nearby.

"I guess that does it, Jay," the expressman said, collecting the last of Jay's parcels. Jay stacked the Cheyenne-bound ones on his handcart, nodded, and let the expressman slide the door shut. Huckleberry stared.

The train tarried another ten minutes, but Jay swiftly wheeled the parcels to his express room, and began checking addresses and bills of lading. He would soon load the parcels, lock his office, and start delivering.

Even as Huckleberry watched.

Jay logged the parcels in a ledger, hoping Huckleberry would vanish, but the redhead lingered there. Huckleberry Jones was plainly after something.

"I have parcels to deliver," Jay said. "I'm locking up."

"Yeah, well, I'll keep you company," Huckleberry said.

"I can't do that. Deliveries are confidential, and by employees only."

"So who's gonna stop me?"

Jay had a dozen parcels, none of them weighty this time, and chose a two-wheeled cart for the job. He thought if he ignored the claim jumper, he'd drift off. But Jones stayed glued to Jay, watching as Jay loaded up and headed into Cheyenne. There were parcels for several merchants, which Jay delivered, and two more destined for residences.

"Okay, Huckleberry, you've been following me around. What do you want? Spell it out now or quit me," Jay said.

"I don't want anything. Just learning the business," Huck said. "You sure put in a lot of work for nothing."

Jay ignored him, and uneasily delivered the last two parcels, collected signed receipts, and went back to the express agency, with Huckleberry glued to him. He figured whatever was coming would happen once they got back.

A young man was waiting at the train station.

"You the boss here? I'm looking for work," he said.

Jay unlocked. Huckleberry slid in.

"Mr. Jones, this is a confidential interview."

For once, Huckleberry backed off, and the kid came in, and Jay closed the door.

"Tell me about yourself," Jay said.

"I hopped a freight. I'm from Topeka, and got bored. My folks, they don't know how to live so I took off."

Another dud, Jay thought. "What sort of work are you looking for?"

"Anything keeps food in my belly."

"This is a job with a lot of responsibility, sir. I didn't catch your name."

"Just call me Boxcar. I don't want my pa chasing after me."

"Well, Boxcar, you'll be meeting trains, handling parcels, delivering them and picking them up from people here, mostly merchants. You'll be working odd hours. We have no set hours; we meet every train carrying express packages, day and night. And the pay's a dollar a day, but goes up fast when you prove yourself."

"I'll think about it," Boxcar said. "You mind lending me two-bits for some chow?"

Jay didn't mind. Hightower had done that for Jay, not long before. He'd give the kid a meal and never see him again. "Here. Go eat. Beanery down the street. And let me know."

Boxcar fled. Huckleberry materialized instantly. The claim jumper had been observing everything.

"Look, I'm busy," Jay said.

"No, you're not. This is no big deal, this job of yours. You can do better."

Here it comes, Jay thought.

"Lots of valuables sent express," Huckleberry said. "Banks, they want a hundred thousand from the Treasury, it goes in Express cars."

"I don't know anything about that," Jay said shortly.

"I think you do. It sure is nice, knowing all that stuff. You could retire, knowing things like that."

"I said I don't know. So are you gonna get out of here now?"

Jay didn't actually know. Only when cash was destined for a local bank was he informed, so he could arrange a safe transfer of the pouch to the bank. Not once had he been informed, or gotten wind of, large shipments elsewhere.

"Jay, old pal, you're playing your cards too close. There's a great future for you. All you need to do is tell me when a big shipment's going out the rails, give me the train and the time, and you get a third."

There it was. "And who gets the two-thirds?"

"Your old friends, you know them all. Jake Bones, for starters. Me, Cassidy, Boggs, we're all glad to share our good fortune with you."

"I'm locking up. You want to come with me?"

"Wherever you're going, I'll go, old pal."

Jay locked the agency, and started walking west and then north, with Huckleberry tagging along. It was an overcast day that matched the gloom inside of Jay.

He turned right at the sheriff's office.

"Come on in," Jay said.

Huckleberry stood, staring. "You walk in there, Jay, and you're dead," he said.

"Come with me, Huck. We'll have a visit with the sheriff. His name's Jones, like your name. Joneses should all talk to Joneses."

"You go in there, you're dead," Huckleberry said. He jammed a hand into his coat.

Jay ignored him and walked in. He turned at the door, and saw Huckleberry walking away as swiftly as his legs would carry him.

He found Sheriff Walt Jones snoozing in a cell, sat down, and told him the story, not leaving out his own youthful days as a claim jumper, and naming names.

"That was a fine thing to do, Warren. I don't think they'll be stopping any trains around here now. But watch your back!"

"They think I know when shipments like that come through, but I don't, sir. That sort of shipment's done as quietly as possible. I don't even know for sure how fresh greenbacks get from the Treasury to the banks. Or any other securities."

"They'll make a stab at it, you can count on it. But up or down the line, most likely. As I say, fella, watch out. And if you get any tips, let me know."

"I will do that," Jay said.

Jay walked back to the agency and found Boxcar waiting. Jay opened up, and they went inside.

"That was a good meal, beans. First I've had in two days," Boxcar said.

"Boxcar, I don't think I'll hire you."

"Try me. Just try me."

"I think you're mostly interested in getting as far from your pa and ma as you can, and you see a job here as nothing but a meal ticket."

"Just try me, sir. Give me a chance."

"Why?"

"Because I'm ready."

Damned if that didn't appeal to Jay. He thought about how unready he had been when his father had kicked him out and sent him west. But that was his father's reason for doing it.

"All right, Boxcar. You're on."

Jay again remembered Hightower's kindness to him when he needed help. "And I'll pay you at the end of the day, so you can eat. And maybe I can do more, if I like what I see."

Boxcar was nodding, and wiping away the wetness around his eyes.

Chapter Thirty-Five

Boxcar set to work with a fury that Jay could scarcely imagine, much less understand. The boy delivered every parcel off the next train within an hour, even though he didn't know his way around Cheyenne. And he did it well, with signed receipts. He got the outgoing parcels loaded on the hand truck. On his own, he swept the floor and washed the windows, making the express agency shine for the first time in months.

Jay guessed Boxcar was a runaway, maybe sixteen or seventeen, a kid who had gotten too much of a strict home and headed out. Jay wondered whether the boy was running away from something, or toward something, maybe toward a dream. Boxcar mastered each task with one run-through, and seemed to know intuitively what needed doing. Jay gave him the night-man cubicle, and told him to meet the night trains, which delighted Boxcar all the more. A room of his own. He stared in wonder at the iron-framed cot, and dresser with the pitcher and bowl on it.

Jay didn't know how long it would last. He wasn't expecting Boxcar to linger more than a few days, and then the boy would skedaddle somewhere else, looking for something he scarcely knew. The boy stayed quiet about his past; Jay never got anywhere trying to find out who the kid was, and why he ditched his folks. At the same time, Boxcar seemed to brim with the future. Would there soon be more passenger trains? Would there be new express agencies opening up? Was Cheyenne growing?

The day came, though, that Jay would need a real name for his personnel records. He could slip temporary labor a greenback, but not an employee. And Boxcar was ready for full employment.

"Boxcar, we've got some business to transact," Jay said.

"You gonna fire me?"

"No, you're hired. You'll be a regular employee now."

"It's my first job, except selling newspapers."

"If I make you an employee, I have to have a real name. The company wants that," he said.

"Then maybe I should just quit!"

The boy's vehemence startled Jay. "Don't do that. I want you here. You're the best man I've had in the job."

"Yeah, and I tell you a name, you ship me back east to my ma and pa."

That clarified things some. "No, I won't. You've started out in the world as an adult, and I won't turn you around. I spent a long time getting to where you are right now. You got something I'd never destroy."

"They can come and get me. I'm not old enough."

"How long until eighteen?"

Boxcar stared. "I'm not saying."

"Are you indentured? Pledged for seven years to a tradesman?"

Boxcar struggled with that. "My pa wanted me to be a cooper."

"That's a good trade. People need barrels."

"You on his side? I'm getting out of here."

"Boxcar, I'll keep you on as day labor for a while. When you're ready to take the job, tell me your name, and I'll employ you. That way you'll get raises, get a paid holiday, and all that. I want you here. I want you to give the express company a chance."

Boxcar stared, and then nodded. He'd stay on, at least for a while. Jay hoped he'd take the job and settle down.

The boy surprised Jay with a grin a mile wide. "Maybe," he said. "I like Cheyenne."

That was more than Jay could say about Cheyenne. Jay liked the freshness, the dry prairie breezes, the hustle and bustle, and the way the huffing and puffing trains poured through, bringing new people each day to the young territory of Wyoming. But it wasn't a place to settle down, raise a family, and grow old. He couldn't say why. Some places seemed like home; others never could. Was his home still

New Haven, or the mansions of Newport Beach?

The boy headed out with a handcart loaded with parcels, mostly wares for Cheyenne merchants, and Jay settled into the routine of book-work. The express business involved an uncommon amount of time keeping ledgers updated.

That's when Fairweather Foley walked in, along with a dapper gent, dressed in a gray summer suit, with a black bowler. Jay took one look at the stranger, and knew this would be about money.

"Mr. Warren, I believe?" Foley asked.

Jay nodded. It had been some months since the two had any contact.

"I'm glad I found you. I've caught a word now and then, and knew you were with American Express."

"Better part of a year, sir."

"This gent has asked me to locate you. He has word for you. He's come all the way from the East, looking for you, knowing only that your last address was Cheyenne. May I present Clive Carter?"

"Someone looking for me? Oh, sir, welcome. I'm Jay Warren."

"Jay Tecumseh Warren," the man said.

Foley and Carter exchanged glances. "There's your man, Carter. I'll leave you to your business."

Foley eased out the door.

"A seat, sir?" Jay motioned him behind the counter, where there were two swivel chairs.

"I'm grateful to have located you. We had word you were in Deadwood, or that vicinity, and I spent a few days there, but you were unknown, except for some mining claim ledgers, where your name appeared. . . . I represent your family."

Jay had suspected as much, but that didn't allay the rush of feeling he felt contemplating the easterner.

"There is painful news, sir. Two things. Your father's suffered a stroke that has carried him to a different world. He's alive, but has left this one, and is not expected to last. In fact, he's failing, and it may be for the best, since he cannot speak, is paralyzed on his left side, and can barely track a visitor with his eyes. He doesn't respond to anything anyone says."

A turmoil rose in Jay. Some of the old bitterness, some of the love, and a disappointment too. He wanted to see his father again. He wanted to meet his father, not as father and son, but as an adult.

"I'm sorry, sir," Clive Carter said, gently.

Jay sighed, and felt his spirits sink. "Am I needed there? Is my mother all right?"

Carter looked troubled. "There is more, Mr. Warren. Some months ago some corporate raiders, pirates in starched white collars, began buying stock in your father's shipping company, and won control. It was a fine company, well managed, offering coastal shipping from Maine to Texas, and these raiders, whose names you might know if you're familiar with Wall Street, swiftly gutted the company and forced it into bankruptcy. Your father lost everything."

"You mean, everything? Everything?"

"Not quite. The house remains. It's been sold, and the proceeds will support your mother for a while."

"It's gone? Did that destroy him?"

"He collapsed one week after the company was forced into bankruptcy. The pirates had cleaned over a million dollars out of it in various ways. I'm afraid, Mr. Warren, that led to his current state."

"Is nothing left? Is his stock worth nothing?"

"Less than nothing. Creditors are filing suits against him."

Jay felt a flood of something he could not define. His world had vanished.

He eyed the clock. "Mr. Carter, sir, please wait. I've an express car arriving in a moment, and I must take care of it."

"Certainly. I'll bide my time in the station until we can continue."

Jay hurried his handcart to the platform just as Westbound Number forty-one hissed to a stop. The expressman had a dozen parcels for him; he handed six to the expressman, and the train wheezed west.

Carter was watching.

"You have made a living at this?"

"Yes, sir. I'm managing the agency, and have a young man working for me."

"We had word that you were in the goldfields."

"Was, sir." He smiled wryly. "It was an education."

"You have large responsibilities, Mr. Warren."

"Yes, and I'm bringing along a boy to take my place when the time comes. And that brings me to a question, sir. What do you advise me to do?"

"You may wish to see your father while he lives. He won't recognize you. You'll hold the hand of a stranger. But he lives, for the moment. And you may wish to see your mother. The circumstances have been, well, very hard for her."

"Is she at the family home?"

"No, she's in a flat in New Haven. I have her address here—ah, right here."

"So I have a decision to make."

"You do."

"Who sent you here?"

"I've been your father's attorney for three decades, Mr. Warren. I came on my own initiative. It seemed the thing to do."

"You did that? Will you be paid?"

"My pay, Mr. Warren, is finding you, finding you grown and productive and secure."

"How long have you been looking?"

"This is the third week. One to come west, a long while in Dakota, and finally back here."

"Mr. Carter, I've put a little by, and I plan to pay you."

"I'm well paid, Jay—may I call you that?"

"I am pleased that you do. What would you advise?"

"The doctors gave your father a month. And that was three weeks ago. I know your mother would rejoice. She's beset with grief and worry. She still has Matilda serving her—for the time being."

Boxcar burst in, eyed Carter, and started loading up parcels.

"Boxcar, I want you to meet an old friend of my family, Clive Carter," Jay said.

The boy paused, shook hands hesitantly.

"I like your name. Don't change it," Carter said.

"Don't change it?"

"It's the best name a young man could have. Much better than Caboose."

Boxcar broke into one if his huge smiles, that lit his face and then the whole room. Then he hastened his parcels out the door.

"Since he's been here, we've delivered most of our parcels within an hour of the time we've unloaded them," Jay said. "And the customers like it."

"The boy has a future. How'd he get that name?"

"He hasn't told me."

"Well, that winds it up, sir. I'll be catching the nine-twenty east."

Carter left addresses and a card with Jay,

hastened to pick up his bag, and headed for the platform as the eastbound chuffed in.

They shook hands. Jay watched him climb up the Pullman steps, and vanish. When the train chuffed away, Jay was flooded with a strange sorrow, akin to loneliness.

Jay settled deep into the swivel chair, unable to sort out everything or make sense of it. But one thing he knew: he wanted to reach his father while he could. Even if the man couldn't see or sense anything, Jay wanted to hold that hand, and be with his father, who had given him a gift larger than an inheritance. And then visit his mother, make sure she was well cared for, let her know that her son had come into his own, and was doing well, and was proud of her and all the ways she had nurtured him during his earlier years.

But he was trapped by responsibility. He could not leave the agency untended. He had no replacement, no subordinate who could manage for two weeks. It would take five or six days to go east, over several lines, sometimes not connected directly. Even with express trains going forty or fifty miles in a single hour, it would be a five-day trip each way. He needed two weeks, and that could not be managed.

As much as he yearned to go, needed to go, needed to see his failing father, that was not possible—unless he quit. And he knew he wouldn't. He would not abandon the company and leave it with a crisis. He would do his duty, no matter what the consequences.

Late the next day he received a telegram from Omaha, sent by Clive Carter:

REGRET INFORM YOU
TECUMSEH WARREN DIED
PEACEFULLY YESTERDAY EVE.
CARTER

Jay studied the yellow sheet, unable to stem the flood of grief that swept him. He sat down in the squeaking swivel chair, staring out the express agency window, not knowing what to do, wishing he had gotten back there while his father still had breath. But it was always too late. By the time Carter found Jay, Tecumseh was breathing his last. Jay sat and stared and tried to fathom life, but couldn't.

Chapter Thirty-Six

It was time to buy the ticket. Jay wanted to go east before winter set in. Boxcar had toiled steadily, and knew the business, but still lacked the seasoning that comes with experience. And he was still a boy. So Jay stayed, running the express agency, making sure all was done right, and all customers were happy.

The days and weeks droned by. Boxcar remained a day laborer, until one morning he approached Jay. "It's my eighteenth birthday. No one can come after me now. Do you want to hire me?"

Jay did. Boxcar said his name was William Boxer. One could call him Boxcar and he was simply answering to his own name.

"Don't call me Bill, Billy, or William," he said. "I don't like my given name."

Boxcar was soon on a fifty-a-month salary, a good wage for a youth starting his first job. And he continued to live in the night room and meet trains. And he continued to do as fine a job as anyone could.

Everything was in place. "I hope to travel for two weeks. Go east. Can you handle it alone?" Jay asked.

Boxcar beamed. "I think you'll find everything in good order when you get back."

That sounded fine to Jay, so he went to the ticket window at the station, and ordered a round trip ticket to New Haven, which proved to be a yard long, the same as his outward bound ticket. He let his Denver supervisors know, and assured them the express agency would be in good hands. Boxer was the sort of man companies dream of.

He packed. Nothing going into his portmanteau had come west with him earlier. It was all new clothing, purchased in Cheyenne by his own means. He boarded the morning eastbound, found his Pullman berth, and settled himself as the train huffed its way out of the city where he had struggled and succeeded and was making friends.

The prairies, golden in the fall light, shone under a broad heaven, where one could see clear to tomorrow. He realized he loved the West. This wasn't the breathtaking West, but a land of shining prairie, rich with life and promise. That was the thing: he was living a life of promise.

The wheels clicked east, clattering over switches, thundering over an occasional bridge. He wasn't bored. Herds of pronghorns startled and raced. The prairie shimmered as afternoon came and went, and then the train pulled into a Nebraska station for a dinner stop. Some trains had diners; this one stopped for twenty-minute meals. These places were usually called beaneries, and could serve up a bowl of edible bean stew in seconds. You always paid first, so you didn't have to settle up as the train was pulling away.

Nebraska, Iowa with its tall grass, Illinois, trees and streams, a smaller sky, and settled towns. Chicago, bustling and odorous, smoke in the air, and then the Pennsylvania Railroad, Indiana, Ohio, Pennsylvania, New York, and finally New York City, city of brigands who stole his father's company. Then the local train, stopping and starting its way to New Haven. The air was moist, and he didn't care for it. The seats were sticky, and he wondered how any mortal could live in such a place. The dry west was almost always comfortable.

He should have rejoiced. Home at last, after months of desperation and struggle. But his heart was heavy as he lifted the portmanteau and carried it into the station. He checked it there and would look for a hotel room later. There seemed to be people everywhere, crowded close, jammed into smaller rooms. But he was as lonely as he ever got. New Haven had once been home, but now it was a moist, cramped, hard place and he was the alien on its streets.

His mother's flat was only a mile or so away on Whitney Avenue; a pleasant walk along elm-canopied streets lined with century-old brick buildings tight against one another. The street was pleasing to the eye, but made him claustrophobic. He needed air, big skies, and space. Elbow room. The West had seared that into him.

The flat proved to be on the second floor of a four-apartment building. He found a brass knocker and rapped, expectantly. A reunion! He had never been close to his mother, but even so, this surprise visit filled him with delight. This was home.

Matilda answered, the same as ever, in black with starchy white collar and cuffs.

She eyed the stranger at the door, recognition lighting her graying features.

"Why Mr. Jay!" she said, a thin smile suffusing her lined face.

"Surprise, eh?"

"Yes, sir. Surprise. I . . . presume you wish to see your mother."

There was an odd reluctance, maybe a hesitation, in her.

"Of course. Is she up? Is she about?"

"She's in the parlor, Mr. Jay. I suppose you know . . ."

"Know what?"

Matilda's welcome vanished. "You'll see," she said.

Jay left his hat at the foyer, and followed the old family retainer through a narrow hall and into a sunlit, small parlor, quietly furnished with a few pieces from the great, and gone, brick pile he had grown up in.

She was there in the morning sun, a lap robe covering her as she sat quietly in a small rocking chair. Her gaze followed Jay as he approached.

"Madam, your son is here," Matilda said.

"Oh," said Jay's mother.

Jay took her small, veined hand and held it, but what he was seeing sent cold straight through him. She was not recognizing him.

"Pleased to meet you," she said.

"How have you been, mother?"

"I don't know," she said.

"Are you comfortable here?"

"Where?"

"Here, where you're living now."

"Oh," she said, and folded her hands together on her gray lap blanket.

And so it went.

"Would you like tea, Mr. Jay?" Matilda asked.

"Why, yes. May I come choose it?"

He followed her into the prim kitchen.

"Forgive me, sir. She's been like this ever since your father died. She seems to have slipped into her own world."

"Did she recognize me? I saw no sign of it."

"She lives in her world, sir. Mr. Carter comes regularly to check up. And he handles everything."

The hour he spent with his mother went very slowly and quietly. He absorbed her condition, knew that communion with her was no longer possible, asked about her physical comforts, and finally realized this flat was simply a vestibule, a waiting room to the beyond.

He thanked Matilda, smiled at his lost mother, and left. Motes of dust danced in the sunlight. He stepped outside, an orphan.

Clive Carter's firm was only a few blocks away. He met the old family retainer and soon had the story of his mother's decline. The very day they buried Tecumseh, she began to fade into the wallpaper, her own life done. It had, actually, been a sweet and close bond, but the reality was that both of Jay's parents had departed.

"Is she secure?" Jay asked.

"For two or three years. After that . . . no."

"I can help some." Jay wondered how much, and whether fifty a month would go far.

"That would be valuable, Jay. It would help put off the day. And Matilda has no place to go, you know."

From Clive Carter, Jay got directions to the cemetery where Tecumseh lay, and Jay found a horse trolley that would carry him there, well inland and west of central New Haven. The memorial park was gracious, canopied by giant elms and mighty oaks, the lawns verdant, and the graveled walkways immaculate. It was the resting place of the affluent, a place of great sepulchers and classical vaults, announcing the grandeur of those who rested within. But Tecumseh's grave was not like that. It was not among the memorials of the fortunate. There was a simple double headstone, half of which had been completed with his name, birth and death. The other half would soon bear its own legend.

Jay stood before the grave of his father, sorry that he had not made it back in time to commune with him. There would have been much to talk about. And both Tecumseh and Jay might have found great reward in the reunion.

He took his hat off. He wished he had brought a dozen roses to lay upon the grave.

He knew what he wanted to say, and did not hesitate. "I missed you by a few months. I hope your spirit is here and can hear me," Jay said. "It's simple. You gave me a great gift, even if I didn't know it, and resented it at the time. You gave me the means to make my way in the world. You knew what I lacked, and what I needed. For that I thank you. It took me a long time to fathom what you gave me, and only now, when I see it was the gift that endured, do I think of it as my true inheritance. I'm making my way, father. And I'm very glad you were my father."

He couldn't think of anything else to say, so he stood there, absorbing the quietness of the place, seeing grass far more verdant than any in Cheyenne, seeing stately trees that threw shade over the good earth. He sensed that somehow he had conveyed his message. All of that was a mystery, something felt rather than understood.

He was content. He felt less loss, and grieved less, than he had supposed. Instead, he felt himself to be an extension of his father, the man's beliefs and values embedded in him. He had fought bitterly against those things, preferring a life on Easy Street, but now those things were his salvation. If he ever had children, he would try to imbue each one with the same ideals and understandings.

He stood a while more, absorbing the place and the moment, and the simple marker. He probably would never be back. So he wanted this to live in his memory.

He was done in New Haven, Connecticut.

He checked out of the hotel, walked to the railroad station, the very station where he had started his western odyssey so long ago, and caught the local to New York, watching the teeming East slide by through grimy windows. In New York, he caught the Pennsylvania Railroad west.

The other passenger in his Pullman suite, in the seat facing him, was a handsome young woman in a green travel suit with a white jabot at her throat. Her eyes were green, and matched the suit. He intuited that the suit was not her preferred dress. For some reason, she looked familiar. Jay examined her attentively, first checking her left hand for any sign of commitment. But it was bare. She eyed him as attentively as he was eyeing her, but refrained from saying anything, and her face revealed nothing of her thoughts. She had a copy of Godey's Lady Book with her, to instruct her in the arts of womanhood. But she was only pretending to read.

"You look western," he said.

"You look like a masher," she said.

"I don't think you ride sidesaddle," he said.

"I don't think you like the East," she said.

"I was born there, but the clouds parted, and sun came out, and I was sent to Cheyenne, in the Territory of Wyoming."

"I'll be damned," she said. "That's home. I was sent east to a finishing school and it pretty near finished me."

"Where's home?"

"Wherever there's prairie and sunshine and promise."

"I am Jay Warren," he said.

"Elizabeth Foley."

"Daughter of Fairweather?"

"I'm me; he's him. Watch what you say."

"Will you marry me?" he asked.

"I thought you'd never ask," she said.

Center Point Large Print
600 Brooks Road / PO Box 1
Thorndike, ME 04986-0001 USA

(207) 568-3717

US & Canada:
1 800 929-9108
www.centerpointlargeprint.com